BENEATH A BLUE MOON

CRESCENT CITY WOLF PACK BOOK TWO

CARRIE PULKINEN

Beneath a Blue Moon

Contact Information: www.CarriePulkinen.com

First Edition, 2018
ISBN: 978-0-9998436-3-5

CHAPTER ONE

CHASE BEAUCHAMP ROLLED HIS HARLEY TO A STOP outside the morgue on Earhart. He let the engine idle, the low rumble filling the humid night air with its sultry song. The stale stench of death seemed to ooze from the pores in the brick building, undulating into the parking lot like a suffocating fog.

He killed the engine and stared at the heavy, metal door, a chill creeping up his spine as the memory of his last trip to the morgue played in his mind. He still had nightmares about the twenty minutes he'd spent in the cold locker, hiding from the same cop he was about to meet now. Exhaling a curse, he dismounted his bike.

Go in. Check out the body. Get the hell out. That's all he had to do. At least he wasn't trying to steal the damn thing this time.

He heaved open the door and blinked as his eyes adjusted to the stark white reception room. Though what kind of reception one could give to anyone who came to identify a body, he had no clue. The sharp tinge of bleach in the air did nothing to mask the sour, musty aroma of dead flesh. He tried to keep his facial expression neutral as he scanned the empty room, but the smell was more offensive than a Saturday night on Bourbon Street. Something about preserved dead people gave him the creeps.

And where the hell was Macey?

The door swung open, and a man with clean-cut, light-brown hair ambled in. If his shoulder holster didn't give him away, his cocky gait screamed cop. Chase had seen this guy before. Macey's partner, Bryce.

"You Chase Beauchamp?" He raked his gaze over Chase's tattooed arms before lingering a little too long on the piercing in his right eyebrow.

Chase nodded and returned his stare.

"Detective Bryce Samuels." He held out his hand. "I'm Detective Carpenter's partner."

Chase shook his hand, and not a hint of magic seeped from his skin. This guy was all human. "Where's Macey?"

"She's checking up on a lead. Asked me to show you the body. Apparently, you might be able to *pick up* on something she didn't." He made air quotes with his fingers and looked toward the front desk. "Where's the mummy?"

A scrawny kid with shaggy red hair typed something into his computer and shot to his feet. "Locker twenty-six. Did you prepare him?" He cut his gaze toward Chase and grimaced.

Bryce slapped Chase on the shoulder and walked toward a swinging door. "She's a mummy. Prepared?"

"As I'll ever be." He followed Bryce down a narrow hallway illuminated in sickly-green fluorescent lights. The putrid color did nothing for the ambience. Then again, a storage house for the freshly dead didn't need to be warm and cheerful.

They turned a corner, and Bryce lowered his voice.

"Macey tells me you have a similar ability to her spirit sensors."

"Something like that. I'd say mine's a little more pronounced." How much did this guy know about his partner? Macey was the alpha's mate and the only werewolf on the New Orleans police force. Being second born, she lacked the ability to shift, but nearly all werewolf offspring possessed some sort of power.

Bryce stopped outside a door. "So you can see ghosts? Or spirit energy? I think that's what she calls it."

"Sort of." *Not at all.* Macey suspected the victim died of supernatural causes, but she didn't know enough about the paranormal world to make the call. She'd had no idea she was a werewolf herself until a few months ago. Whether or not the pack got involved in this case would be up to Chase. Then it would be Macey's job to make sure the police never discovered the truth.

Bryce pushed open the door and strode toward a locker. Chase followed, trying his best to *not* think about how it had felt to be inside one. Suffocating. Cold. Morbid. Another chill spiraled from his tail bone up to the base of his skull.

Sliding the drawer open, Bryce pulled back the sheet to reveal the corpse. Dry, brown skin stretched tight across the boney figure, as if someone had wrapped a science class skeleton in leather and slapped a bleached-blonde wig on it. Thin lips stretched back into a torturous howl, and the sunken cheeks looked like they'd crumble to bits if he touched them.

But the most haunting aspect of all was the gaping, hollow eye socket.

Though his skin crawled like a swarm of spiders skittered across the surface, Chase leaned in closer to the shriveled corpse. "Any idea what happened to her eye?"

Bryce pinched his brows as if looking at the body caused him pain. "No clue. Can't you ask her ghost?"

"Right. Let me see if I can pick up anything." He closed his eyes and took a deep breath, trying to mimic the way Macey acted when she read energy.

Big mistake.

The rancid death stench made his stomach turn. How could humans not be bothered by this smell? He swallowed the sour taste of bile from his throat and raked his gaze over the body. "Looks like something sucked the life right out of her."

"No kidding. Autopsy says her blood has turned to powder. Pretty much all her insides have."

"Hmm. A vampire wouldn't have left any blood behind at all, so it's safe to rule that out."

Bryce blinked.

Crap, he shouldn't have said that. Chase shoved his hands in his pockets and forced a smile. "I'm kidding."

He chuckled. "You never know in this town. A few months ago, we had so many people trying to convince us werewolves were involved in a case that Macey started to believe it was true."

Chase shook his head, laughing off the statement. "Women."

"Right. So, no lingering spirits then?"

"None that I can see." Not that he could have detected one if it were there. Like most first-born weres, Chase's only powers were massive strength and the ability to shift into wolf form. "Does she have any other markings? Punctures or cuts?"

"She has a tattoo beneath her collar bone. It's hard to

tell, the way the skin shriveled up, but it looks Celtic." Bryce pulled the sheet down to reveal a warped, black design on the woman's chest.

He could see how a human would mistake the twisting, knot-like pattern for Celtic, especially in this distorted condition, but the tattoo had nothing to do with the Irish. This woman belonged to a witch's coven, though which one, he couldn't be sure.

The sour taste returned to the back of his mouth. *Damn witches.* They were a bunch of selfish pricks who didn't give a shit about the rest of the supernatural community. This woman had probably pissed someone off high up in the coven, and they'd discarded her like trash, leaving the mess for the werewolves to clean up. It looked like the pack would be getting involved after all.

Bryce covered the body with the sheet and shoved the drawer shut. "Recognize the design?"

"No. You're right. It's probably a Celtic knot. Sorry I couldn't be more help."

Bryce narrowed his eyes, studying him. "Don't you need to touch something? Or meditate?"

"Pardon?"

"Macey always puts her hands on the walls and closes her eyes and starts swaying like she's hypnotized."

Damn, this guy was perceptive. If Macey had given Chase a head's up, he might have been prepared to put on a show. As it stood now, he just wanted to get the hell out of that stinking cesspool of death. "My ability doesn't work that way."

Bryce lifted a shoulder and nodded toward the door. "Whatever you say, boss. I won't even pretend to understand what y'all can do. Frankly, it's a little weird."

If he only knew the half of it. "I can see how it would

seem that way." He followed the officer to the reception area, the tightness in his chest loosening now that a solid wall stood between him and the bodies.

Bryce stopped at the desk and signed his name on a clipboard before turning to Chase. "We rely on Macey's ability a lot."

Chase nodded. "Reading spirit energy is a handy talent."

"She said you'd fill in for her while she's on her honeymoon in a few months. Help us out if we need it." He raised his eyebrows, silently asking for confirmation.

"Did she?" Strange the alpha himself hadn't told him about this new assignment. Chase would need some lessons on pretending to be psychic if he was going to keep this charade up.

Bryce popped a piece of gum into his mouth and clenched it between his teeth. "That okay?"

"You get any more weird cases, give me a call. I like weird."

Bryce nodded curtly. "Will do."

Chase shook his hand and shoved open the door. Thick, sultry air enveloped him as he treaded through the parking lot to his bike, breathing deeper now that he'd gotten away from the damn morgue and its foul stench. Thunder clapped in the distance, and his arm hairs stood on end as the storm clouds gathered above.

He glanced at his watch and cursed under his breath. Luke would expect a full report, but he didn't have time to swing by the bar. Bekah had a class tonight, and the one thing Chase liked better than hunting demons was babysitting for his sister.

A text would have to do. *Victim's a witch. Insides turned to powder. Never seen anything like it. Babysitting tonight.* He mashed the send button with his thumb, shoved the phone in his pocket and then headed home.

He'd be happy if he never stepped foot inside that morgue again, but something told him he'd be spending a lot more time there, thanks to the alpha's mate.

Rain Connolly sat at a table in the darkened bakery and stared out the window. Using the side of her hand, she wiped the condensation from the pane and leaned toward the glass. Fat water droplets danced across Royal Street, pooling near the sidewalk and cascading down the storm drain, washing the sludge from the road. She'd always loved a good thunderstorm, and not just because of her name.

The cleansing act of water from above rinsing away the impurities on the ground soothed her. If only her own sins were so easily washed away.

The sudden showers had sent tourists and locals alike scattering for cover. Now the rain and the streetlights had the stage to themselves, and they created a choreographed routine Rain could've watched for hours. The boom of thunder interrupted the musical cadence of the shower, but the droplets found their rhythm again, falling individually before becoming one with the steady stream running down the street.

She sighed as a woman rounded the corner, stomping her heavy, black boots through the puddles, disrupting the dance of the downpour. Though the hood of her jacket hid her face in shadows, the woman's deep-magenta aura and purposeful strides couldn't be mistaken. Rain leaned away from the window and clutched the pendant hanging from her neck. Though the goddess seemed to have abandoned her, a quick prayer wouldn't hurt.

The woman banged on the door as a bright bolt of lightning flashed across the sky, followed by a massive clap of thunder so loud it rattled the windows of the nineteenth-century building. She squealed and knocked harder.

As tempting as it was to leave her landlord out in the storm, Rain rose from her chair and opened the door. "I'm closed, Ingrid."

"I'm not here for cake." Ingrid folded her umbrella and left it on the front steps before striding inside and slipping the hood off her head. She shook out her crimson curls and huffed as she examined the wet ends of her hair. "Your rent is late, and your fees need to be paid."

"Fees for a coven to which I don't belong." Rain walked deeper into the storefront, but Ingrid lingered in the doorway.

"Do we have to have this conversation every month? If you want to operate as a witch, you either join the coven or you pay the fees. It's not a difficult concept."

She put her hands on her hips in a challenging pose. The *concept* wasn't the difficult thing. "Then let me join the coven."

Ingrid rolled her eyes. "Only real witches can join."

The corner of Rain's mouth twitched as a spark of heat flashed through her body, and she inclined her chin. "I am a real witch."

"You're cursed."

"Then let *me* join." Snow padded in from the back room and set a stack of freshly-washed plates on the counter.

Ingrid let out an irritated sigh and wiped the dripping

hair from her forehead. "We're not taking chances with your sister either. You two don't know when to quit, do you?"

"Connollys never quit." Snow stood next to Rain and crossed her arms, her platinum blonde hair swishing as she shook her head.

Rain would argue to her last breath with any witch who challenged her heritage. Yes, she was cursed, but magic did flow through her veins. Unfortunately, though, even joining the coven wouldn't help her current situation. She sat on a barstool. "I don't have the money."

"Why not?"

"Business has been slow, but I have a potential wedding client coming in tomorrow. If they book, I can pay the rent or the fees. Not both. Not now. Can I have an extension?"

Ingrid opened her mouth as if to speak, but she closed it again. "You know I can't show you any kindness. Renting the building to you is all the risk I'm willing to take. I wouldn't have even let you sign the lease if I'd known about your curse beforehand."

Rain cringed inwardly. She'd been required by law to inform the coven priestess of her curse when she moved here, but she'd purposely signed the lease on the shop before she did. It wasn't a selfless act, but what else could she have done? She needed the prime location if her business would ever take off. "It's not a kindness. Decent landlords give their tenants extensions all the time. One more month."

"I'm not even going to chance being decent. Late fees started accruing last week. If I don't receive your payment in two weeks, you'll be evicted." Her eyes softened. "I'm sorry. I don't like being this way. It's not you…"

She stiffened. "It's my curse. I understand."

Ingrid attempted a sympathetic smile, but her mouth merely twitched as she opened the door. "Don't take it personally."

Rain returned the gesture with a faux grin. "How could I not?"

Snow locked the door after the landlord left and turned to her sister. "She's right, you know? You shouldn't take it personally. I bet they'd all love you like I do if they got to know you."

"It's not about being loved. Or even liked." She sighed and shook her head. "The second people find out about my curse, they act like I've got a contagious disease." And she deserved the punishment. She was lucky she'd gotten settled in before word of her curse spread through the community.

"They're being cautious."

She folded her hands in her lap and picked at her pale-pink nail polish. "What am I going to do? If I lose the bakery, I'll be on the street."

Snow sat on the stool next to her and wrapped her arm around her shoulders. How long had it been since another witch had gotten close enough to touch her?

Leaning into her sister's side, Rain let the affection calm her. "Careful comforting me. Don't be too kind."

"Don't be silly; I'm comforting myself." She laid her head on Rain's shoulder. "We can stop selling enchanted cookies. If we're a human bakery, you won't owe the fees."

Rain let out a dry laugh. "The spells are what pay the bills between weddings."

"True. Spellbound Sweets wouldn't be much without the spells." She sat up straight. "Let me pay the fees. I'm the one operating as a witch anyway. I should be the one paying for the license."

Rain rose to her feet and shuffled around the counter to put the plates away. She'd drained her savings account to get the place up and running, not allowing her sister to pay for something as small as a can of rainbow sprinkles. It was the only way to make certain her curse didn't affect Snow. "It's a witch's bakery. *My* bakery. If you paid, it would be a kindness. I won't let you take that risk."

"What's the worst that could happen? Pneumonia for a week? A sprained ankle?"

Rain closed the cabinet, her heart sinking at the thought of what her curse could do to her sister. "You could get run over by a streetcar. Or struck by lightning. Or worse."

"Yeah, okay. Good point. The appointment tomorrow sounds promising, though. Werewolves tend to stick together, so if you can land the alpha's wedding, we'll have our foot in the door with their pack. They could bring in a lot of business." She spun a circle on the barstool and grinned. "Werewolves like to eat."

A tiny flame of hope flickered in her core before dying out. Her shoulders drooped. "Until another werewolf opens a bakery. They prefer to do business with their own kind. Don't get your hopes up."

"Well, there aren't any werewolf bakeries now, and now is all that matters at the moment." Snow leaned her elbow on the counter, resting her chin on her fist. "Let's focus on landing this gig, and it will solve half your problems."

"And the other half?"

She shrugged. "We're Connolly witches. We'll figure something out."

Rain smiled at her sister. Snow risked so much by being here every day, and gratitude didn't begin to describe the emotions Rain felt for her. "*You're* a Connolly witch. I'm just a Connolly." Or so everyone seemed to believe.

"Your powers may be bound, but there's magic in your blood." Snow leaned her forearms on the counter. "How many ingredients are left to find?"

She'd received an unbinding spell from the national witches' council in the mail three months ago on enchanted paper. Each time she retrieved an ingredient, the next one revealed itself. "I've got two ingredients left. As soon as I get my hands on some Bauhinia harvested by a priestess beneath a full moon in Peru, the last one will be revealed, and we'll be good to go. Do you really think it will work?"

Snow lifted an eyebrow. "Are you doubting my powers, sister?"

She laughed. "Of course not. But the council said only an ultimate act of selflessness could break the spell and unbind my powers."

"Then they said seven years of repentance is enough."

"I know that's what the letter said. It seems strange that they'd change their minds though. I bet Mom had something to do with it."

"So what if she did?" Snow lifted her hands as she shrugged and dropped them to her sides. "Maybe they weren't specific enough in what an 'ultimate act of selfless-ness' is. Maybe they feel like you've learned your lesson."

She traced the marble pattern on the countertop with her finger. "I guess." If the lesson was to put others before her powers, she hadn't had a choice but to learn. She'd been powerless for seven years. "Whatever their reason-ing...I want my magic back."

"I understand. This will work." Snow stepped around the counter and gave her sister a hug. "I'm going home. Can I have today's pay so I don't get run over by a streetcar on my way?"

Rain chuckled and took two twenties from the cash register. "Be safe."

"Always."

After her sister left, Rain locked the door and turned off the lights before padding to her storage closet-turned-bedroom in the back of the shop. If this unbinding spell worked, and her curse could be broken, she might be able to save the bakery.

Bauhinia itself was easy to come by, but the stipulation that it be harvested by a priestess beneath a full moon made it difficult to find. She'd located a shop in Peru who could fill the order, but the cost of the ingredient, plus international shipping, had set her back several hundred dollars. But if she could get rid of this curse and be accepted into the witches' community again, she'd have more than enough business to pay all her bills.

Though she'd never achieve a spot on the national council after what she'd done to earn the curse, she might be able to work her way up in the coven once they let her in. At least she could hold a position of power within the community. It was better than nothing.

CHAPTER TWO

CHASE SAT BEHIND A MASSIVE OAK DESK AND EYED the whimpering rule-breaker. The lanky teen couldn't have been more than seventeen, and he shifted in the green vinyl chair like his ass was sore. His dad most likely had torn the kid a new one the moment his little sister blabbed about what he'd done. Now he had to face the punishment from the pack.

With one elbow resting on the desk, Chase leaned his mouth into his hand, trying to hide the involuntary curve of his lips. Truth was, he saw a lot of himself in the rebellious teen. Growing up, he'd never been one for rules. Now his job for the next twenty-plus years was enforcing them. Who would've thought?

"What the hell were you thinking, Landon?" His smile under control, Chase steepled his fingers beneath his chin—a move the old alpha had pulled when Chase got in trouble himself—and leaned back in the squeaky leather chair. "You don't show your wolf form to humans."

Landon lifted his hands and started to speak, but he

dropped them in his lap and let out a dramatic sigh. "You wouldn't understand."

He arched a pierced eyebrow. "Try me."

"He was kissing my sister in the back of his truck. In the swamp. *The swamp.* Who does that?" He fisted his trembling hands on the arms of the chair. "I was trying to save her."

The corners of Chase's mouth tugged upward, so he shot to his feet and paced around the desk. "Save her from what?"

Landon cowered in his chair. "He's going to break her heart. Dude's got a new girlfriend every week."

He stood behind the chair and peered through the mini blinds at the empty stone corridor. The kid's mom and sister waited in the bar down the hall, probably cowering in their chairs like rebellious Landon here.

The kid peeked over his shoulder and caught Chase's gaze. As soon as he made eye contact, he jerked his head forward and stared at his hands in his lap. "What are you going to do to me? Are you going to kill me?"

Now he didn't fight the smile. "For a first-time infraction? We're more civilized than that." He ran a finger across the back of the chair, and the kid froze. The hum of fluorescent lights and Landon's rapid, shallow breaths filled the otherwise silent room. The red numbers on the digital clock display flipped from eleven forty-five to forty-six. Forty-seven.

A little flush of fear ought to keep the kid in line for a while. It always worked on Chase when he was young. A pair of work boots thudded on the concrete outside, and Landon dropped his head into his hands. Being drilled by the second in command was intimidating enough. Now he'd have to hear it from the alpha.

The door flung open, and Luke sauntered in. He wore paint-stained jeans and a gray T-shirt, and his light-brown hair was tied back at the nape of his neck. Chase liked to think his own tattoos and piercings made him intimidating, but Luke held an aura of authority only members of the first family had.

The alpha dropped into the leather chair and leveled his gaze on Chase. "What did I miss?" Landon let out a whimper, and the corner of Luke's mouth twitched.

Chase crossed his arms and stood next to the kid. "Showed his wolf form to a human to stop him from making out with his sister."

"Did he now?" Luke pinned Landon with a hard stare. Both men had their own little sisters, so they could sympathize with Landon's need to protect his sibling. But the kid didn't need to know that.

The alpha rested his hands on the desk. "And what's the verdict?"

Chase strolled forward to lean against the desk. "Thirty hours of pack service and an apology to his sister."

Luke nodded. "Sounds good to me."

Landon lifted his head. "Thirty hours? That'll take forever."

Chase put a heavy hand on his shoulder. "We could put you in the pit. Or kill you."

His eyes widened. "No, no. Thirty hours sounds fair."

"Great." Luke smirked and took an old toothbrush from a desk drawer. "You can start by cleaning the toilets."

"Yes, sir." Landon took the toothbrush and sulked out of the office.

As the door clicked shut, Chase laughed. "That the same one your old man made me use when I screwed up?"

Luke nodded. "That toothbrush has seen more toilets than a frat boy during rush week."

Chase flopped into the chair and ran a hand through his hair. As second in command, his main job was to deal with rogues and rule-breakers. Lucky for him, Luke kept the pack under tight control. Rules were rarely broken.

Luke opened the laptop on the desk. "How's it feel being on the other side of the interrogation?"

"If you'd have told me ten years ago I'd be your second, I'd have laughed in your face."

The alpha chuckled as he punched the keyboard with his index fingers. "You've grown up a lot since we were kids. So have I."

"Yeah, but you knew you'd be alpha from day one. Responsibility's in your blood."

"It's in yours too. Just took you longer to figure it out." He hit the enter key and closed the computer.

"I suppose." Responsibility occupied ninety-nine percent of his time lately, but surprisingly, he didn't mind.

Luke's phone chimed, and he pulled it from his pocket. "Oh, shit." He scrubbed a hand down his face. "I forgot about that. Come on, I need a beer." He paced out of the office before Chase had a chance to ask what was up.

He followed him up the short flight of stone steps into the bar, where Luke's sister stood behind the counter, polishing a beer mug. Amber wore the standard O'Malley's uniform—jeans and a black button-up—and she'd swept her light-brown hair into a high ponytail.

"It's about time you got here." She set down the glass and picked up a stack of notebooks. "I have to get the stock orders done. Just because you have rank now, it doesn't mean you get to make your own schedule. I own this bar." She winked. "I run the show."

Chase glanced at the clock. "I'm ten minutes early."

She lifted a section of counter top and sashayed toward him, a playful grin lighting on her lips. "Good." She glanced at Luke. "Keep him in line. I'm sensing change in his future."

Chase narrowed his eyes. "What kind of change?"

She shrugged. "Don't know yet. The feeling's building." She dropped into a chair at a table and opened the books, ending the conversation.

Luke settled onto a stool, and Chase slipped behind the counter and poured a tall glass of Blue Moon beer, sliding it to his friend. "Your sister's gift isn't very useful."

"She has her moments. Empathic premonitions are never exact."

He shook his head. She had helped a bit with the recent demon infestation, but change in his future? No, thank you. He liked his life the way it was. "What's going on?"

Luke took a swig and gripped the glass on the counter. "Damn cake tasting."

He cocked an eyebrow. "Cake?"

"For the wedding. Macey's dragging me to the bakery to taste the damn cakes for the reception. Like I give a shit if she chooses almond or butter cream. Cake is cake."

He laughed. "Better you than me."

The alpha narrowed his eyes. "It'll happen to you one day, my friend, and I plan to enjoy watching you squirm when it does."

Chase huffed. "You had to mate. I don't." And until recently, he didn't plan to. Ever. He had enough responsibility in his life without having to answer to a mate too.

"When you meet the right woman, you'll want to."

He crossed his arms. "I've met plenty of women. I don't want to."

Luke chuckled and downed the rest of his beer as his mate walked through the door. His entire demeanor shifted, and he shot to his feet and then sauntered toward her. Macey's smile reached all the way to her emerald eyes as she gazed up at Luke and wrapped her arms around his waist.

"Hi, beautiful. How's your day been so far?" Luke ran a hand over her head and tugged at the tight bun she wore at the nape of her neck.

Chase looked away from their affectionate display. Since Luke and Macey had gotten together, Luke had been the happiest he'd ever seen him. Apparently, love did that to a guy; not that Chase would know. But he'd reached the age where his mating instincts were kicking in hard. He wouldn't mind waking up in a beautiful woman's arms every morning, but he damn well wouldn't admit it to the alpha. It was hard enough admitting it to himself.

"Good." Macey pulled from Luke's embrace. "Hi, Chase."

"Afternoon, ma'am."

"How did it go with Bryce?"

"Oh, fine. A heads-up would've been nice. I didn't know I'd have to put on a show."

She turned to her mate, her eyes widening. "You didn't tell him I wasn't going to be there?"

"It may have slipped my mind." Luke chuckled. "Sorry about that, man."

Slipped his mind, my ass. He probably forgot on purpose to keep him on his toes. It wouldn't be the first time. "No problem."

Macey kissed Luke on the cheek. "Bryce is in the car waiting for me. I got called to a scene."

"So, no cake tasting?" Luke's voice sounded way too hopeful.

"I need you to go without me."

The alpha's mouth hung open, and Chase stifled a laugh.

Luke shook his head. "Reschedule it. I'm not going to pick a cake without you."

"I've already rescheduled on her three times." Macey walked her fingers up his chest. "You can do it, baby. I trust your taste." She kissed him on the cheek and headed for the exit. "Roberta says Spellbound Sweets is amazing. Just make sure nothing tastes gross." She waved goodbye and disappeared through the doorway.

Luke spun around, a look of terror freezing his features.

Amber shook her head. "Don't look at me. I've got a shipment coming in half an hour, and I have to finish balancing the books." She glanced at Chase, a sly smile curving her lips. "But I can man the bar if you want to take your second."

"Oh, hell no." Chase crossed his arms. "I'm not going to a witch's bakery. I'd rather go back to the morgue."

Luke raised his chin. "If another mummified body shows up, you will. Right now, you're tasting cake. Let's go."

Rain took a deep breath to calm her racing pulse as she arranged the cake samples on the platter. After they'd rescheduled the tasting so many times, she'd begun to worry this appointment would never happen. Snow had fielded all the calls from the alpha's mate, and they both stared at the phone, expecting it to ring any second with another cancellation.

"I think they're going to show this time." Snow drummed her lilac nails on the counter.

"Goddess, I hope so. I either get this deposit or I'll be sleeping on the streets." She eyed her sister. "Please be on your best behavior."

Snow pressed a hand against her chest, feigning shock. "Me? You think I'm going to screw this up?"

"Don't even pretend like you've cast a spell. And watch your temper. This is an alpha we're dealing with."

Snow smirked. "The hot temper runs in the family, love. I could say the same to you."

Rain huffed. Her sister had a point. Her temper had been what got her into this mess to begin with. "We've been here six months and haven't had any trouble with the werewolves. I don't want to start now."

Snow furrowed her brow. "What makes you think we're going to have trouble?"

"The Miami alpha's daughter went to culinary school with me, and we talked. Alphas are rough, no bull-shit men." She set the tray of samples in the fridge. "I guess they have to be in order to run a whole pack of were-wolves. I hear their mates aren't any nicer." While she'd never met the New Orleans alpha, she couldn't imagine him being much different.

Snow blew her bangs off her forehead with a huff. "Jeez. They sound like the clients from hell."

"Yeah. But if we get this job, we'll be in. You said yourself how loyal werewolves are. Once the alpha accepts us, the whole pack will. I might be able to keep this place afloat after all." She dusted the powdered sugar from her pants. "At least I'll have a place to sleep for another month or two."

Snow rolled her eyes. "You'll sleep at my place before you'll be on the streets. I'll take my chances with the curse."

Rain pressed her lips together and peered at her sister. Snow would knock her out with a sleeping spell and drag her to her house before she'd let her end up homeless. And she could imagine the wrath her curse would bring down on her sister if she did. "That will never happen." She couldn't let it.

The front door chimed before Snow could argue, and a hummingbird took flight inside Rain's ribcage. She could do this. Be nice. Don't piss off the werewolves. Hope they like the cake. She took a deep breath, plastered a smile on her face, and sashayed into the storefront.

The alpha stepped through the door first, his deep-orange aura screaming power like nothing she'd seen before. He stood nearly six-foot-four and had light-brown hair and bright blue eyes.

He stepped aside for the next werewolf to enter, and Rain's breath caught in her throat. Another male, a few inches shorter than the alpha, shuffled into the store and shoved his hands into his pockets. His shiny, dark-brown hair was cut short on the sides, long enough on top to cascade to one side and curl down to his eyebrow where it accented a circular, silver piercing in his skin. He had a full, dark beard, and a series of intricate tattoos covered both his muscular arms, disappearing into the sleeves of his black shirt.

His deep-orange aura wasn't as strong as the alpha's, but he radiated sex and power. The man was scrumptious.

His hazel eyes brightened as he caught her gaze, and one corner of his mouth tugged into a cocky grin.

Crap. He'd caught her staring.

Straightening her spine, she stepped toward the men. "Hi, welcome to Spellbound Sweets." She glanced to the door, expecting a female to enter, but the men appeared to be alone. Pausing, she cocked her head. The taller man was obviously the alpha, so did that make the sexy one his mate? Was that even allowed?

She cut her gaze between the two men, stretching the silence into awkwardness. Snow had never mentioned the mate she'd spoken to on the phone was male. Everything Rain knew about werewolves she'd learned from her friend in culinary school. Alphas had to be blood relatives of the first family, and they were required to keep the bloodline flowing. How could he continue the family legacy if his mate was...? She held back a sigh. All the hot ones were either gay or married, and this one was about to be both. Not that a cursed witch could afford to take a chance on any man, but still...

The alpha cleared his throat. "I'm Luke. This is Chase. We're here for a cake tasting."

Luke, that's right. Snow had written down their names, but Chase didn't ring a bell. She shook Luke's hand, and a jolt of magical energy shimmied up her arm. "I'm Rain. This is my sister, Snow. Thanks for coming."

Snow shook both their hands, and as Rain reached for Chase, a similar electric sensation danced from his skin, but it sent an extra jolt straight to her chest. He tightened his grip and furrowed his brow. "I thought this was a witch's bakery."

She pulled from his grasp. "It is. My sister is the witch. I'm the owner."

He narrowed his eyes. "That doesn't make sense."

"Snow? Do you want to bring out the samples?" She motioned to the table she'd set up with forks and water glasses. "Please, have a seat."

If they found out about her curse, they'd tuck tail and haul ass out of there before the sugar ever touched their lips. She'd have to do everything she could to steer the conversation away from the reason they didn't feel any magical energy emanating from her skin.

They settled into the chairs, and an amused grin lit on Luke's face. He looked at Chase. "This isn't so bad, is it?"

Chase's gaze slid over her body, feeling way more intimate than it should have. He was gay for goodness sake, and about to marry the alpha. But when he looked into her eyes, she couldn't stop her tongue from slipping out to moisten her lips.

Where the hell was Snow?

She needed to say something. Anything to break the awkwardness of his enticing gaze. If the alpha thought she was coming on to his future husband, she'd be toast. The first thought that crossed her mind tumbled from her lips before she could stop it. "I thought alphas had to ensure the continuation of the bloodline. How will you do that taking another male as your mate?"

A look of bewilderment flashed in Chase's eyes. "Your job is to make the cake. Pack business isn't your concern."

Luke crossed his arms. "I didn't realize you were *that* kind of bakery."

"I'm not." Oh, goddess, what had she done? If she had a shovel she'd dig a hole and bury herself for the rest of eternity. She mumbled a little prayer to the Earth Mother, asking for the ground to swallow her whole, which of course went unanswered.

She stepped to a display cabinet and took two cake toppers from a shelf, holding them up so the men could see. "I've done same-sex weddings before. You can marry a goat for all I care, as long as the goat consents."

The corner of Chase's mouth twitched. "A goat?" He crossed his arms, and Rain couldn't stop her gaze from sweeping over his muscular biceps.

Sweat slickened her palms, and she returned the cake toppers to the display. Why was she letting herself get so flustered? Sure, they were both powerful werewolves, but she'd been a powerful witch before the curse. She needed to pull herself together. Hold her ground.

Crossing her arms to mirror their posture, she shifted her weight to one foot. "You're half-animal yourself." She shrugged and returned to the table. "Pack business isn't my concern."

"Oh, Rain." Snow stopped in her tracks, gripping the cake tray in her hands.

Luke pressed his lips into a hard line.

Dear goddess, please don't let them shift in my store.

Fantastic. She'd pissed off the werewolves—exactly what she'd warned her sister not to do. Why couldn't she learn to think before she spoke?

She looked at Luke. If she could make peace with the alpha, maybe she could salvage the situation. "I'm sorry. My comment was out of line. I really take no issue in who you choose as your mate."

The alpha's eyes sparkled as his mouth split into a grin and he laughed. "Chase isn't my mate; he's my second."

She ducked her head. "Your second…mate?"

"Second in command." Chase leaned his forearms on the table. "Do I look gay to you?"

"Yes." *Damn it!* "I mean…you're hot, so…" *Jeez!* She

covered her mouth with her hands before she could say anything else stupid.

"You'll have to excuse my sister." Snow dropped the tray onto the table, clanking the forks and shaking the water glasses. "She has no filter between her brain and her mouth."

Rain sank into her chair, afraid to make eye contact with the werewolves. Afraid if she opened her mouth again something even stupider would slip from between her lips and ruin her chance of getting this wedding...if she hadn't ruined it already.

Luke laughed again, and the corners of his eyes crinkled as he smiled. "No harm done; I'm sure it was an honest mistake." He winked at Rain and the tension in her muscles loosened. "My mate is Macey. She had to work and didn't want to cancel on you again, so Chase is here to help me pick the cake. His palette is a little more refined than mine. Right, buddy?" Luke clapped him on the shoulder, and Chase let out his breath in what could've either been a chuckle or a huff. It was hard to tell.

She caught Chase's gaze, and his hazel eyes held hers. Light greenish-gold with little golden flecks dancing around the pupils, they drew her in, pulling the breath from her lungs. She tried to look away, but her eyes ignored the command from her brain.

As his lips curved into that cocky smile, Snow cleared her voice. "Tell them about the cakes, hon, before they dry up."

Rain blinked, coming back to herself. Maybe the werewolves' power wasn't what had her flustered. Maybe it was the man. "Right, the first one is a vanilla-almond cake with classic buttercream frosting. It's the most popular for weddings because of its light flavor and moist texture." She needed to pull herself together. An attractive man shouldn't have made her this flustered. She'd never gotten this goo-goo eyed over one before. Not without the help of a spell.

Snow placed a sample of the cake in front of each man. Luke popped the whole piece into his mouth and grinned. He sure smiled a lot for a hard-ass alpha. "Tastes great to me. Chase?"

Chase used a fork to slice off a small bite and mushed it around in his mouth. He looked thoughtful for a moment before training his gaze on Rain. His piercing glinted as his eyebrow arched. "Too much nutmeg. What else you got?"

She straightened. Too much nutmeg? Was he insane? The nutmeg was what *made* this cake. How dare he insult her most delectable dessert? "There's only a pinch of nutmeg to enhance the almond and offset the sweetness of the vanilla."

Chase shrugged. "Whoever pinched it has a heavy hand then."

Heat flashed through her veins, her family's signature hot temper flaring to life. She'd won more awards with that recipe than she could count. No one ever picked up on the nutmeg. She couldn't help but glare at the man. He may have been as sexy as sugar was sweet, but his taste buds worked about as well as a busted kitchen scale.

Snow rested a hand on her shoulder. "Let's try the next one."

Rain let out a slow breath as her sister served the men the next slice. "This one is Italian cream cake with a cream cheese frosting. It has a stronger flavor and a denser texture, but it's also popular for weddings."

"This one's great too," Luke said with the food in his mouth.

Chase shook his head. "Way too dense. Shouldn't have to chew it this much."

Rain bit her tongue to stop from spouting off. She served them two more rounds of cake—raspberry-almond and lemon cream—and both men had their usual reactions. The alpha loved them all, but Chase found something negative to say every time.

Rain curled her hands into fists under the table. He was messing with her, getting her back for the goat comment. He had to be. Her lemon cream was divine, and he did *not* nearly choke on too much zest...because she didn't put any zest into the damn cake. "Are you this critical of everything you eat?"

Chase cracked his knuckles. "I know good cake when I taste it, and this isn't it."

"If you're upset because I questioned your sexuality, that says more about you than it does me." Clamping her mouth shut, she tried to keep her expression neutral. She should have clamped it shut before the insult tumbled out, but like Snow said, she had no filter. Words seemed to shoot from her thoughts to her lips, completely bypassing the rational part of her brain.

Luke made a strange sound in his throat that could've been a laugh or a choke. Chase leaned back in his chair. "You don't know a thing about me."

She arched an eyebrow. "And I don't care to." Unless it involved examining all those tattoos more closely...with her tongue. *Stop it, Rain.* What was she thinking?

The alpha rose to his feet. "Thank you for letting us sample your cakes. I'll talk to Macey, and we'll be in touch." He slapped Chase on the shoulder and shuffled to the door.

"Rain..." Snow whispered in her ear. "Stop them."

What was the point? The alpha wouldn't hire her for his wedding after that debacle.

Rain narrowed her gaze as Chase stood and gave her a curt nod. "Have a nice day, Rain. It was nice to meet you, Snow." He turned, and she caught a nice view of his backside as he sauntered out the door.

What the hell was her problem? He'd insulted her baking...several times...but all she could think about was what he looked like under those clothes and how much of him was covered in tattoos.

CHAPTER THREE

CHASE KEPT HIS GAZE TRAINED ON THE SIDEWALK AS they exited the bakery, fighting the urge to turn and catch a glimpse of the insolent witch.

"You want to tell me what that was all about?" Luke stared straight ahead, giving him ample time to formulate an excuse for turning a simple cake tasting into a fiasco.

He nodded and paced through the intersection, out of earshot and any magical enchantments the witches may have put on the bakery. He wouldn't have put it past them to cast a hunger spell on the sidewalk outside the shop to entice people to go inside and buy one of those mouth-watering cakes. Every damn one of them had melted on his tongue like an orgasm for his taste buds.

Stopping on the sidewalk, he glanced at the shop. "She's hiding something."

"Who? The owner?"

"Rain." Her name tasted as good on his lips as that lemon cake. Sweet and creamy and slightly tart.

Luke followed his gaze toward the yellow building. "Everyone's hiding something. Either tell me why you acted like an asshole, or I'm going back in there and picking the damn cake myself."

"She's hiding her magic. Didn't you notice when you shook her hand? Her sister's magic felt like a deep vibration. Strong. When I touched Rain, I didn't feel anything." Correction: he didn't feel any magic. When her delicate fingers wrapped around his hand, he'd felt plenty of other things. And damn him for feeling them for a witch.

Luke shrugged. "So? Maybe one of their parents was a human, and her sister got all the magic. I didn't sense any need to be on alert, and that bakery comes highly recommended."

"Recommended by another witch."

"Macey trusts Roberta, and so do I." He inclined his chin. "The owner is pretty, isn't she?"

He clenched his jaw. "Gorgeous." Could his nerves be on edge because of the way his body had reacted to the woman? Maybe the years of self-imposed celibacy were catching up to him. He shook his head. "She's a witch. She can't be trusted."

"I understand your aversion to witches, but they're not all bad." Luke shifted his weight to one foot. "Neither was the cake, was it?"

"Best damn cake I've ever tasted." Possibly the most beautiful woman he'd ever seen. And the way her temper flared and she bit back when he'd baited her...he could almost see the storm brewing in her dark-gray eyes.

Luke crossed his arms. "So you acted like an asshole because you're attracted to a witch who doesn't have any magic?"

"I was protecting the pack." And maybe his heart, but Luke didn't need to know that.

The alpha chuckled. "I see. Well, since you're so

concerned about my mate's choice in bakeries for our wedding, you've earned yourself a new job."

"What's that?" Wariness stretched out his words. Whenever Luke got that look in his eyes, it usually meant trouble.

"You're in charge of all things cake."

A brick settled in the pit of his stomach. He'd been trying to avoid ever having to see the beautiful woman again, not end up as the cake liaison for the alpha's wedding.

"You're going to haul your ass back to the bakery, apologize for being a dick, and sign the contract so I can make my mate happy, understood?"

He met Luke's eyes briefly before shifting his gaze downward. "Yeah." What the hell kind of mess had he gotten himself into?

"And, since you're so concerned about her lack of magic, you're going to do a thorough investigation into her and her background."

He ground his teeth. "Damn it, Luke."

His friend laughed. "You're on witch duty until the wedding is done. Hopefully, by then, you'll get over your prejudice."

Second in command of the sixth largest werewolf pack in the United States, and he'd landed himself on witch and wedding cake duty. *Fantastic.* He grumbled under his breath as they walked away from the bakery.

Luke nodded to the left and crossed the street. "C'mon. We've got another appointment before you head back to apologize."

They rounded a corner to find a couple in the alley in the middle of what appeared to be a heated argument. The woman clutched her purse to her stomach, gripping the strap so tightly her knuckles turned white. The misaligned buttons on her waitress shirt indicated she'd gotten dressed in a hurry, probably trying to get away from the asshole pursuing her.

The guy's blond hair was slicked back from his face, his suit an Armani knock-off, his Rolex fake. He had a cocky grin and predatory eyes, and as he grabbed the woman's elbow, she jerked away. "Come on, baby. How many times do I have to tell you I'm sorry? She didn't mean anything."

The smooth insincerity of his voice raised Chase's hackles. He'd known plenty of assholes like this. Hell, he'd almost turned into one himself.

"We're through, Alan. Leave me alone." The woman turned to walk away, but Alan grabbed her bicep, spinning her to face him.

Chase strode into the ally and stood next to the woman, careful not to touch her—she'd been manhandled enough today—but close enough that Alan could feel the power in his aura. "Is this guy bothering you, ma'am?"

She glanced at Chase, her posture straightening. "He's leaving, aren't you, Alan?"

Alan flicked his gaze from the woman to Chase, and back to the woman again. The muscles in his neck worked as he swallowed whatever snide remark he was about to make and released his grip on her arm. "Yeah. I'm going." Maybe he wasn't as stupid as Chase thought. "See you around, Jamie."

Jamie inhaled a shaky breath and smoothed her crumpled shirt down her stomach. Her fingers trembled over the misaligned buttons for a moment before she fisted her hands and turned to Chase. "Thank you."

"Any time. Need me to walk you to work?"

She tugged on her blonde ponytail. "I'm already

there." Nodding to a doorway a few feet away, she adjusted her purse strap.

"If you don't feel safe heading home after your shift, ask someone to escort you."

"It's fine. He won't try anything." She shuffled toward the door. "Thanks again." She cast a pained glance at Alan's back before disappearing into the building.

"You done playing Captain America?" Luke jerked his head, motioning for Chase to follow.

"Not quite." He intended to make sure the asshole never bothered Jamie again. "Hey, Alan."

"What do you want now?" As the man turned, Chase caught a glimpse of the tattoo on the side of his neck—a fleur-de-lis designed from a trinity knot. A coven crest.

Goddamn witch. His hands balled into fists as he barreled toward Alan. Grabbing him by his fake-Armani lapels, Chase twisted the material in his hands and slammed him against the wall.

Alan's eyes widened as his head made contact with the brick. "What the hell, man?"

"Chase." Luke growled a warning.

"He's a witch," he said through clenched teeth, never taking his eyes off the asshole. "Leave the woman alone."

Alan glanced at Luke, and a look of recognition flashed in his eyes. He lifted his arms, trying to shake Chase off, but Chase pressed him harder into the wall. "All I did was sleep with her friend. Aren't werewolves supposed to fight real monsters?"

"What do you think I'm doing?" He tightened his grip.

Luke moved toward him, but Chase didn't let up.

"You'll use her until she stops giving you what you want, and then you'll leave her. Or worse. I know your kind." Heat rolled through his body, his beast feeding off the emotions as memories flooded his brain.

Alan scoffed. "Sounds like you're speaking from experience."

Chase sucked in a breath to respond, but Luke's hand landed squarely on his shoulder, a silent order to end it. He pried loose his fists and released his hold on the man, taking a step back to surrender control to the alpha.

Luke straightened to his full height and looked down at the witch. "Actions always have consequences. Tread carefully."

"Yeah." Alan dusted off his jacket and narrowed his eyes at Chase before strutting out of the alley.

"This is exactly what I'm talking about," Chase grumbled. "Witches can't be trusted. None of them."

Luke crossed his arms. "This ends now."

"I just wanted to scare him. I know how it's going to end. He'll move on to the next woman, and Jamie will be left with the consequences." He glanced at the door the woman had disappeared through.

"They're not your concern." Luke uncrossed his arms, his eyes softening. "She's not your sister."

He let out a slow breath, the anger cooling to a mild burn. "I know. I got carried away. Sorry."

Luke nodded for him to follow him out of the alley. "You need to get over your aversion to witches."

"That won't happen any time soon." After everything he'd been through, it was ingrained in his soul.

"Then you're going to have to fake it." Luke hung a left on Ursulines and headed toward Rampart. "We need to pay a visit to the coven priestess."

Chase stopped short. "More witches?"

"We have to find out if the mummy is a one-off thing or if we should be expecting more victims."

Chase grumbled under his breath, but he followed the alpha to the coven house on the outskirts of the Quarter. Built in the 1800s, the three-story brick building once housed one of the most influential families of the nineteenth century. The wrought-iron galleries adorning the second and third floors overflowed with ferns and ivies and every other kind of plant imaginable. What was it about witches and nature? They could grow sunflowers in a frozen tundra if they had the mind to. Chase could barely keep the aloe vera plant Bekah brought home alive.

Luke knocked three times on the door, and Chase flanked him, standing a step behind his right shoulder. The sound of boots thudding on the hardwood floor seeped from inside, and Chase tensed. Witches and werewolves weren't mortal enemies. They had quite a bit in common if he paused to consider it. Magic in their blood, a shared affinity for the moon. Hell, some witches could even shape-shift.

But they were too powerful. With their spells, controlling the elements, the ability to bend people's will to do their dirty work for them... A chill crept up his spine.

"Relax," Luke muttered over his shoulder as the lock disengaged and the door swung open.

Like hell he would. His disdain for witches was purely personal, and he'd be damned if he'd ever let his guard down around one again. He'd learned his lesson. Twice.

"Can I help you?" A look of recognition flashed in the man's blue eyes before he cut his gaze to the left.

Getting a visit from the alpha werewolf would be enough to make any supernatural being nervous. Chase crossed his arms and widened his stance, adding to the intimidation effect.

"Is Calista here?" Luke asked.

The man swallowed. "Do you have an appointment?" His voice was thin, like it was a standard question he had to ask, but he knew what the answer would be.

Luke inclined his head. "Do I *need* an appointment?"

"No." He opened the door wider, motioning for them to enter. "Come in."

Chase's boots thudded on the floor as he stepped into the foyer, quieting as he reached a plush, green runner. A crystal chandelier hung in the entryway, casting golden light on the cream-colored walls. To the right lay a great room with a raised ceiling and polished wood floor. In the old days, the space would have been used for entertaining and could double as both a dancefloor and a massive dining room, depending on the occasion. Now, it housed some kind of altar, and the overpowering scent of incense made his nose burn.

"Have a seat in here." The man waved a hand toward a sitting room to the left. "I'll let Calista know you're here."

Chase shuffled into the sitting room behind Luke and lowered himself into a straight-back chair. Oil paintings adorned the dark-wood walls, and a baby grand piano occupied the corner of the room. The extravagant coven headquarters was a far cry from the squat Irish bar the pack called home base. With its low ceilings and bare brick walls, O'Malley's Pub would have these witches curling their lips in disdain.

What would Rain think of the bar? Or his tiny shotgun-style house for that matter? With her polished look, shiny hair, and perfect complexion, she probably came from money. Hell, she owned her own business. She wouldn't give a second glance to a rough-around-the-edges werewolf bartender.

He scrunched his brow. Why the hell was his imagination treading down *that* path? He shouldn't have given a second thought to a witch who was hiding her magic, but damn it, if he wasn't on the fourth or fifth.

Luke leaned forward, resting his elbows on his knees. "You okay?"

Chase blinked, banishing the image of the feisty witch from his mind. "Yeah. This place gives me the willies."

"Maybe someone's trying to cast a spell on you. Make you fall in love with a witch."

The sensation of a thousand ants skittering across his back made him shiver. "Don't even joke like that."

"Spells affecting free will are forbidden." A tall woman with long, dark hair and four-inch heels clicked into the sitting room. "Surely, you're aware of that, Mr. Mason."

Luke rose to his feet. "So is murder, but there's a dead witch at the morgue. Not everyone follows the rules."

Her eyes widened in shock for a split second before she composed herself. She opened her mouth to speak, but she hesitated as a pair of witches in Harrah's uniforms sashayed to the door. "Bye, Calista," the blonde called from the foyer. "See you tomorrow."

Calista waved over her shoulder and turned to the werewolves. "Let's have this meeting in my office." She motioned for them to follow her down a hallway and through a set of oak double doors.

A heavy wooden desk sat in front of a large window overlooking the courtyard, and the witch slinked behind it to lower herself into a tan leather chair. "How do you know it's a witch in the morgue?"

Luke sat in a chair across from the desk. "Tell her what you saw."

Chase settled into the one next to him. "She had a tattoo under her collarbone. Trinity knot with a coven crest."

Calista folded her hands on the desk. "Which coven?"

He huffed. "How the hell should I know?"

"No one in my coven has been reported missing." She took a sheet of paper from a drawer and offered it to him. "Do you remember what it looked like? Can you draw it for me?"

"Sure." He snatched a pen from the holder on the corner of her desk and leaned forward to sketch the design. The pen made a scratching sound on the paper as the crest came into shape. A trinity knot situated in a crescent moon with a string of six stars connecting the ends to form a circle.

As he finished the drawing, an honest-to-God black cat jumped on the desk and hissed before slinking across the surface. *Typical.* He pushed the paper toward Calista and glanced around the room, almost certain he'd find a pointy hat and a broomstick hanging on the wall.

He didn't.

Calista shooed the cat off the desk with her hand and pressed her lips together as she gazed at the sketch. "This witch belonged to the Miami coven. Her death doesn't concern us. Or you."

Luke straightened his spine. "It does when the cause of death was supernatural."

The cat jumped into the witch's lap, and she stroked its back. "How did she die?"

Chase cringed as the image of the mummified corpse flashed in his mind. "Something sucked the life right out of her. Took her eye as souvenir. Any of your minions have that ability?"

Calista bristled. "That's a weighty accusation to make." She shifted her gaze to Luke. "You need to keep this one on a tighter leash."

"No one's making accusations." Luke flashed him a warning glare. "But if you have any information, we'd appreciate your cooperation. It's our job to protect the secrecy of supernatural beings."

She inhaled deeply, cutting her gaze from Luke to Chase and back again. "You're looking for an energy vampire, and no, I don't know anyone with that power."

Chase shook his head. "The veins contained powdered blood. If it were a vampire—"

"Not the blood-sucking kind." She set the cat on the floor. "An *energy* vampire. Someone who can drain the magic and the life force from another being. Witches can develop the power by practicing the black arts, but I can assure you none of my witches would dare. We are a peaceful, goddess-worshipping coven."

"Thank you for your time." Luke stood, and Chase followed his lead.

Calista walked ahead of them toward the exit, her heels clicking on the wood in a melodic rhythm. She opened the door. "If I can be of any more service…"

Luke stepped through the door, but Chase paused in the threshold. "Actually, you can."

"Oh?"

"What can you tell me about the witch who runs the bakery?"

A strange look flashed in her eyes. "I'm afraid I can't tell you anything. She doesn't belong to the coven."

He rubbed the back of his neck. "Why doesn't she belong?"

"I'm afraid I can't answer that either. Have a nice day, gentlemen." She all but slammed the door in Chase's face.

Rain was hiding her powers *and* she didn't belong to the coven. She didn't look like the type of woman who'd drain the life from someone, but he'd learned his lesson giving witches the benefit of the doubt. Something wasn't right in that bakery, and he planned to figure out exactly what it was.

Rain leaned her elbows on the table and held her face in her hands. "What am I going to do now? I'll never be able to pay the rent without the werewolf wedding."

Snow rubbed a hand across her back. "I'm sure it'll work itself out. You put so much kindness out into the world; it's going to come back around to you soon."

"Sure." Like that could happen. She hadn't acted the slightest bit kind toward Chase. "Something tells me I'm not through making up for the bad things I've done."

"Bad *thing*. Singular. We all make mistakes."

"I'll be paying for mine for the rest of my life." Pinching the bridge of her nose, she squeezed her eyes shut. Why couldn't she have kept her temper in check? The alpha seemed to love every bite of cake he tried. But Chase...

Snow folded her hands on the table. "You have to admit, those werewolves were kinda hot."

"They were not..." Her stomach fluttered. "Yeah, they kinda were."

"Especially the tattooed one. What was his name?"

"Chase." Why did her voice sound so breathy, the S stretching out into a hiss? And why did his name taste so good to say?

"That's right." Her sister gave her a strange look. "Dark hair, ink, smoldering eyes."

"Mm-hmm." His eyes did smolder, didn't they?

"Exactly your type of guy."

Rain sat up straight. "He is *not* my type. I don't have a type. Anyway...he insulted my baking skills."

"I don't think he meant it." Snow smirked.

"He meant it. He was out to get me from the moment he stepped into the bakery."

Snow rolled her eyes. "Think about it. He knows enough about baking to taste the nutmeg in your classic vanilla-almond. You have to admit that turns you on. At least a little bit."

She wanted to argue. To insist his sensitive palate didn't interest her in the slightest. But she couldn't. "Yeah, okay. You made your point, but it doesn't matter. There's no way I'll be doing the werewolf wedding after that fiasco."

"You never know." Snow shrugged. "Maybe the alpha will bring his mate back and let her choose. We're the only supernatural bakery in the Quarter, and they seem like busy people."

"Maybe." Probably not.

The door chimed as a DHL delivery man carried a small cardboard box into the shop. Rain's heart sprinted as he shuffled toward her. "Rain Connolly?"

"That's me." She plastered on a fake smile to hide her nerves.

"Sign here please." He handed her a tablet. "My stylus broke, so you'll have to use your finger."

She scribbled her name on the device and wiped her sweaty hands on her jeans. "Thank you." Now if he would leave the store so she could open the box.

He shuffled toward a display case and gazed at the bite-sized delicacies beneath the glass. Snow padded behind the counter and jerked her head at Rain, a silent order to snap out of it and try to sell the guy something.

"Are you hungry?" Rain stood and joined her sister behind the display. "We've got a variety of mini cakes and cookies you can snack on while you're making deliveries."

"Not really." He shoved his hands in his pockets.

Damn. It seemed she couldn't even make a dollar today.

"These are interesting, though. What do the symbols mean?" He nodded at Snow's contribution to the bakery —cookies with a magic spell for clarity baked into them.

Rain gazed at the treats. They all contained the same spell, but the intent of the person eating it always focused the outcome.

"Oh, you have a discerning eye." Snow laid on the charm thick. "We're a witch's bakery, you know? And you were drawn to our spellbinders. They're magical cookies that help you realize your dreams."

He chuckled. "Is that so?"

Snow waved her hand over the glass in a flourish. "Need help finding your dream job? This is the cookie for you." She pointed to a green-iced cookie with a dollar sign frosted on the top. "Not doing so hot in the love department? We've got what you need." She indicated the cookie with a red heart. "If you're having trouble making a decision, this one can help." She used a piece of tissue paper to take a cookie with a blue question mark from the tray and offered it to him. "Clarity in a cookie for the bargain price of two ninety-nine."

He laughed unconvincingly. "If I give that heart one to the girl I like, she'll fall in love with me?"

"Oh, no." Rain pressed a hand to her chest and feigned offense. "Spells that hinder free will are forbidden. But if *you* eat it, it will help you realize if she's really the one for you."

"Hmm…" He narrowed his eyes. "I'll take the question mark one."

Snow slipped the cookie into a white paper bag and took his money. "Have a nice day."

"You too." He looked at the bag and shook his head before shuffling outside.

As soon as the door fell shut, Snow raced across the room and locked it. "Open it!" She scrambled back to the counter and gripped Rain's arm. "It's the Bauhinia, isn't it?"

"I think so." Her heart pounded. With a trembling hand, she grabbed a knife from a cutting board. The cool, steel handle slipped from her grasp. Like an idiot, she tried to catch the utensil midair, and the sharp end bit into her finger before it clattered on the floor.

"Crap!" A bead of warm, red blood pooled on her fingertip, and she gazed at it, mesmerized by the dim, magenta glow. She couldn't really call it a glow. It was more like a shimmer, proving her magic resided there and she'd moved one step closer to unlocking it.

"Are you okay?" Snow wiped her finger with a paper towel and wrapped a bandage around it, bringing Rain back to the present.

"I will be soon."

Snow handed her the knife. "Don't drop it."

Rain smirked. "Thanks." Pressing the sharp tip against the tape, she sliced down the center of the package where the two halves of the lid met in the middle. The flaps sprang open, and she yanked out the wad of paper sitting on top. There, nestled in a bed of packing peanuts, lay the Bauhinia.

She gingerly lifted it from the box and examined the container. A glass jar held a single pink flower attached to a stem with six green leaves shaped like a cow's hooves. Medically, the herb could lower blood sugar and treat diabetes. Magically, it could be used to resist the effects of controlling magic, like love spells and, more importantly...binding spells.

Excitement made her stomach turn. Two weeks and three hundred dollars later, and she finally held in her hands the second to last ingredient to unbind her powers and break the curse. "Get the bowl."

"One step ahead of you." Snow set the copper container on the counter and gently pried off the lid. A gelatinous mixture of mango, long pepper, agarwood, and a slew of strange liquids coagulated in the bottom of the bowl. She held out her hand. "Pay me first."

"Right." She yanked a twenty out of the cash register and pressed it into her sister's hand.

Snow shoved the bill into her pocket. "You're lucky this spell was written specifically for you. I hear I could get ten grand for one of these on the black market."

"Sure. Get caught and you'll end up with your powers bound like mine. Trust me. It's not worth it. Nothing is." Rain peered at the concoction, careful not to touch it for fear of contamination, and handed her sister the Bauhinia. Snow dropped the new ingredient into the bowl and crushed it into the mixture with a cast-iron pestle.

Holding her breath, Rain waited, anticipating some spark of magic or glowing aura to form from the potion. Nothing happened.

Snow set the pestle on a towel. "Huh."

Rain's shoulders drooped as she leaned her hip against the counter and shook her head. Could this entire spell be someone's idea of a sick joke? It hadn't been *that* long since she'd had the ability to make potions, and every time a new ingredient joined the mix, its magical properties changed the components of the spell, altering the appearance. She might as well have been staring at cake batter for all it mattered because this potion was as mundane as vanilla frosting.

Snow returned the lid to the bowl. "I'm sure the last ingredient will activate it. Unbinding potions are super powerful, and since this one takes so long to make, it probably requires the final step for the magic to galvanize."

The heaviness in her shoulders lifted, and she straightened her spine. Her sister's hypothesis made sense. "Let's find out what the final ingredient is." She padded through the kitchen to her bedroom in the back of the store and pulled a wooden box from beneath her bed. Retrieving the key from the closet, she opened the lid and took out the spell. The thick parchment felt like hope in her hands, and she ran a finger over the list. It had taken her three months to gather all these ingredients. Hopefully the last one would prove less difficult.

Returning to the storefront, she laid the enchanted paper on the bowl and chewed her bottom lip as she waited for her final task to appear.

"I can't look." Snow turned her back to the counter and pressed her fingers to her temples. "Tell me what it says."

Rain peered at the paper. The magic shimmered, a silvery mist swirling on the parchment as the words appeared on the page. Her heart sank. "Oh, no."

"That's a good 'oh, no,' right? Like, 'Oh, no. That's so easy to find.' Right?" Snow turned around.

A sour, burning sensation crept up Rain's throat. "Easy to find. Impossible to obtain."

"Oh, goddess, what is it?"

Rain sucked in a sharp breath and blew it out hard. "Two drops of blood from a first-born werewolf, given willingly, beneath a blue moon."

"You're joking. You have to be." Snow snatched the paper from her hands, her mouth hanging open as she read it. "How the hell are we supposed to manage that? No supernatural being is going to willingly give her blood away. Especially a werewolf. That's where our magic resides."

"No kidding." Rain looked at the bandage on her finger. Blood magic was a risky practice. Too little and the spell might only partially work...if at all. Use too much, and the consequences could be dire. "It must be the transformation and healing abilities that are needed to complete the spell."

"Maybe we can make a substitution. Maybe if we mixed this with a healing potion..." Snow drummed her nails on the granite.

"That won't work. This spell was written by a witch on the council, and it's a one-time deal. If we screw it up, that's it. Even if we did it exactly right the second time, it wouldn't work. They made that very clear in the letter that came with it." She carried the paper to her bedroom.

"So that's it then?" Snow followed on her heels. "You're giving up?"

Rain locked the spell in the box and slid it under her bed. "What else can I do? I've already pissed off the alpha, so the Crescent City Pack is out of the question. I won't go back to Miami. It's useless." She plopped onto her bed and rubbed her forehead. "Why did they have to throw the *given willingly* clause in there?"

Snow crossed her arms. "They're not going to make it easy for you, but you can't give up."

It was hopeless. Werewolves considered their blood sacred, and it was highly illegal for them to get it anywhere near another person. First-born werewolves weren't even allowed to go to the hospital. "Tell me what to do then, oh wise sister, who's only a year and a half older than I am."

"I'll tell you what you're going to do." She leaned a shoulder against the doorway and crossed her legs at the ankles. "You're going to the alpha and apologizing. You didn't piss *him* off. It was his sexy second who had the problem with you, and he's not the one getting married. Take a box of samples. Ask him to give them to his mate and let her decide."

"What good will that do? Maybe I'll get to do the wedding, but it won't help me with the spell." She sat up straight. "But maybe I'll get the wedding. Then I can pay my bills." Maybe she'd never be rid of her curse, but at least she wouldn't be on the street. "That's a great idea, wise one. I'll stop by their headquarters tomorrow morning."

Snow arched an eyebrow, and the corner of her mouth tugged upward, almost as if it were connected by a string.

A knot of wariness formed in Rain's stomach. That look only meant one thing. "There's something more sinister lurking inside this plan, isn't there?"

"Not sinister." Snow pushed from the doorway and

settled on the edge of the bed. "I saw the way Chase looked at you. He wants you."

A fluttering sensation formed in her stomach before it sank to her knees. "I don't like where this is headed."

"You're attracted to him, right?"

"Who wouldn't be? The guy is like sex on a stick. But...even if I did apologize to him, you know what happened last time I fell in love. That's not something I care to go through again. Ever."

"First of all, you and I both know something *else* was going on last time...whether you can prove it or not." Snow grinned wickedly. "And anyway, who said anything about falling in love? Flirt with him. Earn his trust. I hear werewolves will do anything for their mates."

"I am *not* going to be his mate."

"Then be his friend. I may not be able to see magic like you, but I did see a spark between you two."

Rain chewed her bottom lip. She had to admit there'd been *something* between them. Was it a spark? It was hard to say. She had felt a bit of heat, which was more than she'd felt for any man in years. Then he went and insulted her cake. "I don't know..."

Her sister put a hand on her knee. "Everything happens for a reason. Chase coming into your life might be the end of your bad karma. Think of him as a gift from the universe. From fate."

"He does come in a nice package, doesn't he?" It wouldn't hurt to be nice to the man. Maybe they could be friends, but that was as far as she'd take it. She could enjoy his sex appeal from a safe distance, earn his trust, and when the time was right, she'd ask him for a small favor.

Yeah, right. Like that would work. No telling what

kind of punishment he'd endure from his pack if he granted her request.

"It doesn't hurt to try." Snow stood and glided to the door. "I'm going to unlock the shop in case we get any customers."

Rain returned the key to the closet and straightened her sheets. It was the craziest, stupidest plan her sister had ever come up with, but it was the only one she had.

CHAPTER FOUR

CHASE SHUFFLED UP ROYAL STREET TOWARD
Spellbound Sweets and glanced at the time on his phone.
Five-fifty-nine p.m. He'd caught a glimpse of the store
hours posted on the door when he'd been there that afternoon, and the shop was scheduled to close at six. With
any luck, the place would be empty when he got there.

He hadn't been avoiding talking to the witch. Not
really. After their meeting with the coven, he'd spent the
afternoon planning the bar menu for tomorrow and
making sure they had enough ingredients in stock for the
barbeque nachos he had planned. It wasn't his fault he
didn't finish until five-forty-five. Sure, he could've taken
care of the cake issue beforehand, but he'd dealt with
enough witches for one day. Hell, he'd dealt with enough
for the rest of his life.

Mumbling a prayer to whatever gods might be listening, he scrambled to find a way to approach the situation.
He had to apologize for being a dick, number one. Even if
the cake had tasted as bad as he'd pretended it did, he'd
been out of line.

But there was something about the way her temper had flared that caused something to burn inside of him. And when the clouds gathered in her eyes, he couldn't help but want to experience the storm.

She was sexy as hell, and that was the problem. There were too many mysteries surrounding her. Too many red flags in his mind. But it was his job to get to know her—thanks to Luke—and he always followed through on his orders, no matter how ridiculous and scheming they may have been.

At five after six, he tried the door. Warm metal greeted his palm as he gave the knob a twist. *Damn.* Unlocked. Rain's dark curls bobbed as she snapped her head up and pinned him with a heated gaze. The gray in her irises seemed to swirl, undulating like a whirlpool, making the rest of the world disappear. She wiped her hands on a towel and glided around the counter with the grace of a swan.

"Can I help you?" She caught her bottom lip between her teeth, and the strength in his knees wavered.

He gripped the door knob tighter, his own body heat —combined with the sun-warmed metal—making his palm sweat. "I see you're about to close. I'll come back tomorrow."

"Please don't go." She reached toward him then dropped her arms to her sides. "I want to apologize for the way I acted. It was unprofessional."

"No. I want to apologize." He let the door fall shut behind him. "That's why I'm here."

The corner of her mouth twitched. "You *want* to apologize? Or were you *told* to?"

"Both. I was out of line. I'm sorry."

Her pink lips curved into a smile, revealing a set of

perfectly straight, white teeth. He could imagine the way they'd feel nipping at his neck, gliding down his stomach to... *Whoa. Stop right there.* He cleared his throat and shoved his hands in his pockets.

"Apology accepted. I'd offer you a snack, but since my baking skills are apparently lacking..." She crossed her arms.

"Yeah, about that..." He stepped toward her. "Your cakes were amazing. Luke and Macey would like you for their wedding."

Her eyes widened briefly before she blinked away the surprise. "Why did you say they were terrible?"

"As second in command, it's my job to protect the pack. You being a witch made me wary. Then there was this." He took her hand and held it between both of his. Her lips parted as she sucked in a small breath, and then her eyes locked with his. What was it about her eyes?

He released her hand. "Why don't I feel your magic?"

She lifted her chin. "I don't have any magic."

"You have to. If your sister is a witch, that means at least one of your parents is. Magic is in your blood, but I don't feel it. Why is that?"

She lifted one shoulder as if to dismiss him and glided behind the safety of the counter. "I'm a dud, okay? Let it rest." She glared at him, daring him to press the issue.

He'd hit a sore spot. Maybe she was telling the truth. Some second-born weres didn't have special abilities, though he'd hardly call them duds. They had the magic in their veins, and they could continue the supernatural bloodline. He stepped toward the counter. "Is that why you aren't part of the coven? Because you don't have powers?"

"I'm not part of the coven, either." Snow's heels clicked

on the tile floor as she approached her sister and wrapped her arm around her shoulders. "There's no requirement to join." Rain gave her a harsh look, and she dropped her arm to her side. "Sorry. Not helping?"

"Not really."

"Here." Snow handed Rain a stack of papers. "The wedding contract. I'll be in the back if you need me." She cut her gaze between Rain and him. "It's good to see you again, Chase." She strutted to the back before he had time to respond.

Rain slammed the papers onto the counter and paced to a glass display case. Now he'd hit a nerve. Hard. Would the coven deny someone entry because she didn't have powers? Leave it to witches to turn against their own.

"I'm sorry if I upset you."

"I'm not upset. Anyway, my sister and I belong to our old coven." She yanked a tray of cookies from the case, and it fell from her hands, scattering the confections across the floor. "Crap." She dropped to her knees, disappearing behind the display.

"Let me help you with that." He rushed around the counter and joined her on the floor.

She snatched the cookie he reached for. "I don't need help. Thank you." Scrambling for the rest of the cookies, she tossed them on the tray.

He reached for one that had landed halfway beneath the cabinet, but she grabbed his wrist. Her fingers were soft and warm wrapped around his arm, and while he didn't detect a magical signature from her skin, another kind of electricity shot straight to his heart. Why was he drawn to this woman? Was it her secrets? The mystery and danger brewing in her eyes? Or was it something else entirely?

Keeping a firm grasp on his wrist, she used her left hand to snatch the cookie and toss it on the tray. "Please don't show me any kindness." She released her grip and rose to her feet before carrying the tray to a waste bin and dumping the crumbling cookies into the trash.

What an odd thing for her to say. He spotted a cookie she'd missed and picked it up, examining the blue-frosting question mark drawn on the top. "Does the five-second rule apply?" He flashed a grin, hoping to get a smile out of her, and held up the cookie.

"I wouldn't."

Damn. No smile.

She set the tray on the counter. "You're already wary of witches. Those were clarity cookies. Snow makes them with magic."

He tossed it in the trash and wiped his hands on his pants, hopefully wiping away the damn spell before his skin absorbed it. "You sell spells to humans? That's allowed?"

She rolled her eyes. "It's a simple clarity spell, and they know it when they buy it. All it does is help them see their goals more clearly. Yes, it's allowed."

"Does it work?" He sauntered toward her and leaned a hip against the counter.

"Depending on the person's intent, yes." She moved toward him. Her eyes held a curious look as she dropped her gaze to his mouth briefly before flicking it back to his eyes.

A strange magnetism danced between them. Was she as drawn to him as he was to her? She seemed to be. But she was a witch, and his sudden urge to take her in his arms and kiss those soft, pink lips blasted a warning alarm in his brain. He had a job to do, and getting involved with the person he was supposed to protect the pack from wasn't part of it.

Then again, with the dead witch in the morgue and Rain without powers, maybe she was the one who needed protecting. Possessiveness coiled in his core as if his body had already decided she was his to take care of without consulting his mind first. Where the hell had this unwelcome emotion come from, and how could he get rid of it?

She cleared her voice and stepped back. Damn it, he'd been staring at her. And she'd been staring right back at him.

"Are you a chef?" She blinked twice, and her composure returned, the moment they'd shared dissolving as if it had never happened.

"No. Why do you ask?"

"No one has ever noticed the nutmeg in my classic vanilla-almond. And your comment about the zest in my lemon cream...There was no zest in it, but you must be familiar with cooking to make such an accusation."

"I'm self-taught. I do the menus for the bar and cook for my sister and niece." A pang of guilt spread through his stomach, and he rubbed the back of his neck. "I am sorry I said those things. All of the samples were delicious. Luke liked the vanilla best, so they're going with that one."

Her lips curved into a smile, and his heart slammed against his ribs. Damn, she was beautiful.

She scribbled something on the stack of papers and handed them to him. "If you can ask your alpha to sign this and bring the deposit by tomorrow, I'll add them to my calendar."

Chase grabbed a pen from the counter and signed his own name, adding the number for the bar and his personal cell to the form. "I'm on cake duty, so my signature will work. I can bring the money tomorrow."

She took the papers. "I'll look forward to seeing you."

"Me too." He shoved his hands in his pockets. That was his cue to leave, but he couldn't make his legs carry him to the door. He wanted to know this woman, but damn it, he didn't trust her. In the forty-five minutes he'd spent with her, his mind and his dick had waged a war inside his body. "Do you want to go to dinner?" *Crap.* It looked like his dick won that battle.

She opened her mouth to respond, but her brow furrowed, the storm in her eyes brewing as if she fought her own battle. "I..." She clamped her mouth shut and chewed her bottom lip. "Thank you, but no."

Snow emerged from the back of the store and flashed her a strange look, but Rain shook her head.

This cue to leave he didn't miss. "Right. Well, be careful heading home. I love this city, but it's not the safest place in the world."

"Don't worry. I live right here." Rain opened her arms, indicating the bakery.

"I'll bring the deposit by tomorrow. Good evening, ladies." He shuffled out the door and rubbed his chest, trying to rub away the sting of rejection. What the hell was he thinking asking her to dinner?

He wasn't thinking, and that was the problem. Not with the head on his shoulders anyway. The clicking of heels on concrete grabbed his attention, and he turned around to find Snow prancing after him.

"Chase, wait." She stopped a few feet in front of him and glanced at the bakery. "Rain's in the back. She doesn't know I'm talking to you."

"Okay." Why did that matter?

"My sister is a really great girl."

"I don't doubt that."

"She's kind of a tough nut to crack, though. I know she turned down your offer for dinner, but if you keep trying, she'll come around."

He held her gaze, trying to figure out her motivation. Was she attempting to play match-maker for her sister, or did she have an ulterior motive? He never knew with witches. "Thanks for the advice."

"She eats lunch in Louis Armstrong Park near the statue when the weather is nice. Tomorrow's forecast is sunny and warm." She smiled and spun toward the bakery.

"Hey, Snow?"

She stopped and faced him.

"Rain said she still belongs to her old coven. Which one is that?"

"We're from Miami. We've only been here six months, so we need to make sure things are going to work out before we change. See you tomorrow." She wiggled her fingers and strutted away.

His mind reeled. Miami? Did they know what happened to the witch in the morgue? Could they have been involved?

The battle to think with the right head raged inside him. He wanted to know every inch of Rain's body and every thought in her mind. The primal instinct to protect her, to make her his, roared inside him. If he listened to his beast, he'd know she couldn't be involved.

Then again, his wolf thrived on emotion. His feelings about the sexy witch could be clouding his judgment. Lord knew he'd been wrong about witches before. He wouldn't make the mistake of trusting one again, no matter how deep these strange, new emotions ran.

First order of business: report the new info to the alpha. Contract or no, Luke might change his mind after he heard the news.

CHAPTER FIVE

Isaac Mercado huddled under a scratchy, green blanket in the back seat of a Greyhound bus headed for Louisiana. Everything felt scratchy against his paper-thin skin, but the thought of his torment ending soon was reason enough to endure it.

Every time the bus hit a bump in the road, jostling him in the seat, sharp pain shot through his joints, threatening to shatter his bones. He shifted to his left hip and leaned his forehead against the window. The coolness of the glass did nothing to tame the fever trying to consume his entire body, and a bruise formed within seconds of the hard surface pressing against his skin. He attempted a sigh as he leaned on the cushioned headrest, but it turned into a hacking, wet cough, his chest threatening to explode with each forced breath.

A woman in the seat across the aisle covered her nose with the neck of her shirt and turned her back to him.

He splayed his fingers against his legs and winced as the knuckles cracked into place. The blue color that previously occupied his fingertips had spread all the way to his wrists. His blood had turned against him, refusing to circulate properly through his veins.

His own magic used as a weapon to defeat him.

He rotated his wrists and wiggled his fingers, encouraging his cursed blood to flow again. A trip like this would require at least two weeks in the swamp to recover. Floating semi-submerged in the murky water eased the pain enough for him to focus his mind. The combination of mud and algae soothed his dry, cracked skin, and the remote location provided the privacy he needed to meditate for hours at a time.

The world thought him dead, and now that his true powers had been revealed, it needed to stay that way.

He closed his eyes and tried to ignore the prickling sensation in his legs. His feet had probably turned purple in the three hours since he'd boarded the bus in Florida. The pounding in his head was only matched by the pain of his predicament.

A witch of his magnitude reduced to meditating in a swamp, surviving on frogs and nutria for nourishment? Well, it was his own fault for tangling with a witch whose power matched—possibly exceeded—his own.

He'd be head of the council by now if his plan had worked, sitting comfortably in a mansion in the mountains. His tulpas—shadow-like entities he created with his mind—serving him, the entire witch community worshipping him.

But *she* had to screw it all up.

His revenge would be well worth the wait. If seven years of living alone in the swamp had taught him anything, it was patience. Two weeks of recovery would be plenty of time to get his body into shape enough to find and drain another witch. He could spend the days focusing on his tulpa, recharging the entity, increasing its power so it could walk the streets of New Orleans and execute his plan.

The witch he'd drained last week had been magnificent. Her life force had been strong like her magic, her gift of sight giving him the temporary ability to finally locate the one responsible for his demise. Too bad he'd burned through all her energy finding the bitch and sending his tulpa to New Orleans to dump the body. Hopefully, by now, his enemy was scared shitless, watching her back and jumping at every shadow. If she wasn't yet, she would be soon.

And then he'd make her suffer.

Slipping his hand into his pocket, he pulled out a small glass jar. The witch's eye sloshed in the liquid as he turned the container and peered at the bright-blue iris. The orb contained enough magic for him to find his target once he arrived in the city.

A small child squealed from the seat in front of him, the shrill pitch of his young voice cutting through Isaac's ears like shards of glass. The boy reached his tiny hand around the seat, grasping the back as he squished his tear-streaked face between the seatback and the window. His eyes widened as he looked at Isaac, his mouth falling open, his body freezing in shock.

Isaac reached for the boy's hand, gripping the soft, life-filled skin in his frigid grasp. Warm energy flowed into Isaac's hand, restoring the tawny color to his skin as it cascaded up his arm to fill his chest. He inhaled the first deep breath he'd been able to take since he drained the witch and closed his eyes for a long blink to revel in the healing sensation.

The boy fell slack, leaning against the window before

collapsing into his mother's lap. Isaac released his hand and stretched his arms over his head. What was it about young life that felt so damn good? He attempted a smile, but the shriveled skin of his upper lip split, and the coppery taste of his traitor blood oozed into his mouth. He hadn't drained nearly enough energy from the kid to make smiling worth it. Any more, though, and he'd have killed him. Now the boy would sleep for the rest of the trip and wake up with a vague memory of the monster in the seat behind him. He'd done the kid's mother a favor.

CHAPTER SIX

RAIN GLIDED UNDER THE ARCHWAY AT THE ENTRANCE to Louis Armstrong park and passed the life-size bronze marching band statues on her way to her favorite bench. Settling onto the seat, she gazed out over the man-made lake, admiring the fountain flowing in the center of the water. The sound of the spray and the splash of the drops as they hit the surface caused a familiar ache inside her chest. As much as the sound brought comfort to her ears, it also reminded her of how much she'd lost.

A couple strolled along the brick path, pausing on the footbridge to steal a kiss before continuing on their way, and a woman spread a blanket beneath a massive oak while three small children played tag on the lawn behind her.

The early autumn sun warmed Rain's skin, and she closed her eyes for a moment, basking in the peaceful serenity of the scene. She smiled as she unwrapped her sandwich and took a bite. Not only had she won the were-wolf wedding, but the pack's sexy second-in-command had been tasked to handle the cake.

Her knee bounced in anticipation at the thought of seeing Chase again. Him asking her to dinner had come as such a shock that she hadn't been able to form a proper sentence. Her first instinct had been to say yes. To go to dinner with him and hope he intended to have *her* for dessert. Thankfully, her brain had taken over before her mouth could react, and she'd said no. With her luck, he'd only asked her because he was suspicious about her lack of magic.

In fact, the more she thought about it, the more that seemed to be the case. He'd probably been assigned to watch her. To make sure she didn't pose a threat to the pack. The flitting elation at seeing him again that she'd felt a moment ago fizzled out like a can of soda left open overnight. Either she'd imagined the smoldering way he'd looked at her yesterday or he'd been faking the attraction.

Either way, it didn't matter. Her curse made getting close to people impossible. She wouldn't risk hurting anyone else. And with what happened the last time she fell for a man—whether she'd fallen on her own or had been pushed—getting anywhere near love was out of the question.

She'd go along with whatever charade he had planned. Build a friendship like Snow suggested. With the blue moon a few weeks away, she didn't have much time to earn his trust.

She sighed and took another bite of her sandwich. The cool cucumbers crunched between her teeth as she watched the colorful auras of the people in the park. Even humans had life energy that created a muted tone surrounding their bodies. Usually pale blue or green, it didn't sparkle with magic like that of a witch or werewolf.

Across the pond, stretched out on a blanket, a woman

with a deep-orange werewolf aura lay next to a human. The man glided his fingers up her bare arm before leaning in and kissing her. Did the man know he was dating a supernatural creature? Most humans didn't know they existed.

Another orange aura caught Rain's eye, and she nearly choked on a cucumber as Chase came into view. A small girl, around six or seven years old, squealed in delight as she clutched his arm with both hands and he lifted her from the ground, setting her on her feet in front of him.

"Do it again," the little girl cried, and Chase beamed a smile, lifting her into the air once more.

Rain's mouth hung open, so she forced it shut. If Chase hadn't been scrumptious enough before, seeing him playing with a child—and enjoying it—made him mouthwatering. There was no pretense to his smile, no ulterior motive behind the sparkle in his eyes. He was simply happy, and the beauty of it whisked the air from Rain's lungs.

He caught her gaze and waved, and she swallowed the bite of sandwich she'd been grinding between her teeth since he came into view. She lifted her hand to return the wave, hoping to act aloof. He was just a client, after all. But her lips betrayed her, curving into a smile she couldn't have fought if she'd tried. If he had been sent to keep tabs on her, at least she could enjoy the view.

The girl had dark hair like Chase, and as he tugged her closer, Rain could see she also had his hazel eyes. He handed the child a pink plastic bottle and pointed to a group of children playing beneath an oak tree. She ran toward the kids, and Chase sat next to Rain.

"Coincidence seeing you here." He grinned and ran a

hand through his hair. Did she detect a bit of nervousness in his movements? Surely not.

"Is it a coincidence? Or did my sister send you?"

He cleared his throat and glanced at the girl. "She might have mentioned you'd be here."

She'd have to have words with Snow later. Although... she did have a smokin' hot werewolf grinning at her, so maybe she should thank her sister. *No. He's here because his alpha ordered him to keep tabs on me.* She needed to remember that. "Is that your daughter?"

The same genuine smile she'd seen earlier returned to his lips as he glanced at the little girl again. "She's my niece, Emma."

"She's adorable." A flush of what she wanted to call relief washed through her body. Was she relieved? If the girl had been his daughter, then he might have been... "Are you married?" *Damn it!* Why did she ask that out loud?

He cast a sideways glance. "No, I'm not."

Oh, goddess, is that a good thing or a bad thing?

"Have you ever been?" She squeezed her lips together. The next question dancing through her brain involved whether or not he liked chocolate and from which part of her body he'd like to lick it, and she would not allow herself to speak that one aloud...no matter how curious she was for the answer.

He gave her his full attention, pinning her with his heated gaze. "I have never been married." He chuckled. "And I thought I'd be the one doing the interrogation."

"I'm not sure I like the sound of that." Unless it involved handcuffs and his detailed exploration of her body. *Stop it, Rain...*

Stretching his arm across the back of the bench, he

shifted toward her. His position gave him view of both Rain and Emma playing in the grass behind her, and that was obviously why he moved, but when his knee brushed her thigh, her stomach clenched as if the touch had been intimate. She tried to hide her reaction, but his sly glance down at her leg and the crooked grin curving his lips said he knew exactly the kind of effect he had on her.

"Snow said you're from Miami."

"We moved here six months ago." She shoved her half-eaten sandwich into its wrapper and tossed it into her bag. "What about you? Have you always lived in New Orleans?"

"Since I was a teenager. Are there any other Miami witches here?"

That didn't sound like a getting-to-know-you question. She narrowed her eyes in suspicion. "None that I'm aware of, but I don't pretend to know every witch in this city. Do you know every werewolf?"

He straightened. "Of course I do. It's my job."

"Uncle Chase!" Emma pranced toward them, swirling a plastic wand in her pink bottle. "Watch this." Pulling the wand from the soapy solution, she blew on it softly, creating a bubble nearly as big as her face. "Toby taught me if you're gentle, you can make it grow big without breaking it."

Emma waved the wand, and the bubble detached to float in front of them. Rain reached out a hand, and the bubble landed on her fingertips. "And if you're really gentle, you can catch them."

"Wow! How'd you do that?" Emma reached for the bubble, cupping her hands around the soapy sphere.

"Careful." Rain smiled as the girl tried to grasp the

bubble, giggling as it popped in her hands. "My sister can make them freeze. She turns them into ice bubbles."

Emma's eyes widened. "Really?"

"Mm-hmm." She leaned closer and whispered, "She's a witch."

"Cool! I'm going to be a werewolf when I grow up, like Uncle Chase. My mom says I might not, but I know I am. Werewolves are the best."

"Witches are cool too." Chase said it to his niece, but his gaze locked with Rain's before lowering to her lips. She was definitely not imagining the attraction now.

She forced herself to look at Emma. "Maybe your uncle will bring you by my bakery sometime, and she can show you."

"Can we, Uncle Chase? Please?" She blinked at him expectantly.

Chase rubbed his beard as his gaze danced between Rain and Emma. "Sure, squirt. Anything for you."

"Cool!" She trotted off to play with the other kids.

Chase cast her an unbelieving look. "Snow can freeze things? Did she change her name after she came into her powers or is it a coincidence?"

"Nothing is coincidence. Our mother knew what her powers would be when she was pregnant. It's one of her gifts." A gift that had landed her mom a seat on the national council as foreign ambassador. She could read anyone's magic, tell exactly what they were capable of and whether or not they posed a threat.

Rain had been her protégé, and she'd learned the importance of power from her mother. Her chest tightened at the disappointment and embarrassment she'd caused her family. If she'd introduced her mom to her last boyfriend sooner, all the trouble might never have happened. She looked at Chase, and her heart raced. Could he be the answer to her prayers?

He arched an eyebrow, and the piercing glinted in the sunlight. "And what are your gifts, Rain? Controlling the weather?"

"I told you; I'm a dud." She should get up and walk away. If he continued to pry, she might slip up and tell him too much. Then she'd lose her one chance at paying the bills and lifting the curse. No matter how slim that chance might have been, she couldn't let it slip away. "Why does Emma's mom say she might not be a werewolf?"

His gaze hardened. "Because her dad's not. If both parents aren't weres, there's a fifty-fifty chance their kids won't be either."

"She idolizes you."

He gazed at the little girl. "I'm the only father-figure she has in her life. She and my sister live with me."

"It's nice that you're there for them." Her stomach fluttered. Oh, goddess, what was she getting herself into? The more she learned about this man, the more delectable he became. Helping raise his sister's child. Giving them a place to live. Second in command of an entire pack. He was powerful and kind. A provider. A protector.

"We take care of our own." Though he stated it as a fact, Rain couldn't ignore the jab to her heart, reminding her she wasn't one of them. She didn't belong.

She couldn't quell her curiosity. "It's acceptable for werewolves to date people outside their species?"

He glanced at his niece, keeping a close watch on her, before focusing on Rain again. "We can date anyone we want."

"What about marriage...or I think you call it mating, right? Can you mate with someone who isn't a werewolf?"

"We can mate and marry whomever we choose." The heat returned to his gaze, and his lips tugged into his signature cocky grin. "Are you in the market for a mate?"

She blinked, heat flushing her cheeks, as she realized how her question must have sounded. "No, absolutely not." Why couldn't she think before she spoke? She focused on the couple across the lake. "Take those two for example. Does that guy know he's dating a werewolf? You seem so secretive; I would assume he doesn't."

Chase followed her gaze to the couple on the blanket. "If the relationship becomes serious...if she decides to take him as her mate, she'll have to bring him into the pack. He'll be sworn to secrecy. We have rules in place."

"Interesting." The fluttering sensation returned to her stomach, as if the idea that she could potentially become his mate appealed to her. Did it appeal to her?

His gaze lingered on the couple across the pond for a moment before he shifted in his seat, his knee brushing hers again. "What's interesting to me is how you knew she was a werewolf from all the way across the lake."

What was it about this man that had her body reacting this way? One little brush of the knee shouldn't have sent her heart sprinting, but she couldn't deny the incessant palpitations she endured whenever he was near. "I can see her aura. It's part of my curse."

He leaned in closer. "Your curse?"

Her heart made a quick dip into her stomach before lodging itself in her throat. Oh, goddess, what had she done?

He took her hand, holding it between both of his. "Is that why I can't feel your magic? You're cursed?"

"What? No!" She pulled from his grasp and clutched her hands in her lap. She couldn't let the werewolves find out about her curse. It would ruin her.

And Chase...any chance she had at getting to know him better would crumble like a day-old, dried-out muffin. "I mean...I call it a curse...not having any powers. I guess my gift is that I can see other people's powers. I can see magic, but I don't have any of my own."

He leaned back on the bench and eyed her skeptically. "You can tell by looking at me that I'm a werewolf?"

She nodded.

"How?"

"Your aura is deep-orange, and it glows with magic. The stronger the magic, the more saturated the color." She was about to explain how deeply his aura glowed, but Chase scooted closer, the length of his muscular thigh resting against hers, making it hard for her to breathe.

It had been too long since she'd been this close to a man, and his warm, musky scent made her want to lean into his side. She felt herself drifting toward him, so she straightened.

"What about Emma?" He nodded toward his niece. "What do you see when you look at her?"

"I see a child who hasn't come into her powers yet. Her aura is pale blue like a human's. It could change as she matures." Or it could stay the same if her father was human, but the disappointment in his eyes stopped her from saying the last part out loud.

"Damn."

"I'm sorry."

Chase looked at her, his gaze dancing around her face, curiosity in his eyes. "You are a fascinating woman, Rain Connolly."

If he didn't quit looking at her mouth, she might not be able to stop herself from leaning over and kissing him. "You're pretty interesting, yourself."

A slow smile curved his full lips, and he gazed into her eyes for a moment before looking at her mouth again. Damn it, she liked him way more than she'd planned to. If he hadn't shown up in the park with his niece and acted all kind and fatherly, she could have continued admiring the package, assuming the inside was all testosterone and sarcasm.

Now she wanted to know him, and she wanted to start by finding out what those luscious lips tasted like. "If you want to kiss me, you—"

"Uncle Chase!" Emma climbed into his lap, breaking the trance he'd put on her and saving her from finishing the sentence that never should have left her lips. "Can we see the frozen bubbles now?"

He wrapped his arms around the little girl and kissed the top of her head. "We sure can, squirt. I need to talk to Miss Rain some more, anyway."

Emma took both their hands and tugged them from the bench. "Let's go."

Rain hesitated, her heart and her stomach tangling in a dizzying dance. Had they almost kissed? If he had tried to take her mouth with his, she'd have given it to him willingly. What happened to befriending him so he could help her break the curse? She needed to keep her priorities straight. Getting her magic back was her number one goal, but she couldn't deny the strange feelings stirring in her core.

"Do you mind if we walk you back to the bakery?" Chase asked.

She smiled at him before looking at Emma. "I'm sure my sister will be thrilled to meet you."

They strolled four blocks to the bakery in a line, Emma between them holding their hands. The adults remained quiet as the little girl babbled on about Toby from the park, occasionally hanging back and running forward for them to lift her in the air by the hands.

The whole scene felt surreal, walking hand-in-hand with this child, Chase by her side, glancing at her from time to time, a strange smile lighting on his lips. They must have looked like a family to passersby.

She'd better enjoy it now because this was the closest she'd ever get to having her own family, unless she could lift this curse.

As they crossed Bourbon Street, two boys with flattened soda cans attached to their sneakers performed a tap dance on the corner. The rhythmic beat of metal striking pavement created a percussive melody that drew a crowd of onlookers. The smaller boy rose onto the tips of his toes and spun, waving his arms in a windmill motion and ending the routine in a flourish.

"Cool!" Emma shouted, and she tugged Rain toward Chase, placing her hand in his and leaving them to run toward the boys.

Chase didn't jerk away. Instead, he tightened his grip, yanking her to his body and wrapping his arms around her, saving her from being flattened by a taxi. The driver blared the horn and shook his fist out the window, shouting a string of profanities at the people on the street.

"Best to keep to the sidewalks during the day, even on Bourbon Street." Chase's chest rumbled as he spoke, and with her face pressed against him, she couldn't help but notice the firm muscles beneath his shirt.

"You okay?" His chin brushed the top of her head, and…was that his nose? Did he smell her hair? The tingling, bubbly sensation shooting through her insides could have been an adrenaline rush from being nearly run over by a car, but the man holding her in a tight embrace was more likely the reason.

She peered up at him, and he didn't let her go. "I'm fine." This close to his lips, she could almost taste them on her tongue. Cinnamon, probably. Warm and slightly sweet. "Thank you for not letting me get run over. That was kind of you."

He smiled. "My pleasure."

Oh, goddess no. He'd shown her kindness. In keeping her from being struck by the taxi, he'd unwittingly set himself up for his own tragedy. How could she have let this happen? She'd rather be lying bruised and bloody on the blacktop than for Chase to endure some disaster for helping her. *Crap!*

Jerking from his embrace, she smoothed her shirt down her stomach and scurried away. "I need to get back to the bakery. Stop by when Emma's done playing and give me the deposit." She rushed across the street.

"Rain, stop."

She glanced behind her as Chase snatched Emma around the waist and threw her onto his shoulder before following her through the intersection.

His niece giggled as he caught up and set her on her feet. "That was fun! Do it again!"

He mussed her hair. "In a minute, squirt. Wait up, Rain. What's wrong?"

"Nothing." She continued her trek to the bakery, yanked open the door, and glared at her sister as she marched behind the counter. She needed to get herself under control. Change the subject before he pressed her for answers she couldn't give.

Chase caught the door and ushered his niece through. The girl ran to the nearest display case and stared, wide-eyed, at the treats inside. "Can I have a cookie?" She glanced at Chase before focusing on the desserts.

"Sure." He sauntered toward the counter, casting Rain a quizzical look, and opened his mouth to speak.

She cut him off. "Emma, this is my sister, Snow. Why don't you show her your bubbles?"

Emma's face brightened. "Give me my bubbles, Uncle Chase."

"I don't have them." His gaze lingered on Rain before he looked at his niece. "You must've left them in the park."

"Aw." Her entire body deflated.

Snow cut her gaze between Rain and Chase and grinned. "That's okay. We can make some in the kitchen with dish soap and a cookie cutter."

The little girl bounced on her toes. "And Rain said you can make them freeze."

Snow laughed. "I sure can. Come back to the kitchen with me."

Chase stiffened. "That's not a good idea, Emma. You need to stay out here where I can see you."

Rain crossed her arms, torn between swooning at his protective instincts and being offended that he didn't trust her sister.

"The sink is right here by the doorway," Snow said. "You'll be able to see her the whole time."

"Please, Uncle Chase?" Emma batted her lashes, her hazel eyes imploring him until he crumbled.

"Okay. But stay where you can see me. If you can't see

me, that means I can't see you either, and then I'll have to hunt for you."

Emma curled her fingers into claws and growled at Chase before scurrying around the counter to the kitchen.

He kept his gaze trained on his niece until he appeared satisfied Snow wasn't going to kidnap her. Then he turned his green-gold eyes to Rain and took her hand.

She slipped from his grasp. "Witches don't eat children outside of fairy tales, you know. Emma is safe here."

He blinked. "I know. I'm not worried."

She scoffed. "You could've fooled me."

"Did I do something to offend you? I thought saving you from a head-on collision with a taxi was rather chivalrous of me, but it seems to have upset you."

She let out an exasperated sigh. "I said thank you. What more do you want from me?"

Leaning an elbow on the counter, he slipped his tongue out to moisten his lips before speaking. "I want you to finish what you were saying at the park. You said if I wanted to kiss you, I should…"

Emma giggled as a frozen bubble shattered on the floor. Chase glanced in her direction before focusing on Rain again. He really wasn't going to let this go.

Did she want to kiss him? Goddess yes, she did. She wanted to do a whole lot more than kiss the sexy werewolf, who had managed to inch his way around the counter to stand next to her, but she couldn't. She'd already put him and his adorable little niece at risk by spending the past hour with them. This had to end. Right here, right now.

"I was going to say that if you want to kiss me, you should reconsider. I'm not interested." Lifting a shoulder, she turned her back to him and rummaged through a drawer to make herself look busy. Even if she wasn't cursed, he either had a grudge against her or witches in general, so things would never work out between them. Relationships had to be built on trust, and he hadn't shown her an ounce of it.

His sigh was audible, though she couldn't tell if it was from disappointment or frustration. "How much is the deposit?"

She straightened and slammed the drawer shut. "Three hundred dollars will reserve the date. I'll need half of the remainder one month in advance of the wedding. The second half will be billed after delivery."

He handed her a credit card. "It's got Luke's name on it, but I'm authorized to sign for it."

If this had been a human wedding, she'd have refused the card. With so much credit fraud going on these days, she didn't like to take chances. She had no doubts about Chase, though. If he'd stolen the alpha's credit card, he'd have to buy a lot more than wedding cake to make the punishment he'd likely endure worthwhile.

She swiped the card and handed him the ticket to sign. "That's all I need from you then, unless you're picking out the design as well."

He cringed. "God, I hope I'm not."

"Please let Luke and Macey know I'll need their design decisions in three weeks. It's been nice doing business with you." She inclined her chin hoping to end the conversation.

He didn't take the hint. "Listen, Rain…" He let out a heavy sigh and shook his head. "Are you sure you don't know of any other Miami witches in the area? No friends or family came to visit you or your sister this week?"

No one she knew wanted to be within one hundred

miles of her and her curse. "No one; I'm sure of it. Why do you ask?"

"There's a body in the morgue."

That's what this was about? He'd stalked her in the park because someone was dead and he thought she was involved? She stacked the papers and jammed them into the stapler. "I'm sure there are lots of bodies in the morgue."

He laid his hands flat on the counter. "She's a witch... from Miami."

Her heart thrummed. "How do you know that?"

"She has a coven tattoo on her chest. The high priestess identified it as Miami."

Her throat thickened. If he'd talked to Calista, she might have told him about her curse. But surely, if he knew, the alpha wouldn't want her at his wedding. He wouldn't have paid the deposit... "I didn't know were-wolves and witches worked so closely."

"We don't, unless our secrecy is threatened. She appears to have died from supernatural causes. Do you think you could identify her?"

Goddess, she hoped not. "Miami is a big city, and there are far more witches than werewolves. The chances of me knowing her are slim."

"Maybe you can identify the type of magic that killed her. You can see magic, right?"

She shook her head. "I can, but only in a living person. I don't think I can do much for you in this case."

He laced his fingers together. "Please? I could really use your help. I promise I'll leave you alone after this."

Her breath hitched. Leave her alone? That was the last thing she wanted, though it would be best for him...and for her since he'd apparently been acting interested so she would help him identify a body. Of course, her initial reason for befriending him wasn't exactly virtuous either. Maybe they were both feeling things they hadn't planned to feel.

Her curse specifically stated *witches* would be punished for showing her kindness, but she didn't want to take any chances with Chase. He was a supernatural being, so the curse might affect him.

Then again, she was supposed to be leading a selfless life, and he needed her help. She owed it to him for saving her life. "Okay. I don't know how much help I'll be, but I'll give it a shot."

He smiled. "Great. I'll talk to Macey and see when she can get us into the morgue."

"The alpha's mate?"

"She's a detective." He picked up a business card from the counter. "Is this the best number to reach you at?"

"Let me give you my cell. I don't answer that number after hours." She took the card and scribbled her personal number on the back before handing it to him.

"Thank you. I'll be in touch." He ambled behind the counter to the kitchen, taking his time as if he didn't want to leave yet. "Time to go, squirt."

"Can I take them home?" Emma scooped up an armful of frozen bubbles. "They're so pretty."

He laughed. "They'll melt by the time we get them to the house."

"I gave them an extra-hard freeze," Snow said. "They should be good for at least an hour."

"I guess so, then." With his hand on Emma's shoulder, he guided her to the storefront.

Rain handed him two chocolate chip cookies in a

white paper bag. "Here's that cookie you promised her. There's one for you too."

He eyed the bag skeptically. "These didn't come from that shelf, did they?" He nodded toward the clarity cookies.

Irritation grated in her chest like sandpaper against her sternum. What would it take for him to trust her? "They're completely mundane. I'll take a bite myself to prove it to you if you want."

The look in his eyes said he was considering her offer. Luckily, he shook his head instead. "I'll take your word for it. Thanks."

He opened the door and nodded for Emma to pass.

"Call me," Rain said as he stepped through the threshold. She grimaced. *Why the hell did I say that?*

He paused and grinned. "I will."

As the door clicked shut behind him, Snow giggled. "Call me," she sang in a mocking tone.

Rain closed her eyes for a long blink, trying not to direct her irritation at her sister. "I did not mean to say that out loud."

"What did you mean to say?"

"Go away. I never want to see you again." Those cookies would be tossed into the first trashcan he saw, and the fact that he distrusted her that much when she'd done nothing wrong gnawed in her gut.

Snow laughed. "That's the fattest lie I've ever heard come out of your mouth. You want him."

"So?" She rolled her eyes. How could she be attracted to a man who emanated so much distrust?

"So…the bad boy werewolf turned out to be a family man. How hot is that?"

Then again, he was protecting his niece. She sank onto a stool and slouched her shoulders. "Extremely."

Snow climbed onto the stool next to her, excitement dancing in her eyes. "What are you going to do about it?"

She took a deep breath and drummed her nails on the counter. "I'm going to look at a dead body."

CHAPTER SEVEN

CHASE GRABBED HIS SECOND BLUE MOON BEER FROM the fridge and settled into a chair at the kitchen table.

"You're taking her to the morgue on your first date?" Luke took a swig from his bottle. "Wouldn't be my first choice."

Drumming his fingers on the wood, Chase took a long drink, savoring the way the citrusy effervescence danced on his tongue, tickling his throat as it made its way down to his stomach. He could imagine what Rain's plump, pink lips would taste like…sweet like the beautiful cakes she created, maybe with a hint of strawberry to match their color.

He'd had the chance to taste them at the park that afternoon. Then he'd hesitated, and he'd dodged a bullet. His lips didn't need to get anywhere near the witch.

He set the bottle on the table with a *thud* and wiped his mouth with the back of his hand. "It's not a date; it's business. Anyway, she's a suspect. I'm not getting involved with a possible enemy."

Luke chuckled. "Is she really a suspect? Do we need to find another bakery?"

Chase grumbled. "No. She *should* be a suspect, but..."

"You trust her."

"I'm more afraid she'll be a target." The mere idea of finding Rain in the morgue with the life drained out of her had his beast begging to come out. He'd stalk the perimeter of the bakery, making sure nothing could harm her. Hell, if he had his way, he'd bring her to his house and keep her there until they figured out whether the murder was a one-off thing or they caught the bastard who killed the witch.

Luke nodded. "You feel a deep, primal need to protect her, don't you?"

"Yeah." It didn't mean anything. Ever since Emma was born he'd felt the need to protect his own. His family. His pack. Rain may not have been a werewolf, but the alpha had put Chase in charge of the witch, and he took his job seriously.

Luke clapped him on the shoulder and strolled to the fridge for another beer. "I know that feeling, my friend. Sounds like you found your fate-bound."

Chase stopped mid-swallow, choking and spewing beer across the table. "Bullshit." Fate-bound, his ass. She was beautiful, with a feisty personality. Independent. Strong. There was something inherently sexy about a woman who ran her own business. Who wouldn't be attracted to Rain? She was a witch, though, and that fact would never change.

And Chase would never trust a witch again.

A knock sounded on the door before James, his hunting buddy, let himself in. "What did I miss?" He strode straight to the fridge.

Luke grinned. "Chase was telling me about how he's met his fate-bound."

James grabbed a beer and paused, shaking his head before shutting the fridge door. "Not you too." He plopped into a chair at the table. "I'm going to have to find new hunting partners. Hanging out with a bunch of mated men cramps my style. You'll be slow."

Luke straightened his spine. "Mating does not make you slow. If anything, it makes you stronger."

"I'll take your word for it." James raised his beer in a salute and drained half the bottle.

Chase had just met the woman, and his friends already considered him mated. This nonsense had to stop. "I will not bind my fate with a witch."

Luke laughed. "You don't get a choice. Believe me."

"You're mating with a witch?" James's eyes widened in surprise. "You hate witches."

Chase chewed on the inside of his cheek. Luke was wrong. This was not happening. "I don't hate them; I just don't trust them."

"Except for this one." Luke tossed his empty bottle into the recycle bin. "Which proves my point."

Chase groaned.

The front door opened, and Emma darted to the table. "It's hunting night! Can I go this time? Please?" She hopped from man to man, batting her lashes and tugging on their arms.

Chase's heart swelled with love for the feisty little squirt. She'd be devastated if her witch genes turned out stronger and she didn't inherit the ability to shift. Of course, that was mostly his fault. He'd built up being a werewolf in her little mind and not done a thing to let her know it would be okay if she couldn't shift. That needed to change.

He pulled her into his lap. "You can't hunt gators unless you're a wolf."

"I am a wolf." She squirmed out of his arms and dropped to the floor.

"You might not be, squirt, and that's okay too. You've got magic in your blood, and that's all that matters."

Bekah dropped her purse on the counter and mouthed the words *thank you*. "Go get ready for your bath, Emma. I'll be there in a minute."

Emma let out a dramatic sigh, slumping her shoulders as if the request pained her. "Yes, ma'am." She trotted through the doorway into her bedroom.

Bekah crossed her arms, giving him a questioning look. "Where did that comment come from?"

"His fate-bound is a witch," Luke said.

"Wipe that shit-eating grin off your face, man. It's not happening." He rose and tossed his bottle into the bin. "Let's get this hunt started." At least in their wolf forms, he wouldn't have to listen to them run their mouths. Letting his beast take over for a while would help him clear his mind.

"Hold on." Bekah stepped toward him and grabbed his hand.

He tried to yank from her grasp, but she held a firm grip. Grinding his teeth, he muttered, "I don't need you to read me." His sister's empathic abilities came in handy occasionally, but not now.

She pressed her lips together, fighting a smile as she released his hand. "How about that. My brother has bonded with a witch." She shook her head. "What an unlikely turn of events. Finally letting go of your grudge?"

"I…" He rubbed his forehead. Damn it, why was this happening? "After what happened to me, and what Tommy did to you, I can't…" He couldn't what? Follow his fate? Trust his instincts and make the woman his? None of this made any sense.

Bekah rolled her eyes. "Tommy did what he did because he's an asshole, not because he's a witch. Same thing for your little school friends. They were jerks; you took the fall."

"If they weren't witches, they wouldn't have wanted my blood."

"I don't know what your friends were up to, but I believe that Tommy wanted it for your healing abilities. Healing is his gift."

He scoffed. "And then when I refused, he left you." He'd trusted the guy. Hell, he'd even liked him. But for a supernatural being to ask another for blood…especially to ask a werewolf…was unforgivable. His sister's ex-boyfriend had expected him to break an ancient, sacred law. Shit, it was one of the first and most important laws were-children learned. Rule number one: never fight a human while in wolf form, unless it's a fight to the death. Rule number two: blood is sacred and can never be shared.

Chase ground his teeth. "Witches are assholes."

Willingly giving his blood away would've landed him in the pit for the next twenty years. He'd have been middle-aged by the time he'd served his term in the werewolf prison. And that was if he received the lightest sentence. The national congress condoned death as a suitable punishment for giving blood to a witch.

No way. Not for anyone.

Bekah sighed. "I think his leaving had more to do with Emma than with you. Get over it. You can't fight fate."

Luke stood and cracked his knuckles. "Welcome to the club, man. You're in for a wild ride." He jerked his head toward the door. "Let's hunt."

"Have fun, boys." Bekah grinned as Chase followed Luke and James out the door.

They loaded into Luke's truck and then headed down Interstate 10 toward their favorite hunting grounds. The massive swamp area was ripe with gators, wild boar, and plenty of other animals to satisfy the cravings of a wolf. Unfortunately, the beast inside Chase craved a lot more than the thrill of a hunt and the satisfaction of a meal. He craved a mate, and it seemed only one person would do.

He cranked up the AC, but it did nothing the cool the fire building in his core. "What if I date someone else? Find another mate? Surely this feeling will go away."

"I'm happy to play wingman if you want to hit the bars tonight." James raised his eyebrows, looking way too hopeful. "It's been a while."

Luke laughed. "Good luck with that."

"What's that supposed to mean?" Chase cut him a sideways glance, but he had a feeling he knew exactly what Luke meant.

"If Rain is your fate-bound, being with anyone but her will be unthinkable." He shrugged and pulled off the highway. "Might be a good test though. If you can pick up another female, then it's your hormones making you hot for the witch and not fate."

They bounced down a dirt path, heading deeper into the woods before rolling to a stop next to a massive cypress tree. Chase hopped out of the truck after his friends and gazed up at the half-moon brightening the night sky. Two more weeks, and it would be a blue moon, the second full moon of the month. He could almost feel the extra boost of magic pooling in his blood. Every first-born in the pack would be hunting beneath the blue moon. Their magic would be undeniable that night; the beast would take over whether they wanted it to or not.

Maybe that was what all this was about. His wolf's extra strength and his intense desire to mate had caused him to obsess over the first female he'd found attractive.

A test. That was exactly what he needed. Then he could prove to his friends, and to himself, that his fate was not bound to a witch...or to anyone for that matter.

"What do you say?" James cracked his neck and rolled his shoulders, his anticipation for the hunt evident in his posture. "Want to hit the bars after this? See if we can get you laid?"

"Hell ye—" A lump the size of a baseball formed in Chase's throat, and the *yes* he'd tried to answer got lodged beneath it. *Shit.* Hell yeah, he wanted to sleep with a woman. But the thought of climbing into bed with anyone but Rain Connolly made his skin crawl. He narrowed his eyes and glared at the moon.

"Can't do it, can you?" At least Luke wasn't laughing anymore, but his tone turned too serious. The last thing Chase needed was a therapy session.

"No." He called on his beast, letting the vibrating energy consume him, transforming his body into his wolf. He took off into the trees, putting space between his friends and him. His beast had the instinct to hunt with the pack, but the man needed to clear his head.

Why did he have to find his fate-bound? And why did it have to happen now? He liked his life the way it was. He was busy. Between his position as Luke's second, his job at the bar, and taking care of his niece, he barely had time for a social life, much less a girlfriend. And now he'd met the woman he was supposed to spend forever with, *and* she was a witch?

Fate had a sick sense of humor.

A rustle in the brush to his left yanked him from his thoughts. A shadow darted from behind a tree and disappeared as quickly as it had formed. *What the hell was that?* It had the silhouette of a man...sort of...but it's movements were more fluid, its shape seeming to roll and reform with each step.

He searched his mind for Luke and James. Though they couldn't speak in wolf form, they had a sort of telepathic connection. His friends hunted half a mile away, giving him the space he'd craved. He'd have to handle this one on his own.

Crouching low, he belly-crawled to the clearing where he'd spotted the shadow. It could have been a hunter, which would mean trouble for them all. Though werewolves were exceptionally fast healers, even he wouldn't recover from a bullet to the brain.

Dry leaves crunched beneath his paws as he dragged his body across the ground. Crickets chirped, and a sultry breeze rustled his chocolate fur, but the shadow...and whatever creature it belonged to...had vanished.

He stood and shook the dirt from his coat. Maybe he'd imagined it. He'd been caught up in his thoughts, not paying attention to where he was running. It was probably a trick of the moonlight. He needed to get out of his head and into this hunt before he drove himself crazy.

A high-pitched wail grated in his ears, making them twitch as something splashed into the water a few yards away. Instinct took over, and he dashed toward the sound, skidding to a stop at the water's edge. An air pocket covered in thick, green sludge bubbled to the surface, releasing a putrid steam as it popped.

The ground beneath his back paw crumbled, and he slipped, his right leg sinking in the sludge. He scrambled to grip the deteriorating soil with his left paw, digging his nails into the dirt for traction.

Something grabbed hold of his leg above the paw, and piercing pain shot straight to his bones. Chase yelped and clawed at the ground, but he couldn't get his footing. His other leg slipped into the muddy water, and jerking his head around, he clamped his jaws down on whatever animal had bitten him. Another sludgy air pocket bubbled from the surface, and the creature released its grip.

Using his front paws, Chase dragged himself from the water, letting out a howl he hoped his pack mates would hear. He collapsed on the bank as a throbbing pain spread from his leg, up to his haunches, all the way to his chest.

What the hell had bitten him? A venomous snake? Whatever it was, the poison spread quickly, making his entire body ache like he'd been hit by a truck. As the alpha howled his response, the world went black.

The trill of transformative magic surged through Isaac's veins, half-healing the puncture wounds from the animal's fangs before his own cursed blood vanquished the magic. Had he known it was a werewolf, he'd have put more energy into his tulpa and lured the beast farther into the water where it couldn't have gotten away so easily. The energy he could have gained from draining the creature dry would have more than made up for the amount he would have had to expend.

Even at optimum health, he'd be no match for a werewolf, though. Without his magic as a weapon, the beast could have ripped him to shreds before he had the chance to drain him.

Prying his lids open, he lifted his head above the murky water to peer at his victim. Matted, dark-brown fur covered the wolf's limp body, and it shimmered as he lost control of his magic and transformed into a man.

In the werewolf's current state, Isaac might've been able to take him, but the pain he'd endure dragging himself from the water wouldn't be worth it. He'd focus on his tulpa instead. Stick to the plan. Another week of recovery and he'd exact his revenge. He'd bide his time until then.

Two more wolves appeared in the brush. A light-brown one, the biggest of the three, nosed the body, rolling the man onto his back, while the gray one sniffed around the area. Its enhanced sense of smell led it to the water, and Isaac held his breath, sinking beneath the muck to hide his scent.

His lungs burned for oxygen. His blood barely carried enough to his cells as it was, and his entire body screamed with the need to breathe. Unable to stand another second without breath, he slowly rose from the muck until his nose broke the surface. He stifled a gasp and sucked in a breath as two men carried his victim away.

CHAPTER EIGHT

Rain closed her computer and dialed her landlord's number. After paying the utilities and buying supplies to run her store, she had enough money to pay the rent and the late fees, but the coven fees would have to wait until she got another big order or the werewolves paid the first half of their remainder.

"Hey, Ingrid, it's Rain. I have the rent check whenever you want to come pick it up."

Laughter echoed in the background. "I'm in Mexico until next week. I'll come by for it then."

It figured. Ingrid had rushed her to pay, and now that she had the money, she couldn't give it to her. "That's fine, but I expect the late fees to stop accruing as of today."

Ingrid paused, her voice sounding regretful. "I can't show you any kindness."

"It's not kindness; it's principle. I have the money, and I'm trying to make a payment. It's not my fault you aren't available to collect. I'll take it to your house and put under the doormat if I have to, but I'm not paying late fees anymore."

Ingrid sighed. "I guess you're right. But if you don't have the money when I come by, the fees will be doubled."

While that stipulation was nowhere in her contract, Rain understood Ingrid's position. Showing her kindness would result in a nasty accident or tragedy for her landlord. Rain wouldn't want to risk it either. "That's fair. I'll see you next week."

She hung up the phone and drummed her fingers on the counter. It had been two days since she'd heard from Chase. After the way she'd blown him off, she didn't expect him to show up for lunch again. But he did say he needed her to identify a body in the morgue, and she expected him to follow through on that.

Worry knotted in her stomach, and she chewed her bottom lip as she contemplated what to do. He'd saved her from getting hit by a taxi, and if that wasn't kindness, what was? If his punishment for saving her life were to lose his own, she'd never forgive herself.

Snow carried a tray of fresh clarity cookies to the display case and positioned them on a shelf. "Something's weighing heavy on your mind. Want to talk about it?" She wiped her hands on her apron and slid the case shut.

"Remember how I told you Chase asked me to look at a body in the morgue?"

Snow shivered. "You think it might be someone we know?"

"It's possible, but that's not what's bothering me. He asked me that two days ago, and I haven't heard from him since. If he was really concerned about a witch being murdered, don't you think he would have made an appointment to go to the morgue? Or at least called me?"

A mischievous grin curved Snow's lips. "You really like this guy, don't you?"

Who wouldn't? Simply looking at his sculpted body had her mouth watering and her fingers itching to peel away his clothes. He smelled like a forest after a cleansing rain, and he seemed to genuinely enjoy his niece. He was sexy and kind…

But his kindness could get him killed around her.

"I'm afraid that when he pulled me out of the taxi's path, he may have triggered the curse. What if he's sick… or dead?" Her stomach tumbled to her feet at the thought.

Snow wrinkled her nose. "He's not a witch. The curse doesn't count."

"It might."

She shook her head. "I remember it specifically said any *witch* who shows you kindness will be punished. There's no mention of werewolves."

Rain bit her lip. The curse did specify witches, and the words of a spell were taken literally. She'd found that out the hard way. But still… "He could have some witch blood in his veins. His niece is only half-werewolf. Who's to say his great-great-grandfather wasn't a witch? It's possible."

"Did you see it in his aura?" Snow leaned a hip against the counter.

"No, but he's a strong werewolf. If the witch blood is from a distant ancestor, I might not be able to see it." Her stomach twisted, the guilt churning in her gut.

Snow crossed her arms and drummed her fingers against her biceps. "Did you call him?"

"I don't have his number." She bit the end of her fingernail between her front teeth.

Snow pursed her lips for a moment before raising her eyebrows. "He put it on the contract."

She sucked in a sharp breath. "That's right; he did."

Yanking open the filing cabinet, she grabbed the wedding contract and scanned the page. He'd checked the cell-phone box next to the primary contact number and scribbled the digits on the line.

This was the right thing to do. Even if he told her he'd changed his mind and didn't need her help, at least she'd know he was alive. She took her phone from her pocket and dialed his number. Straight to voicemail. She hung up before the greeting ended. "His phone must be off. It didn't even ring."

Shaking her head and suppressing a smile, Snow uncrossed her arms. "If you're that worried about him, hon, go check on him. I'm sure someone at the bar knows where he is."

Rain gripped the contract in her left hand, wrinkling the pages, as she gnawed on her right pinkie nail. "Do you think I should?"

"You're not going to have any fingernails left if you don't."

Yanking her finger from her mouth, she examined her hand. She'd already chewed the first three nails down to nubs, and it was only ten o'clock. "You're right. I should. It will give me peace of mind."

Snow stopped fighting her smile. "And it will show him how much you care."

She did care, more than she wanted to. But her emotions didn't matter when he'd have to risk his life to be with her. She'd go to the bar, make sure he was okay, and then she'd shove her feelings for the sexy werewolf into the back of her mind and keep them there until the wedding was over. Then she'd forget about him.

Forget about breaking her curse. Willingly giving her his blood would be the kindest thing he could do, and he'd be met with the worst punishment possible…if he hadn't already. It was time to stop pretending she could have any kind of relationship with Chase…romantic or friendly. "I'll be back soon."

"Take your time," Snow sang.

The sun warmed her skin, chasing away the chill in the air, as she strode up Royal and made a left on St. Philip. She walked with purpose, ignoring her surroundings, anxiety tightening her muscles as her long strides carried her toward the bar. Something was wrong; she could feel it in her core.

A stream of cold water pelted her from above, jerking her from her thoughts, and she squealed. Jumping out of the way, she peered up to find a man watering a row of ferns hanging from a second-story gallery. The pots swung in the breeze from their wrought-iron hooks, and the man waved and shouted, "Sorry."

Rain forced a smile and returned his wave before continuing her trek to the bar. She'd passed by O'Malley's Pub plenty of times since she moved to New Orleans, but she'd never ventured inside. With her hand on the door-knob, she inhaled a deep breath and braced herself. With any luck, Chase would be behind the bar, a smile lighting up his handsome face as she entered the room.

But luck never was on her side.

As she stepped through the threshold, a crisp curtain of air blasted her skin. She made her way toward the bar, and a woman with light-brown hair and bright blue eyes greeted her.

"Welcome to O'Malley's. What can I get you?"

Rain gripped the edge of the bar. "Is Chase here?"

The woman tilted her head, studying her. "Are you Rain, the baker?"

"Yes." Her heart thrummed. Had Chase talked about her? Was that why the woman assumed she was Rain?

The woman smiled. "It's nice to meet you. I'm Amber. Luke is my brother."

Why was she giving her such a curious look? "It's nice to meet you too."

Amber wiped her hands on a dish rag. "Chase is at home. He got a nasty snake bite while he was hunting. Knocked him on his ass."

Icy tendrils of dread spiraled up her spine to squeeze her heart. Her curse had gotten him too. "Is he...will he recover?"

She shrugged. "Werewolves are fast healers. Must have been one hell of a snake, though. I've never seen him take this long to recover from an injury."

She lowered herself onto a barstool. He was hurt because of her. She had to see him...to do something to make this right. "I don't suppose you could tell me where he lives, so I could drop by and check on him?"

Amber grinned as she scribbled his address on a green Post-It Note. "I think he would love that. Here." She handed her the paper. "And tell him I said 'change is good.'"

"Okay." Rain gave her a quizzical look. Was that some kind of werewolf code?

"He'll know what I'm talking about."

Chase lay on the couch, flipping channels on the TV and cursing himself for falling into the water. The pounding in his head had subsided to a dull ache, and his vision had finally cleared, but at the rate he was healing, he'd be useless for another twelve hours minimum.

His mom had stayed with him yesterday while Emma went to school and Bekah worked, but he'd finally convinced the women he'd survive if they left him alone. That didn't stop his sister from taking an early lunch break to come home and check on him.

"You're sure you're going to be okay if I go back to work?" She refilled the water glass on the end table and rested her hand against his head. "You still feel like crap."

"Thanks, I hadn't noticed." He didn't need his sister to tell him what a wuss he was.

She sank onto the edge of the couch. "You can't fake feeling better around me. I'm an empath, remember?"

"You never let me forget."

She clutched his ankle, and shoving his sweats up to his knee, she turned his leg from side to side. "You don't find it strange that the puncture wounds healed when the rest of you is this sick?"

"Maybe they healed before the venom took effect." He turned off the TV and dropped the remote next to the water. "Can you get me a beer?"

Giving his leg a pat, she stood. "You can have a beer when you feel well enough to get off the couch and get it yourself."

"Gee, thanks."

Bekah picked up her purse. "Call Mom if you need anything. She'll be over in a heartbeat."

A knock sounded on the door.

Chase sighed. "Sounds like she couldn't stay away."

Bekah swung open the front door. "Hi. Can I help you?"

With the door half-open, he couldn't see the person on the porch, but Rain's melodic voice melted in his ears like ice cream—sweet and smooth. "Hi. I'm Rain. Is Chase home?"

"He sure is." His sister's evident smile gave her voice a musical quality. "You've got a visitor, Chase. Make yourself presentable."

As if he could haul his ass off the couch if he wanted to. He wore the same shirt and sweatpants Bekah had changed him into two days ago, and he hadn't brushed his teeth since before the hunt. Taking a big gulp of water, he swished it around in his mouth, hoping to wash away the grimy feel, and ran a hand through his disheveled hair.

Hell, maybe his gross appearance would be a good thing. Maybe she'd take one look at him and turn tail and run away. That might be best for both of them.

Rain tiptoed into the room, chewing on her bottom lip and looking at everything in the area but him.

"I'll see you later," Bekah called as she closed the front door on her way to work.

When Rain finally looked at him, it felt like the air had been sucked from his lungs. A possessive growl resonated deep inside his soul, and a single word echoed through his head: *Mine.*

Holy hell. His wolf had claimed her.

He expected his mind to reel with dismay or at least a little shock. Instead, the feeling settled in his core like it had been there his entire life, giving him a sense of completeness he'd never felt before.

She wore skinny jeans and a pink T-shirt with matching Converse, and her hair hung loose, her dark curls tumbling over her shoulders, accentuating her slender neck. As he held her gaze, her stormy eyes shimmered and liquid pooled on her lower lids.

Damn, how bad did he look? He swallowed the lump from his throat and shoved his wolf's desires to the back of his mind. "Hey. Thanks for stopping by."

She covered her mouth with her hand and shook her head. "I'm so sorry."

"It's not your fault." He scooted back on the couch, moving his legs to give her room, trying to keep his face neutral so she wouldn't notice the pain shooting through his limbs as he moved. "Want to sit?"

"Um…sure." Clutching her purse to her chest, she sank onto the edge of the sofa. "I looked for you at the bar. Amber gave me your address."

"Did she?" He wouldn't expect anything less of his boss. Between Amber and Luke, they were probably already planning his wedding date.

"I hope that's okay."

Okay? He felt better being near the woman. He'd had two days to mull over the fact that Rain could be his fate-bound, and no matter how hard he tried to deny it, he couldn't fight fate. She'd been on his mind every goddamn waking moment since he'd met her. "I'm glad you came. I wanted to call you, but today is the first time it hasn't felt like swallowing glass to talk."

"I'm so sorry. I have something that might help, but…" She clutched her purse tighter.

"But?"

She stared at the wall above his head. "It's a spell. A potion Snow made for you when I told her what happened."

"Ah…" A week ago, he wouldn't have entertained the thought of taking a witch's potion. Hell, he wouldn't have entertained a witch in his living room. But now, since Rain was the one offering it…

She looked at him, the tears sitting on her lower lids beginning to dry without falling. "Why don't you trust me?"

"I trust you." He blinked, his answer surprising both of them as the words tumbled so easily from his lips. It had been hard to admit the truth to Luke, and especially to himself, but the way his wolf reacted to seeing her again confirmed it. She was his fate-bound. It went against his better judgement and everything he'd believed since he was a kid, but he trusted this woman to his core.

The muscles in her throat flexed as she swallowed. "Then you've got something against witches."

Rubbing his forehead, he closed his eyes for a long blink. If he planned to follow his fate and let a witch into his life, he might as well tell her the truth. "It's a long story."

"I've got time." She offered him a smile and let her purse drop to the floor.

Oh, hell. He was doing this. He leaned his head back and stared at the ceiling. There was no sense in sugar-coating the story. If she knew the whole, messy truth, maybe she could forgive him for his initial mistrust. "I wasn't born into the pack."

Her brow scrunched as she tilted her head. His explanation would be harder than he thought if she didn't understand how strong the pack bond was.

He blew out a hard breath. "Do you know what a rogue werewolf is?"

"I'm guessing it's someone who doesn't belong to a pack. Like a lone wolf?"

"Exactly. We're pack creatures by nature. We crave the company of others like us, and we stick together. But sometimes we go rogue for various reasons. My parents were rogues."

"Why?" She scooted closer to him, her hip brushing against his leg.

That innocent touch sent a jolt of electricity shooting straight to his heart, easing the incessant ache in his muscles. "My dad had a wild side. Didn't care much for rules."

Her lips parted, but she paused before she spoke. "Had?"

"He died when I was five. My mom joined the pack because of me. To save me." A heaviness settled on his shoulders at the memory. When was the last time he'd talked about this?

"What happened?" Concern emanated from her eyes, and when she rested her hand on his knee, he fought the urge to lace his fingers through hers and bring them to his lips.

"We lived about a hundred miles northwest of New Orleans in Livonia. There was no pack, very few were-wolves around, but even rogues are territorial. We got too close to another rogue's territory, and he and my dad had it out. Argued for years. When I was five, they got into a bar fight. Before they could take it outside and fight as wolves, one of the rogue's human friends shot my dad in the head."

She squeezed his leg. "Oh, Chase, I'm so sorry."

He shook his head. "I don't really remember him. Mostly things my mom has told me." He'd always have an ache in his heart that his father had been murdered. That he grew up without the man's influence. But he didn't lose sleep over it anymore, and it wasn't the point of the story.

He forced a half-smile. "I inherited my old man's rebellious nature, if you couldn't tell."

"No." She feigned shock. "The tattoos and piercing don't give that away at all."

He chuckled, and for the first time in two days, it didn't hurt to laugh. "My mom tried her best, but I was fourteen years old when I got in over my head. A small coven ran most of the town."

She moved her hand to her lap, taking the soothing warmth of her touch with her.

He inhaled deeply, silently wishing she'd touch him again to give him the strength to continue. This was the messy part. "I hung out with a group of kids from the coven, and we got into all kinds of trouble. Kids' stuff like graffiti, skipping school, you know... Anyway, one night we were hanging out, and they decided to do some kind of ritual that involved fire in the back of a store. We broke in, rearranged the furniture, and I watched them do their thing. They gave me a potion. Said it was the only way for me to participate since I wasn't a witch."

"Did you drink it?"

He clenched his jaw. "Remember when I said werewolves are pack animals by nature? I'd have done anything to belong. To fit in somewhere."

She sucked in a sharp breath. "I don't like where this is heading. Did they hurt you?"

"They tried to. Turns out, I was their sacrifice, and the potion was meant to knock me out. They tried to tie me up. They wanted my blood, and when I refused, they tried take it by force and throw me into the fire." A shudder ran through his body at the memory of the betrayal. "I'd come into my own magic by then, so I shifted and tore into them like I was fighting for my life."

She grimaced. "It sounds like you were."

"The fire got out of hand during the fight, and the building burned to the ground. Everyone got out alive, but they were in bad shape."

"And you?"

"Werewolves are fast healers. I didn't have a scratch by the time I got home, but I got blamed for everything. They claimed I ambushed their sacred ritual and started the fire myself."

"Oh, Chase, that's awful." She returned her hand to his leg, this time on his thigh.

"I was arrested for arson and assault. Spent some time in juvenile detention. Parole for a couple of years after that."

"And the other kids?"

"Nothing happened to them. I was blamed for everything." He laughed again, but he couldn't force any humor into it. "They covered their tracks with magic. Whether or not their parents bought their story, I don't know. As soon as I got out of juvenile detention, my mom packed us up and we moved here. She couldn't handle me on her own, so she sought out the help of the alpha…Luke's old man at the time. He straightened me out. If not for the pack, I'd either be dead or in jail by now."

"Wow." She stared straight ahead and chewed her lip. "Those kids were practicing black magic, which is forbidden. I hope you don't hold that against all witches. Most of us are peaceful, goddess-worshipping people."

How could he not? "That was my first run-in with witches. I've had bad luck with them ever since."

"Well…" She shrugged. "Maybe your luck is changing. Oh, that reminds me…Amber said to tell you change is good. She said you'd know what she was talking about."

He knew exactly what she was talking about. The beautiful woman sitting on the couch next to him, absently tracing circles on his thigh with her fingers. Did she even realize how intimately she was touching him? It felt so natural having her there, her gentle caress giving him the strength to tell his story.

She glanced at her hand on his leg and jerked it away. "Where does that leave us then?"

"I told you I trust you." He reached for her hand, and she let him take it. Her skin was soft, her unpainted fingernails stained blue around the edges from frosting. The temptation to bring them to his lips to taste them made his mouth water.

Luke was right; he couldn't fight fate. Didn't want to anymore. He could set his disdain for witches aside for Rain. His wolf wouldn't have it any other way, and if he had to swallow a spell to prove he trusted this woman, that's what he would do. "Tell me about this potion you brought."

She held his gaze for a moment before she took a vial of orange liquid from her purse. "It's a healing spell. It has mango leaves and rue and some other things, and Snow enchanted it with her power. It won't make you one hundred percent better, but it will speed up the healing."

"Give it to me." He held out his hand.

She eyed him skeptically. "Seriously?"

"I already feel better from you being here. If you're telling me this little bit of liquid will make me heal even faster, I believe you." Rain would never do anything to hurt him. He felt it in his core.

The corners of her mouth tugged into a hesitant smile, and she handed him the vial.

Holding her gaze, he popped out the cork and tossed

the liquid back like a shot of tequila, swallowing it all in one gulp. It tasted like honey, and as the potion cascaded down his throat, a cooling sensation spread from his stomach to his limbs.

Rain's smile reached her eyes as she took the empty vial and returned it to her purse. "How do you feel?"

The ache in his legs subsided, and the pressure in his head lightened. "Like it's cooling me from the inside out."

She nodded "Because you're hot."

"Why, thank you." The widening of her eyes told him she didn't mean it that way, but he couldn't stop himself from messing with her. "That's the second time you've told me that."

She arched an eyebrow. "Bless your heart. You haven't seen a mirror lately, have you?" She chuckled and patted his knee. "I should let you get some rest."

What was it about a quick-witted woman that was so damn sexy? He grabbed her hand, not ready for her to leave. The temptation to pull her to his chest and plant his lips on hers built in his core, but he probably did look like hell, considering how he'd felt the past two days. His breath wouldn't be any better. "Can I ask you a witch-related question?"

The humor in her eyes faded to wariness. "Sure."

He turned her hand over and traced his finger on her soft palm. Her breath hitched as she gazed at their entwined fingers, and a battle of emotions seemed to play across her features.

"After I got out of juvenile detention, we moved, and I haven't seen those kids since. Do you know why they wanted my blood?"

"Blood magic." She slipped her hand from his grasp and wrapped her arms around herself. "Werewolf blood has healing and transformative powers. They were probably working on a spell that would elicit change or something that would be painful and would require healing. I can't say for sure." She grabbed her purse and stood. "I really should go. The potion should have its full effect in an hour or two. I hope you feel better soon."

"I already feel better." He sat up and put his feet on the floor for the first time in two days. Expecting the room to spin, he paused, giving his body time to adjust to the upright position, and then he pushed to his feet.

Big mistake. A wave of nausea washed over him, and he managed to catch the arm of the sofa to steady himself before he crumpled to the floor. Rain wrapped her arms around his shoulders and guided him to the cushions, getting him situated in his previous prone position before settling on the edge of the couch.

She brushed the hair off his forehead and glided her fingers down the side of his face. Though no magic seeped from her skin, her affectionate touch lit a fire inside his core. She smiled, her gaze drifting from his eyes to his lips and back again. "Not that much better, I guess?"

"Apparently not." What was it about her touch that derailed his thoughts? "I told you about my sordid past; it's your turn to tell me something."

She folded her hands in her lap. "What do you want to know?"

"Why do you know so much about black magic if you don't practice it?"

"Not all blood magic is black magic. Anytime blood is used in a spell, the practitioner has to be extremely careful to avoid contamination and to use the exact amount. I'm glad those kids didn't succeed, because if they'd screwed up their spell, the results could have been even more devastating than they were."

He sat up again, scooting to rest his back against the arm of the couch. For a powerless witch, she knew way too much about all this. "Have you ever practiced blood magic?"

She opened her mouth to respond but paused midbreath. Pressing her lips together, she shook her head. "If you're trying to catch me in a lie, it won't work. I don't have powers. I can't cast spells."

Damn. Had his motive been that transparent? If she wasn't lying about her powers, what was she holding back? And *why* was she keeping it from him?

"I'm sorry." He rested a hand on her knee. "Here's the thing, Rain. I find you fascinating and alluring. I want to know you, but I can't shake the feeling that you aren't telling me everything. I already feel like a sentient being again from drinking your potion, which I think proves that I trust you. So, I've opened up. Now it's your turn."

She held his gaze, studying him, as she covered his hand with hers and gave it a squeeze. "You know everything you need to know." Moving his hand to his own lap, she patted it twice before standing. "I need to get back to work." She shuffled to the front door.

"Are you free tonight?"

Shaking her head, she turned to face him. "Chase..."

He wasn't about to let her shoot him down again. "I need you to take a look at the body in the morgue. If I can get Macey to meet us there, are you free around eight?"

Her chest rose and fell as she sighed. "Sure. I'll see you at eight." She opened the door and paused in the threshold, running her finger over the chipping paint on the jamb. "I did lie to you about something."

Swinging his feet to the floor, he rested his elbows on his knees. He'd have preferred to stand and face her for the admission, but he didn't dare risk nearly passing out in front of her again. He held her gaze, his silence encouraging her to continue.

"At the bakery, when I told you that I was going to say I wasn't interested and you shouldn't kiss me…That's not what I was going to say."

His heart slammed against his ribs. "What were you going to say?"

The corners of her mouth twitched into an almost-smile. "I was going to say that if you wanted to kiss me, you should do it, because I wanted to kiss you too. I'll see you tonight." She stepped through the door and closed it.

CHAPTER NINE

RAIN LEANED TOWARD THE MIRROR AND APPLIED A final swipe of mascara. As the brush reached the tip of her lashes, it slipped from her fingers and painted a thick black stripe down her cheek before clinking into the sink.

"Damn it." She glanced at the clock. Seven-fifty. No time to start over. Grabbing a washcloth, she wrapped it around her finger and held it under the faucet before swiping the smudge from her face. Ever since she'd left Chase's house that afternoon, her nerves had been on edge. What did one wear on a trip to the morgue with the man of her dreams?

She applied a fresh coat of powder where the smudge had been and jabbed the mascara wand into the bottle. This wasn't a date; she was doing him a favor, so she'd opted not to change clothes. It didn't hurt to freshen up her makeup and run a brush through her hair, though.

She tossed her makeup into its storage box and shoved it under the sink. Her tiny living quarters didn't leave room for clutter, so everything she owned sat either under the bed or in a cabinet or closet.

Chase's house was small, but what she'd seen of it had been clean. Cozy. Definitely not the bachelor pad she'd imagined him in before she found out his sister and niece lived with him. She smiled and flipped off the light switch before shuffling to the storefront to wait for him.

Hopefully, if her curse had caused his accident, she'd more than countered the effects. She hadn't expected him to actually drink the potion. And the way he'd tossed it back without hesitation did prove he was starting to trust her. But at what cost?

He could tell she kept secrets, but there was no way she could reveal her curse. She absolutely could not admit to needing his blood to break it. Not after everything he'd told her. The trust he'd shown today would dissolve into oblivion if he knew she needed him for the same reason his so-called friends had attacked him when he was a kid. She'd either have to find herself another werewolf or forget about breaking her curse.

The thought of living the rest of her life without her magic sat sour in her stomach like expired milk. What else could she do?

She caught a glimpse of Chase sauntering by the window, but he didn't stop at the bakery door. She hurried to the front and watched as he pressed the buzzer for the apartment upstairs. Her heart fluttered as she fumbled with the lock. *This isn't a date. Why do I have to keep reminding myself of that?*

She leaned out the door and admired his broad shoulders. When no one answered the buzzer, he stepped back and peered at the apartment above. The streetlights illuminated his strong jaw and high cheekbones. The color had returned to his skin, and his hair appeared washed and combed into that messy-chic style that was meant to look natural but he probably spent an hour perfecting. He looked scrumptious.

Not that he'd looked *that* bad at his house earlier. She'd only said he did to turn the tables on his cocky flirtation. He may have been a badass werewolf, but he wouldn't get the upper hand with her. Not if she could help it.

"Looking for someone?" She pulled the door shut and locked it. "No one lives up there at the moment."

He smiled and strode toward her, stopping short of wrapping his arms around her. Instead, he shoved his hands into his pockets and glanced up at the balcony. "I thought you lived there."

"I live in the back of the bakery. I can't afford the storefront and the apartment."

"Oh." He stared at her, and his magnetism made her lean toward him.

She slipped her hands into her own pockets to stop from reaching for him. "You look like you feel better."

He blinked, seeming to come out of whatever trance had been drawing them together. "I do. That potion you gave me was incredible. Tell Snow, 'Thank you,' for me."

"I will. It only worked that quickly because you're a werewolf, though."

"I guess I'm lucky to be a werewolf."

She smiled. "I guess you are."

"We better not keep Macey waiting. You ready?" He motioned toward the black motorcycle parked on the curb.

Sleek yet masculine, the bike sported black leather and shiny chrome. The closest Rain had ever come to a motorcycle was the one she made out of fondant and gum paste for a ten-year-old's birthday cake last year. It was so much sexier in person. Almost as sexy as the man who owned it.

She suppressed the giggle trying to escape her throat. "Seriously? That's your ride?"

"You didn't think I'd drive a Subaru, did you?" He unhooked a helmet from the back of the seat and tossed it to her before pulling a matching one onto his head. Maybe his hair did look that good naturally.

"A fast healer like yourself needs a helmet?" She shook her hair behind her shoulders and stuffed her head into the helmet, buckling the strap beneath her chin.

"I don't know anyone who can recover from having his brains splattered on the pavement." He swung a leg over the seat and straddled the massive machine.

Heat pooled below her navel as she ticked off the items on her mental hot-guy checklist. Tattoos? *Check.* Amazing body? From what she could tell with his clothes on, *check.* Kind, funny, caring, compassionate. *Check, check, check, check.* He got her motor running every time he looked at her, and now she was about to be painfully close to him. She'd have to press her body against his to hold on. His tight backside would fit snugly against her front. Goddess, help her.

"You coming?"

"I've never ridden a motorcycle before." She gripped his shoulders and swung her leg across the seat.

"Hold on tight, lean into the turns, and trust me to keep you safe. If you fight it, we could crash." He revved the engine and looked straight ahead, so she couldn't see his eyes, but the intensity in his words felt like he was talking about more than the motorcycle ride.

She wrapped her arms around his waist and rested her

chin on his shoulder. "Contrary to what you think, I do trust you."

His chuckle vibrated into her chest. "You'll have to prove it."

They took off down the street, and Rain tightened her arms around Chase's firm body. At the slow speed they traveled through the French Quarter, she didn't have to hold him too tightly, but she'd have been an idiot not to take advantage of their close proximity.

His muscles were solid, and his woodsy, natural scent danced in her senses, making her head spin. She rested her nose against the back of his shoulder and took a few deep breaths. Sitting there, holding him, breathing in his intoxicating scent, her insides melted into goo.

Pheromones. His had to be so strong because he was a werewolf. No human—or witch for that matter—had ever affected her this way. Chase was, at heart, a pack animal. And pack animals drew others to them and were drawn to others in return. Instinct explained why the rest of the world slipped away when she was near him...and she couldn't fight instinct.

"Watch where you put your hands, *cher*. I might think you're trying to come on to me."

His deep, velvety voice roused her from her thoughts. They'd stopped at a light, and as her grip loosened, she'd unwittingly allowed her hands to rest on his crotch. Her heart rate kicked up, and she fought the urge to rub her palm across the mound in his jeans.

"Maybe I am." She slid her hands to his thighs and squeezed them before returning her grip to his stomach. With this giant machine rumbling beneath her and her body pressed up against him, how could she not be turned on?

He missed a beat in his reply, as if her response had derailed his thoughts. Good. Remind him he wasn't the only one with sex appeal.

"Hang on. We're heading onto the highway now." He took a left and zipped onto the road.

The speed and the wind rushing against her skin made her pulse quicken in exhilaration. They whizzed past cars and street lamps until they turned into a dizzying blur of light and shadow. Too bad the helmet kept the wind from whipping through her hair. That was the only thing that could have made this moment better.

He eased into the turns, and she tightened her grip as the bike leaned with the momentum. Chase commanded the machine like a man in control, as if it were an extension of his own self. The slight hint of fear she'd felt at the beginning of the ride drained away, leaving behind nothing but the thrill of excitement and the lust for the man. She could've done this all night long.

Chase pulled into the morgue parking lot and killed the engine. That ride had ended way too soon. Rain pried her arms from around his waist and yanked the helmet off her head, but she couldn't make her body move away from his. Being close to him felt way too good. Everything about this man had her mouth watering to taste him.

"You're hot, you're sweet, you ride a badass motorcycle… You must have a new girlfriend every week." She clamped her lips shut. She really needed to work on that filter.

He slid off the bike and set his helmet on the seat. Narrowing his eyes, he put his hands on his hips. "Is that what you think of me? Because I was a screw-up as a kid, I can't be faithful to a woman? Having tattoos and riding a bike automatically makes me an asshole?"

Uh oh. Way to piss off a werewolf again. She set her helmet on the seat in front of her and took a deep breath as she composed her answer. "I don't think you're an asshole. I assumed, based on how you make *me* feel, that a lot of women are attracted to you."

Something sparked in his eyes, and his entire demeanor softened. The edges of his lips curved into a tiny smile as he crossed his arms over his chest. "How do I make you feel?"

Oh, goddess, she did not need to get into her complicated emotions with this man. He made her feel more alive than she'd felt in years. Like maybe there was more to life than power and position. For the first time since she'd been cursed, she had more on her mind than getting her magic back. "We don't want to keep Macey waiting. Let's get this over with."

She swung her leg over the seat and stumbled as she rose to her feet. Her legs felt numb, her knees weak, and Chase caught her by the hips to steady her.

"Careful. Your legs might be wobbly." And there he was, close to her again, his face a few inches from hers.

How easy it would have been to lean in and taste his lips. To feel his beard against her face. Would it be scratchy or soft? She straightened, grabbing control of her thoughts before they spiraled into all the other places she'd like to feel his beard against.

With her equilibrium returning, she stepped back before her desires overshadowed her rational thoughts. "How do you walk so easily after riding this thing?"

"You get used to it." He smiled, and taking her hand, he led her toward the brown brick building.

"Thanks for the ride. Having a man and a machine between my legs at the same time was exhilarating." She sucked in a sharp breath as heat crept up her cheeks. "That did not come out right."

He cast her a sideways glance, one corner of his mouth pulling into his signature cocky grin. "Sounded good to me. I'd like to take you for a longer ride when we're done here."

"I'd like that too." Way, *way* too much.

They stopped outside the door, and he turned to face her. "This body we're about to see is in bad shape."

She put a lid on the pot of emotions boiling over for Chase. As much as she'd enjoyed the ride over, this wasn't a date. It was time to be serious. "How bad?"

"She looks like a mummy. Dark, leathery skin. Missing an eye. If it's too much, let me know and we'll leave."

"I'll be fine." She wasn't about to show weakness in front of him. After everything he'd been through as a kid, for him to show her even the slightest bit of trust proved his emotional strength. But he hadn't gotten over it, and he'd need a strong witch to help him come to terms with his past and let go of his prejudice. She would be strong for him.

"All right then. Don't say you weren't warned." He opened the door and motioned for her to enter.

Bright fluorescent lights hummed from above, giving the plain reception area a clinical feel. Four empty chairs sat against one wall, and a petite, blonde woman leaned against the counter, chatting with a tall man with light brown hair. They both wore business casual clothes, but the guns holstered on the woman's hip and the man's shoulder gave away their occupations.

Chase placed his hand on the small of Rain's back and guided her toward the detectives, his touch sending a flood of warmth through her veins. "This is Macey and her partner, Bryce."

Rain shook Macey's hand. "It's nice to finally meet you. I'm Rain."

Macey smiled. "I hope Chase has been treating you right. I've heard good things about your cakes."

Chase crossed his arms and shifted his weight to one foot, casting Macey an unreadable look. The alpha's mate winked at him, letting him know whatever message he'd tried to send had been received.

Rain looked back to Chase. "We're getting along." That was an understatement. She turned to Bryce. "Hi."

"Nice to meet you." He shook her hand. "I seem to be the only person in New Orleans who doesn't have some sort of psychic ability."

"I'm not a psychic. I'm a witch."

Bryce scowled and looked at Macey, who shifted uncomfortably and glanced to the man behind the counter. "Is the body ready for us?"

"Yes, ma'am. Y'all can head back."

"This way." Macey whispered something to Chase as she strode for the door.

Werewolves may have kept their true identities secret from humans, but witches were well known, especially in New Orleans. They kept their more powerful abilities hidden, like Snow's ability to freeze things, but the practice of spells and rituals were common knowledge.

Bryce followed after Macey, and Chase put his hand on Rain's arm, holding her back a few steps. "Macey's partner doesn't know about us. He thinks I talk to ghosts."

"You could have warned me about that before we got here." She couldn't be expected to keep the right secrets if she wasn't made aware of which secrets she had to keep.

"Sorry." He gave her a sheepish look. "Having your arms wrapped around me for so long distracted me."

Her heart did this weird *thud...thud-thud-thud* thing, and she plastered on a smile. "I won't give your secret away." She moved toward the door, trying to put some distance between them before she wrapped her arms around him again.

"I trust you."

His words stopped her in her tracks, and she lowered her gaze, unable to meet his eyes. He had no reason to trust her. She'd been hiding things from him since the moment she met him, and it killed her to know their entire relationship was built on a lie. She wasn't worthy of his trust, but damn it, she wanted to be. Coming clean about her curse would be the first step. He deserved the truth. At least a little of it.

When she didn't respond, Chase brushed passed her and pushed open the door, leaving her alone in the reception area with the heaviness of her lies weighing her down, making it hard to move. She had to tell him. If she lost the wedding because of her admission, so be it. She couldn't lie to him anymore.

Rain followed the sound of their voices down the hallway and into the heart of the morgue. Her shoes squeaked on the white tile floor as she stepped in the room, and the sickly-sweet smell of decaying flesh made her wrinkle her nose as she took in her surroundings. Row after row of square metal doors lined three of the walls, all of them sealed shut, except one. Chase, Macey, and Bryce stood by the open door, waiting for her.

"Did you prepare her?" Bryce asked Chase.

He gave a quick nod. "She knows what to expect."

Macey reached for the drawer, but Bryce put a hand

up to stop her. "Hold on. Before we do this, I've got to know. What's the difference between a witch and someone with psychic powers like Macey or Chase? You do Voodoo magic or something?"

Rain closed the distance between them and looked at both Macey and Chase, doing her best to assure them with her gaze that she wouldn't say too much. "Most witches are Wiccan. It's a religion; so is Voodoo. We worship a goddess and try our best to be one with nature."

Bryce arched an eyebrow. "Do the spells you cast work?"

A skeptic. Most humans were, but they rarely argued with her logic. "Casting spells is a lot like prayer. Do you believe prayer works?"

He shrugged. "Sure I do."

"Then why not spells?"

Bryce furrowed his brow as he contemplated her words. "I'm not even going to pretend to understand what y'all do or how you do it. The less I know, the better."

Rain gave him a reassuring smile. "I'm not going to cast any spells. I'm here to identify the body. She belonged to my old coven."

Bryce blinked.

"A coven is like a church."

"Hmm…" He rubbed his chin. "Witch church. If you say so." He pulled out the drawer to reveal the body.

Macey moved back the sheet, and Rain's breath caught in her throat at the sight of the remains. Based on the hair and nail polish alone—the only things left intact—she didn't recognize the woman. Her skin had shriveled on her bones, masking any features she might have had while alive. Rain's stomach twisted, and she swallowed the sour taste creeping up her throat. This woman wasn't mummified. She'd had the life sucked out of her, and Rain had only met one person with that ability.

"Here's the mark I told you about." Chase pointed to the coven crest on the woman's chest below her collarbone. "Calista said it was Miami. Do you recognize it?"

Rain nodded. "It's Miami. This is what it used to look like." She slid her shirt off her shoulder and turned her back so they could see the crest on her shoulder blade.

As she turned around and looked at Chase, his eyes held so much compassion, her heart thudded against her ribs.

"Do you know who she is?" His hands twitched as if he fought the urge to reach for her.

"Based on what I can tell from what's left of her, she's no one I was close to. I may have known her in passing, but it's difficult to say." She wrapped her arms around herself to chase away the chill penetrating her bones. Visions of the corpse would be invading her nightmares for weeks. "I've seen enough."

This time, Chase didn't hesitate. He wrapped his arms around her and tugged her to his chest, and the firmness and strength of his embrace warmed her from the inside out. She didn't know the dead woman on the table, but that didn't make it any less disturbing. He guided her out of the building and stopped on the sidewalk out front. The detectives followed on their heels.

"Thanks for your help, ma'am," Bryce said. "We better get back to the station, Mace."

Macey tugged her bottom lip and cut her gaze between Rain and Bryce. "Give me a minute. I need to talk to Rain about my wedding cake."

Bryce chuckled. "I'll be in the car."

As soon as her partner walked out of earshot, Macey

turned to Rain. "Is there anything else you can tell us about the woman? I heard something about an energy vampire mentioned. Could you pick up on anything at all?"

Rain inhaled a shaky breath and leaned into Chase's side for support. Could her ex be alive? Surely not after what she'd done. "It does appear to be the work of an energy vampire, though I've never seen one drain a victim so thoroughly. In my experience, they usually take a little at a time...whatever they need to accomplish their task or recover from overusing their magic."

Chase stiffened. "In your experience?"

"I knew an energy vampire once, a long time ago. I was unwittingly his victim for more than a year before I caught on to what was happening." She shivered.

He tightened his arm around her protectively. "Do you know where this guy is now? Could he have done this?"

"I don't think so." Should she tell him the truth? What would he think of her if he knew what she'd done? "The last time I saw him, he was...ill. He was in no condition to perform any kind of magic, and I doubt he survived."

Bryce tapped on the horn and made a winding motion with his hand, telling Macey to hurry up.

She held up a finger. "Should I notify Miami we have one of their witches?"

Rain chewed the inside of her cheek. Surely it was coincidence the dead witch came from her hometown. If the Miami coven got involved in the investigation, they'd drag Rain into it—probably blame her or Snow. She'd lose the wedding *and* the werewolf she was falling for. "Can you wait? Let me see if my sister can scry for the attacker. She's good at locating people." She looked at Chase.

"Having another coven in your territory could get sticky."
How thick could she make this layer of lies?

Bryce honked again.

"Let me know what you find out. I'll have to contact
them eventually." Macey turned to leave but paused. "And,
Chase, I know this goes without saying, but…"

"I'll keep her safe."

Macey smiled. "I know you will." She climbed into the
car with Bryce, and they pulled out of the parking lot.

"Are you okay?" Chase loosened his grip on her
shoulder and moved to look into her eyes.

"I'm fine. A little creeped out, but I'll get over it." She
had to. While the woman's death was tragic, it had
nothing to do with her. The little wriggling sensation in
the back of her mind was nothing. Isaac was dead. Her ex
couldn't have been responsible for this.

"Will you tell me more about this energy vampire you
encountered? How did he victimize you for so long
without you knowing?"

Her stomach sank. She needed to tell him the truth.
He deserved to know at least some of it, but first she
needed to gather her thoughts. To figure out how much
she was willing to risk. How much she should share. "Can
we get out of this parking lot? How about that ride you
promised me?" She flashed a weak smile.

"Rain…"

"I know. I will tell you, but it's not an easy story to
share." Especially since what she'd done to Isaac had been
a hundred times worse than what he'd done to her. "Take
me for a ride, and I promise I'll tell you."

He arched an eyebrow. "I'll hold you to that promise."

"I hope you do."

CHAPTER TEN

THE BARK OF A CYPRESS TREE DUG INTO ISAAC'S BACK as he closed his eyes and leaned his head against the trunk. The hard ground beneath his legs did nothing to ease his aching muscles, but this would all be over soon. Once the witch was dead, the spell would lift and his body could repair itself...and stay that way.

The temptation to send his tulpa to kill her now was palpable. He could end his own anguish, but death was too easy for the one who did this to him. She deserved to suffer one thousand times worse for what she'd done.

He took the jar from his pocket and gazed at the orb rolling around in the liquid. This little act of magic would require another week of recovery, but he'd endure the agony in order to watch her suffer.

His knuckles cracked as he gripped the lid and twisted it from the jar. Sharp pain shot up to his elbow, the rotating movement threatening to rip it from its socket. Dropping the lid, he poured the contents into his palm, allowing the liquid to flow through his fingers. He closed his hand around the eye and concentrated on the magic within it.

"May the magic inside be my guide." His voice came out in a croak. "I call on her sight to lead me through the night. Show me Rain, who has caused me insufferable pain."

The eye warmed in his hand, sending tingling energy up his arm and into his core. He closed his own eyes, allowing the visions to swim through his mind. Blurry at first, as his concentration focused, they came into crisp view.

"There you are, my little Rain. My, how you've grown." She hadn't been much more than a girl when he'd met her all those years ago. Powerful, but immature. She'd been an easy target, and once he'd cast his spell of obsession, she'd been his to manipulate. She was still beautiful, though her features had matured and her hair had grown. A familiar ache seized in his chest. He had cared for her once, but she'd hardly acknowledged his existence. Always focused on her magic and starting her business, power and position in the coven had been her main concerns.

His spell had taught her to love. To care for *him* above all else. He'd made her a better person, and she'd repaid him in the most inhumane way. The ache in his heart turned to a stab of anger, and he pushed the thoughts out of his mind and focused on her image.

But seeing her face didn't help him with her location. He concentrated on widening the vision. She was with a man. Tall with dark hair, he looked at her as if he wanted to consume her. The smile on her lips said she'd enjoy being eaten.

Isaac paused, his ragged breath catching in his throat as he looked closer in his vision. Though the man's face no longer contorted in pain, his features couldn't be mistaken. The werewolf from the swamp had caught Rain's eye.

Pain shot through his temple as he ground his teeth, and he lifted his injured arm. Cursed blood oozed through the moss bandage, and the burning from the beast's teeth had never ceased. Of all the men his Rain could have latched onto, why did it have to be the werewolf?

He closed his eyes and looked at her in his vision. The moment her wicked spell had taken effect on Isaac, his control over her had broken. He'd get her back, though. The little witch belonged to him, and she'd learn her lesson soon enough. He'd make the man suffer first. Then her sister and anyone else she cared about.

She would fear him, and in her fear, she would respect him. He had once made her eyes sparkle like they did for this man. Perhaps he could make them shine again. If he could drain a witch powerful enough to unbind Rain's magic, he could break her curse. With her magic restored, she could lift the spell she'd put on him and be his forever.

He gazed at her deep-gray eyes in his vision. She would pay one way or another—either sacrificing her life or devoting it to him.

He inhaled deeply, the humid air slicing like razor blades down his trachea, and reined in his emotions. "Show me where she's been."

His vision of Rain swam, drifting through time and space to a house—brown with white trim and green shutters. In his mind, he stepped inside and found her sitting on the couch next to the same man.

With a growl of frustration, he searched the vision again. Another building—bright yellow with a light-green door. A bakery. He peered through the window. Rain wore a blue apron and stood behind the counter, decorating a cake. His lips cracked as they curved into a smile. His pastry chef had made her dream of running a bakery come true.

Forcing his vision to the present, he watched Rain climb on the back of the man's motorcycle. Jealousy rolled through his shriveled veins like fire. The vision wavered as the magic subsided, flickering and losing focus. It was just as well; he'd seen enough. Fisting his hand around the eye, he squeezed until the gelatinous mess oozed through his fingers, ending the horrid vision.

Piercing pain ripped through his body as the magic dissipated, but he found the strength to call upon his tulpa. The shadow figure appeared before him, ready to do his bidding. He didn't need to speak to tell it his intent —*follow the man*. Make them both terrified for their lives.

CHAPTER ELEVEN

CHASE'S HEART POUNDED AS HE SPED DOWN THE highway, but the rush he normally felt from riding on the open road paled in comparison to the way Rain's arms wrapped around him made his body hum. He could've ridden like this for hours, with her soft curves pressed into his back, her hands gripping his stomach.

He drove for half an hour, giving her time to gather her thoughts. Her secrets were about to be revealed, and he wanted to know everything. He took her over the bridge into Algiers and followed the back roads to a quiet spot on the riverbank. When he cut the engine, she tightened her arms around him as if she wasn't ready to let him go. He knew the feeling.

She loosened her grip, and he took off his helmet, hanging it on a handlebar. Climbing off the bike, he held out his hand to help her off. Her chest rose and fell as she took a deep breath and pulled the helmet from her head. Her soft, dark curls bounced as she shook her head and ran her fingers through her hair. She looked sexy as hell perched on the back of his bike...a sight he would love to get used to.

Setting the helmet on the seat, she held his gaze, and the confliction in her eyes tore at his heart. Whatever she was about to tell him wouldn't be easy.

Sharing his secret with her hadn't been a piece of cake either, but they'd get through it, whatever *it* was. It couldn't be any worse than the things he'd done.

She took his hand and swung her leg over the bike, stepping straight into his arms. Holding him tight, she pressed her face against his chest and inhaled deeply. If she was stalling, he wasn't complaining. Damn, she felt good in his arms.

He rubbed his hand across her back and pressed his lips to the top of her head. Her hair brushed his nose, the sweet scent of vanilla tickling his senses, and he tightened his arms around her. There was no denying the primal possessiveness he felt for this woman. His wolf had already claimed her, and now the man had finally accepted it.

Pulling from his embrace, she gave him a half-smile and slipped her hand into his. "I owe you an explanation."

"Then let's talk." He led her closer to the river, and they settled on a patch of grass. Light from the half-moon danced across the surface of the Mississippi, making the muddy water sparkle. The cosmos flowers growing on the bank filled the air with the sweet scent of chocolate, and he inhaled deeply, enjoying the unusual floral perfume.

Rain angled herself to face him, and her knee brushed his thigh. The heat radiating from her body called to him, urging him to take her in his arms again and find out if her lips tasted as sweet as they looked.

She rested her hand on his leg, the simple touch sending his heart racing. As she chewed her bottom lip, she looked into his eyes, her face taking on a mask of resolve. "I haven't always been a dud. I used to have powers."

He suppressed a smile. "I had a feeling you did." Finally, the truth came out. She was way too confident to be a magical being without magic. He'd peeled away one layer of the mystery surrounding Rain Connolly, but it wasn't enough. He ached to know her to the center of her very being. "Why did you lie?"

She let out a heavy sigh. "Let me tell you the story from the beginning. Hopefully you'll understand." She pulled her hand into her lap and clasped her fingers together. "You're not the only one who's had bad luck with witches. That energy vampire I knew...I used to date him."

He clenched his jaw as the feeling of protectiveness gripped his heart. "He took your powers?" If the guy was alive, and if Chase ever found him...

"Not exactly." She dropped her head and stared at her hands in her lap. "I was in love with him. I thought I was, anyway. Obsessed would be a better way to describe it, so I'm not sure if..." She exhaled sharply. "It doesn't matter. We lived together for almost a year."

She looked into his eyes. "I was like you. Second in command of the coven. I was training for a place on the national witches' council."

The fact didn't surprise him. "You must have been very powerful."

"I was. And Isaac...the energy vampire...was using my power without my knowledge. He'd take it, little by little, at night while I was sleeping. It was such a small amount, I didn't notice. I'd feel sick the next day sometimes, but normally I'd recover by the time I woke in the morning."

His jaw clenched. "Bastard." The mere thought of anyone hurting Rain was enough to drive him mad.

"It gets worse. I caught him cheating on me. A friend saw him out with another woman, so I followed him one night, and sure enough, he was seeing someone on the side. When he got home that night, I pretended I was asleep. He stood over the bed and touched my face. It felt like he was draining the life from my body, but I couldn't move. I couldn't stop him. I passed out, and when I woke the next morning, I confronted him."

Chase pried Rain's hands apart and slipped his fingers through hers. The lines in her forehead smoothed as she seemed to relax.

She straightened her spine and took a deep breath. "Long story short, we aren't together anymore. I ended up cursed and my powers are bound. Like I said before, the last time I saw him he was on his death bed. If he were alive, he'd be capable of doing what happened to the woman at the morgue, but I don't see how he could have recovered from his illness." She bit her bottom lip.

Chase ground his teeth as he tried to calm his pounding heart. "He cursed you."

She lowered her gaze to their entwined hands. "I lost more than my powers. And this is why I've been hesitant to get close to you...to anyone. If another witch shows me kindness, something bad will happen. Not to me, but to the person who was nice to me."

Chase closed his eyes and rubbed his forehead. What kind of sick bastard would do this to her? "If he can't have you, no one can?"

She glanced at him before returning her gaze to their hands. The muscles in her throat worked as she swallowed, and she placed her other hand on top of his. "I think that part of the curse was meant to teach me a lesson. I wasn't exactly kind when I confronted him. Now, no one can be kind to me without me unwittingly being *un*kind to them."

That explained her strange behavior. "What kind of bad things happen? And is it if they do *anything* kind? Or does it have to be something big?"

She let out a dry chuckle. "My parents took me out to dinner for my birthday a year after it happened. They both ended up in the hospital with pneumonia for two weeks."

"Ouch."

Nodding, she pressed her lips together, and her eyes shimmered. "The other day, you saved me from being hit by a taxi. Then you got sick when a snake bit you."

"You think the snake bite was because of your curse?"

She drew her shoulders toward her ears, and her bottom lip trembled. "What else could it be?"

Oh, hell no. He had to end this nonsense right now. No way was a stupid curse going to keep him away from his fate-bound. "Rain, listen to me. I was hunting in the swamp; I've been bitten before. That wasn't because of you."

"Have you ever gotten that sick?" A tear spilled from the inner corner of her eye, and he wiped it away with his thumb.

"No, but..." He had to fix this. No wonder she'd been holding back. She thought he'd get hurt if she let him in. "What *exactly* is the curse?"

"Any witch who shows me kindness will be punished."

"Any *witch*. Did it specify that it had to be a witch?"

"Well, yes."

He smiled. "Rain, I'm a werewolf, not a witch. Your curse won't affect me."

She traced her fingertips along the back of his hand. "What if one of your ancestors was a witch? If you have the slightest amount of witch blood in your veins, it could..."

"I don't. I swear, I am one hundred percent werewolf. Look at me." He cupped her cheek in his hand, drawing her face toward his. The sadness in her eyes stabbed at his heart. She'd opened up to him, finally letting him into her world, and now he understood her hesitation. "I'll take my chances."

She shook her head. "If anything happens to you..."

"Then it will be on me. You've warned me. I'm aware of the risks." He leaned closer, the tip of his nose brushing hers.

"Chase."

"I know you won't hurt me. Please let me in." He paused, his mouth lingering centimeters from hers, giving her plenty of time to move away. When she didn't, he brushed his lips over hers.

She responded, leaning into him, running her hand up his thigh to grip his hip. As her lips parted and her velvet tongue slipped into his mouth, fire shot through his veins. She tasted like peppermint, as sweet as the cakes she baked, and he couldn't get enough of her.

He slid his hand into her hair and moved the other to her back, holding her even closer. His entire body hummed, electricity igniting nerves he never knew existed, as if fate were smiling down on him as he held her. She was meant to be his.

Gliding her hand behind his neck, she tugged him toward her as she lay in the grass. He sidled next to her, afraid if he climbed on top of her they might not be able hold back. He wanted her. Needed her...to fill her, to feel her body wrapped around his, to become one with her.

She settled on her side, the length of her body pressed into his, and he closed his eyes to memorize the way she felt. Soft, supple, as if she were made to fit into arms. Tracing the contour of his lips with her tongue, she caught his bottom lip between her teeth.

He couldn't stop the moan vibrating from his throat. His fate-bound mate lay in his arms, and he wanted to taste every inch of her. He trailed his lips along her jawline and nipped at her delicate earlobe. Her breath hitched, and she tilted her head, giving him access to the sweet curve of her neck. He kissed his way down her throat, pausing to feel her pulse race beneath his lips, the intoxicating scent of her skin making his head spin.

He needed this woman, but not here. Not now. He pulled away to look at her, and she met his gaze with so much passion in her stormy eyes he almost gave in to desire. Instead, he took her hand and sat up, tugging her into his side. "A kiss like that is worth twenty snake bites."

She bit her lip and rested her hand on his chest. "Are you sure you don't have any witch in you?"

The warmth of her touch through his shirt made him shiver, and he longed to feel her bare skin against his. "Positive."

A genuine smile lit up her face as she leaned closer and whispered into his ear, "I think I'd like to have a little werewolf in me." She nipped his earlobe, and a flush of fiery heat spread through his chest.

"There's nothing little about this werewolf, *cher*."

She ran her hand down his stomach, moving it over to his hip before she reached the good part. "I'd like to see for myself."

A shudder ran through his entire body. If he got any harder, he'd pass out from the lack of blood flow to his brain. "You're killing me, woman. Let me at least take you out to dinner first."

She sat up straight and studied him, her brow furrowing as if she wasn't sure. Her tongue slipped out to moisten her lips, and he couldn't help himself. He had to taste her again.

Cupping his hand behind her neck, he held her close and kissed her. She opened for him willingly, returning the kiss with as much passion as he felt. Closing his eyes, he drank her in, enjoying the sweetness of her tongue, the softness of her lips against his. He could've kissed her all night long, but she pressed her palms to his chest and pushed him away, laughing.

"Okay, you convinced me. I'll have dinner with you, but not tonight. It's late, and I have to get up early to deliver muffins to a daycare for a teacher appreciation breakfast."

"I love muffins. What flavor?"

"Banana nut and chocolate chip." She rose to her feet and dusted the grass from her pants.

"My favorite." Chase stood.

"Which one?"

"Both." He grinned at the beautiful woman before him. Anything she made would be his favorite. As he reached for her hand, a shadow passed in the corner of his vision. He jerked his head to follow the image, but it vanished into the trees. "Did you see that?"

Rain followed his gaze. "See what?"

"A shadow. It went that way." He pointed to the tree line, and the entity dashed behind a trunk. "Stay here." He took a few steps forward, keeping Rain within arms' reach.

He wasn't about to leave her alone in the dark with no magic to protect herself, but he couldn't leave without investigating the shadow.

It could've been his mind playing tricks, but the sinking feeling in his stomach told him this was the same entity he'd seen in the swamp before he'd been bitten.

Rain stepped next to him and clutched his bicep. "What do you think it is?"

"It might be a demon."

She tightened her grip. "A demon?"

"I thought we got rid of the bastards a few months ago, but someone new might be summoning them." He peered into the trees, but in the darkness, and in his human form, he couldn't make out much. Though his vision was sharper than a human's, in his wolf form he could see fifty times better. If the fiend was alone, Chase could take him and keep Rain safe at the same time. More than one, though, and they'd have problems.

"What should we do?" She loosened her grip and stayed by his side, brave in the face of evil.

He glanced at her before a rustling sound drew his attention back to the trees. "Have you ever seen a were-wolf shift?"

She blinked, a touch of uncertainty flashing in her eyes as she stepped away from him. "No."

"I promise I won't hurt you."

Her doubtful expression faded, and she lifted her chin. "I know you won't." She took a few more steps back, clasping her hands at her chest and watching him with wide, curious eyes.

His body tingled as he called on his wolf, electricity humming through his veins as the magic morphed his form. Dark chocolate fur rolled over his skin as he shifted, and his front paws landed on the ground with a thud.

Rain gasped as the transformation completed, but she didn't back away. Werewolves were massive—at least twice the size of a normal wolf—and his knife-like teeth could easily rip a person to shreds. She had every right to be terrified, but she wasn't. She moved toward him slowly and reached out a hand to stroke his fur. "Should I stay here?"

He jerked his head toward the trees to indicate she should follow him. For now, they were observers. He'd form his plan of attack—if he attacked—once he knew what they were dealing with.

They crept forward, Rain glued to his side, her hand resting on his back. He'd have time to consider how much he respected her bravery later. Right now, he had a demon to vanquish.

As he reached the first tree, the shadow darted from its hiding place and took off in the opposite direction. Torn between his duty to rid the city of demons and his instinct to protect the woman who would be his mate, he chose instinct and stayed by Rain's side. He swept his enhanced vision through the thicket, listening intently for any rustling or out-of-place sounds. Nothing.

He stood utterly motionless, breathing deeply for the scent of death, looking for movement. Still nothing. The fiend had been alone, and now it was gone.

He blew out a hard breath and swung his head around to see Rain. If she was scared, it didn't show on her face. Her eyes were tight, but with determination rather than worry. And he couldn't help but pause to admire her bravery. She'd planned to battle the demon by his side. He nudged her with his head and stepped away from the trees.

"I guess it's gone?"

He nodded. It was possible the demon had planned to attack but changed its mind when it discovered Chase was its natural-born enemy. He'd have to alert the pack, so they'd know to be on the lookout for a shadow.

Rain let out a breath as they walked up the riverbank and away from the trees, her posture relaxing, a sly smile curving her lips. "Are you going to be naked when you shift back to human?"

Thankfully not, or she'd see the raging hard-on she'd given him that was sure to return when he shifted. Then again, with the way she'd kissed him earlier, she might enjoy it. A chill ran through his body at the thought of her enjoying his dick, but that was a thought for another time. He called on his magic and transformed into his human self. Yep, the hard-on came back, tucked away inside his jeans.

Her shoulders slumped. "Damn. How come in the movies werewolves are always naked when they turn back into humans?"

"Because the people making the movies have probably never met a real werewolf. I'm sorry to disappoint."

Her smile widened. "I don't think you could ever disappoint me."

He took her hand and led her to his bike. "Our clothes get absorbed by the magic when we shift. When we change back, everything is in its proper place."

"Fascinating."

He pulled on his helmet. "I need to report this to the alpha. Let's get you home, so you'll be safe."

Rain climbed onto the bike and wrapped her arms around

Chase. Thank the goddess she had a helmet on, or she wouldn't have been able to stop herself from exploring the back of his neck with her tongue. The man was delectable.

And he'd been so confident when he saw the demon. Like he knew he could vanquish it and keep her safe at the same time. Brave, but not cocky about his abilities. A swarm of butterflies took flight in her stomach, and she closed her eyes, letting the rumble of the engine and the smell of his skin seep into her senses, relaxing her. She'd never been in the presence of a demon before, but she hadn't feared for her safety at all. She never would with Chase in her life.

As he stopped in front of the bakery, she tightened her arms around him. She'd been punishing herself long enough. Maybe fate had sent her a werewolf to show her life could still be fulfilling. Maybe the act of selflessness that would break her curse would be *not* asking him for the final ingredient—falling for a man who could end her punishment but caring so much about him that she never asked. But was it worth the risk after what happened before?

She'd been a strong, capable witch at one time before she'd let her emotions overwhelm her, and she'd done the unthinkable to the man she'd thought she loved. Her obsession with Isaac had driven her to use forbidden magic, and she'd been paying dearly for it ever since. What would happen if she allowed herself to fall for Chase? If Isaac didn't have her under a spell years ago, and those insane emotions had been her own, would she turn into a raving maniac this time too?

No, it couldn't happen. She cared deeply for Chase, but the feeling was completely different than before. She loved being near him, but when he wasn't around, she was fine. Sure, she missed him, but she didn't pine away, her thoughts becoming an obsessive whirlwind of anxiety like they had with Isaac.

She'd been young and dumb then. Even if she hadn't been under a spell, the last seven years had changed her, mellowed her. She was capable of having a mature, loving relationship now, wasn't she? There was one way to find out.

They climbed off the bike, and he guided her to the door with his hand firmly planted on her back. She doubted the demon had followed them home, but with Chase's stiff posture, he was obviously on high alert. He had a protective nature, and being near him gave her a sense of security she never realized she'd been lacking. She unlocked the door, and he ushered her inside.

"I'm sure the demon was targeting me, but I don't like the idea of you being here alone."

Was this his way of offering to stay the night with her? The thought of having his warm, hard body next to her in bed all night made her shiver. "What are you suggesting?"

He rubbed his beard and glanced at his bike on the curb outside. "Can your sister stay with you?"

Damn. "That's not the answer I was hoping for." She bit her lip. "I didn't mean to say that out loud."

He chuckled and wrapped his arms around her waist. "You didn't have to. I could see the disappointment in your eyes." He leaned in as if to kiss her, but he pressed his lips to her ear and whispered, "I would love to spend the night with you."

The warmth of his breath on her skin sent shivers running down to her toes. He caught her earlobe between his teeth before moving back to look at her. "But I texted Luke, and he'll have my ass if I don't get out there and stop the damn demon. Can you call your sister?"

"If I asked her, she'd be doing me a kindness. My curse may not affect you, but she would pay dearly for it."

He huffed. "What if I call her? Then she'll be doing *me* a kindness."

She rose onto her toes to kiss him. Her dream of feeling his soft, warm lips all over her body would have to wait, but that was okay. Letting their emotions simmer for a while would sweeten the reward. "There's no need. Snow cast a spell of protection on the bakery. There are totems placed around the perimeter, and as long as the doors are locked, nothing can get in."

He arched an eyebrow, giving her a wary look.

"I'll prove it to you. Go outside, and I'll lock the door. I'll bet you anything you can't get in."

He pinned her with a heated gaze that seemed to suck the breath from her lungs. "Anything?"

She swallowed. "Yep."

Running his fingers through her hair, he grazed her neck with his lips. "If I get in, you'll give me anything I want? Whenever I want it?"

"I will." Her knees weakened. *Goddess, please let it be the same thing I want.*

"And if I can't get in? Not that I won't be able to, but we need to make it fair." The corner of his mouth curved into a cocky grin.

She reached a hand to his face and ran her fingers down the soft hair in his beard. "Then you have to give me whatever *I* want."

"Sounds like a win-win to me."

She ran her thumb across his lips, and tingling magic

seeped into her skin, sending a jolt through her heart. "You're assuming we both want the same thing."

He pulled her close, taking her mouth with his. The evidence of his desire rubbed against her stomach, and she fought the urge to slide her hand between their bodies to feel it. He had to be the sexiest man alive—his body, his scent, his soul—everything about him ignited a fire inside her like an oven on full blast. There was enough heat between them to fuel her entire bakery.

As the kiss slowed, he released his hold and stepped back. "I think we do." He winked and strutted out the door.

She turned the lock and watched as Chase rummaged through the compartment on the side of his motorcycle. Small black bag in hand, he returned to the door, his smile prematurely triumphant.

He held up the kit. "I know how to unlock a door."

How many times had he broken into a building to hide supernatural evidence? He seemed confident he could break in here, so he must have had a lot of practice. He jimmied his tools into the lock, his brow puckering in concentration.

Rain laughed as his smile slipped into a frown. With a huff, he shoved his tools into his back pocket and crossed his arms. He jiggled the doorknob, but it didn't budge.

"Try to break a window," she called through the glass, not even attempting to hide her smile.

He narrowed his eyes. "I don't want to damage your business."

"What's wrong? Scared the big bad wolf won't be able to blow the house down? I've got insurance."

"Oh, now you're asking for it. Stand back." He grabbed a helmet and hurled it into the small, vertical window next to the door, but the glass didn't shatter. Instead, the helmet bounced off the magic force field Snow had created and slammed into Chase's stomach.

He groaned and stumbled to his bike to drop the helmet. "All right. You win."

Rain pressed her lips together and opened the door. "Satisfied of my safety now?"

"I suppose." He rubbed his abdomen as he entered the bakery, absently lifting his shirt to reveal a few ridges of muscle along his stomach. A bird tattoo occupied three inches of space above his left hip, and she was overcome with the urge to explore it with her tongue. To lick every inch of him.

She sucked in a deep, shuddering breath. "Since you have to go, I'll collect my prize later, when you have more time." She'd need at least a few hours to explore his body properly.

He grinned. "I'm looking forward to it. I work at the bar every night until Tuesday. Want to have that dinner date then?"

Running her hands up his chest, she rested them on his shoulders. "I'm not sure if I can wait that long to collect."

"I'm afraid you'll have to, *cher*, if the prize you're looking for is what I hope it is. I'll see you Tuesday." He gave her one last kiss on the lips and slipped out the door.

Rain stood at the window as Chase got on his bike and rode away. As soon as he was out of sight, she plopped into a chair and sighed. She was falling hard and fast for the sexy werewolf, and there wasn't a thing she could do to stop it.

CHAPTER TWELVE

RAIN FINISHED COUNTING THE MONEY IN THE CASH register, and her heart did a little sprint as she prepared the deposit. Once word spread that the alpha werewolf and his mate had chosen her bakery for their wedding cake, business had picked up within the magical community. Pack members had come trickling in over the week, buying desserts and placing orders.

Snow padded into the storefront from the kitchen. "Smiling while you're counting money. That's a good sign."

Rain zipped the money bag shut and leaned against the counter. "It is. I took an order for a five-year-old werewolf's birthday party this afternoon. When they come in tomorrow to pay, I'll have enough for the coven fees."

"Those werewolves are turning out to be a blessing." Snow grinned. "Especially one werewolf in particular."

Warmth spread through Rain's body. Chase had met her in the park for her lunch break every day since that amazing kiss, and tonight would be his first night off. Their first official date.

Snow rearranged the cupcakes in the display case,

filling in the empty spaces with items from the back. "Where's he taking you?"

"To dinner." She clutched the bag to her chest.

Her sister straightened. "And then?"

The heat in her body crept up to her cheeks. "He said, 'We'll see where the night takes us.'"

Snow wiggled her eyebrows. "That sounds promising. Are you nervous?"

Rain forced a laugh. "Me? Nervous? He's a smokin' hot werewolf whose kisses make me feel like a fireworks display with a very short fuse. I have nothing to be nervous about."

Snow wiped the counter with a rag. "You're scared."

"Terrified." She toyed with the zipper on the bag. "I haven't been with a man since Isaac." Her heart sank, a feeling of apprehension settling in her stomach like day-old meatloaf. "It's been seven years."

"I'm sure he'll go easy on you."

"I don't think I want him to." She fanned herself with the bag. Her date with Chase couldn't come soon enough.

"I'm supposed to pick Rain up in an hour. Can't someone else cover the shift?" Chase lowered his voice, using his hand to cover the phone, so his niece wouldn't overhear his conversation with Bekah. He loved spending time with the little girl, but tonight was his date with Rain, and his sister was screwing up his plans.

"No one else can do it. I should be home in an hour and a half." Dishes clanked in the background. "You'll be thirty minutes late. She'll understand."

He ran a hand down his face, muffling his frustrated sigh. "Okay. Get your ass home as soon as possible."

"I love you, big brother." Her voice took on that sing-song tone it always did when she knew she owed him big-time. As a restaurant manager, her schedule tended to be erratic, but it was flexible enough to enable her to go to college at the same time. She'd be graduating at the end of the semester, so her dependence on Chase as a free babysitter should lighten up soon.

"I love you too." He hung up the phone and glanced at Emma sitting on the floor in the living room. She smiled and clapped as the Beast in her favorite Disney movie transformed into a prince, and his heart swelled with love. There were worse reasons for being late.

He dialed Rain's number. "Hey, *cher*, I'm going to be a little late for our date tonight. Someone called in sick on Bekah, and she has to cover until they can find a replacement for the shift. I'm watching Emma until she gets home."

"How late do you think you'll be?" The disappointment was evident in her voice.

"Could be half an hour." He sighed. Might as well let her know what to expect from his sister. "Knowing Bekah, it could be more."

"I see." She paused. "I've already closed the shop. I could come over and keep you company…"

A pleasant ache spread through his chest, and he couldn't fight his smile. "That's a thoughtful offer, but I had better plans than babysitting for our first official date."

"I don't mind. Emma is fun, and I'd…like to spend as much time with you as possible tonight."

The ache extended through his core. "Come on over then. Emma will be happy to see you."

Emma's movie ended, and he made a game of cleaning up her toys, attempting to make the place somewhat presentable for Rain. His niece squealed when the doorbell rang, and he had to jump over the coffee table to get to the door before she opened it. A week had passed with no sign of the shadow demon, but he wasn't taking any chances when it came to Emma.

He put his hand on the knob. "What have we told you about opening the door for strangers?"

"It's not a stranger." She glared at him accusingly. "It's Rain."

"But we don't know that unless we look out the window, do we?" He lifted her so she could see through the glass at the top of the door.

"It's Rain. Let her in!" She kicked her legs until he set her on the floor, and she twisted the knob and swung open the door.

His fate-bound stood on the porch in jeans and a purple shirt. Her dark curls spiraled over her shoulders, and her lips curved into the most breathtaking smile he'd ever seen. She knelt to eye-level with his niece and hugged her before standing and kissing him on the cheek. She stepped back and held his gaze as his heart galloped in his chest. "Are you going to stand there staring at me all evening, or are you going to invite me in?"

"Come in!" Emma tugged her through the doorway, and he followed them into the living room, where Rain settled onto the couch next to his niece.

"You be Belle, and I'll be the Beast." Emma handed Rain a doll and began setting up a scene of other toys on the coffee table.

Chase sank onto the sofa next to Rain. "You don't have to do that if you don't want to."

She scooted closer to him, so the length of her thigh rested against his, and held the doll up to her face. "I don't mind. She kinda looks like me, don't you think?"

He couldn't help himself. Emma had her back turned, so he leaned in and gave Rain a quick kiss. Everything this woman did wrapped him tighter around her finger. She was smart, independent, brave, and beautiful, and she was amazing with his niece. Even if his wolf hadn't claimed her the moment he met her, he wouldn't have been able to stop himself from falling for Rain. She was everything he never knew he wanted.

They played with Emma for the next half-hour, stealing glances at each other as Belle and Beast went on their adventure. Every time Rain's stormy eyes met his, his pulse quickened. His phone buzzed, and he dug it out of his pocket to find a text from Bekah. He bit back the curse that tried to slip from his lips and tossed the phone on the table.

"What's wrong?" Rain had moved to the floor during their play session, so she settled onto the sofa next to him.

"Bekah isn't going to be home until nine. I'm sorry. If you want to leave and reschedule, I understand." Damn his sister. She knew how important this date was to him.

Emma froze. "Don't leave."

Rain smiled at her. "I'm not going to." She laced her arm around Chase's bicep and kissed him on the cheek. "I'm having too much fun."

"Yay!" Emma leaped from the floor and scurried out of the room.

He arched an eyebrow skeptically. "Seriously?"

"I like spending time with you, and the anticipation of getting you alone will make it that much better when it happens." She ran a hand along his inner thigh, stopping halfway up.

His stomach tightened, and he took a deep breath, trying to control the urge to lay her back on the sofa and have his way with her right then and there. He leaned close and touched his lips to her ear. "The anticipation might be the death of me."

He nipped her lobe, and a visible shiver ran through her entire body as her grip tightened on his thigh.

"A little delayed gratification will be good for you." She rose as Emma shuffled into the room, her arms full of coloring books.

"I'm hungry, Uncle Chase."

"I guess I could feed you ladies dinner since we're stuck here all evening." He'd planned to take Rain to his favorite Italian restaurant in the Garden District. Then they'd go for a ride on his bike so he could feel her supple body against his, her arms wrapped around his waist. Something about having her on the back of his bike—and the fact she enjoyed riding it—turned him on to no end.

But it would have to wait. Delayed gratification, she'd called it. He planned to gratify her until she screamed his name.

He shook his head to chase away the thoughts. "How about a pizza?"

"I want mac and cheese." Emma dropped the coloring books on the kitchen table and dragged Rain to a chair.

He followed them into the kitchen. "Don't you think we should offer our guest something a little more... substantial than mac and cheese?"

His niece poked out her bottom lip. "But you make the best mac and cheese in the world. Don't you want to impress your girlfriend?"

He sucked in a breath to respond, but he couldn't get the words past the lump in his throat. He did consider Rain his girlfriend. Hell, he was on a mission to make her his mate, but they hadn't discussed the terms of their relationship yet. He caught Rain's gaze, preparing to apologize, but the look in her eyes stopped him cold.

So much heat emanated from her gaze that it felt like she'd stripped him bare and made love to him with her eyes. Her full lips tugged into a sly smile, and when she slipped her tongue out to moisten them, his knees nearly buckled. "Yeah, Chase." She leaned back in the chair and crossed her arms. "Don't you want to impress your girlfriend?"

His heart slammed against his ribs. Was that a confirmation? "I..." *Get it together, man.* "Let me see if I have the ingredients." He turned around and opened the fridge, hoping the chilled air would cool the heat from his cheeks. It didn't.

He rummaged through the drawers and found the cheddar, gouda, and Colby jack, but the only meat they had in the house was hot dogs. He couldn't feed his *girlfriend* hot dogs.

With his arms full of ingredients, he shut the fridge door with his knee. "You ladies are in luck. I've got all the supplies for my world famous three-cheese mac and cheese, complete with hotdogs for the little one."

Emma stopped coloring and glared at him. "I'll share my hotdogs with Rain."

"That's okay." Rain patted her shoulder. "I'm a vegetarian. I don't eat meat."

Emma scratched her head as if the idea confounded her. "I eat meat. So does Uncle Chase. He catches deer and alligators and sometimes wild hogs..."

"Okay." He dropped a pot onto the stove, hoping the loud *clank* of metal on metal would stop his niece from going into the details of a werewolf diet. "Yes, I eat meat." He looked at Rain. "Is that going to be a problem?"

"I wouldn't expect a werewolf to be a vegetarian. In fact, I would find it rather strange if you were."

"Good." He held her gaze a little longer, building the anticipation, sweetening the gratification his sister had delayed. The things he planned to do to his girlfriend...

He busied himself with his culinary masterpiece, which wasn't much more than some melted cheese and heavy whipping cream mixed with elbow pasta, while Rain entertained his niece with the coloring books. Half an hour later, he carried three heaping bowls of mac and cheese to the table. "Take your stuff to the bedroom, squirt. It's time to eat."

Emma dutifully scooped up all the coloring books and crayons and scurried out of the kitchen as Chase sat in the seat next to Rain.

She picked up her fork and swirled it around in the bowl. "Smells delicious."

"I'm sorry it's not the romantic dinner I promised you."

She reached under the table to rest her hand on his knee. "You cooked for me. I call that romantic." She parted her lips and slipped the fork into her mouth, closing her eyes before sliding it out.

His mouth watered as her jaw flexed, the muscles in her throat moving up and down as she swallowed the food. The woman made eating mac and cheese look sexy. If his sister didn't come home soon so he could get Rain alone, he might spontaneously combust.

"I could be a jerk like you were and find something wrong with it...but I won't."

He chuckled. "I'd call suggesting I mate with a goat a jerk thing to say, but who am I to split hairs?"

She glared at him, but the corner of her mouth tugged into a grin. "It's the best mac and cheese I've ever eaten."

"I told you it was good." Emma climbed into her chair and tore into her dinner as if she hadn't eaten all day.

By the time they finished eating and washed the dishes, the front door swung open and Bekah strutted in. "I'm so sorry I'm late."

"Mommy!" Emma ran to her mom and hugged her.

"Let's go pack a bag," Bekah said. "We're having a sleepover at Grandma's."

Chase arched an eyebrow at his sister. "A sleepover?"

"I owed you one. Now we're even." She followed Emma into the bedroom.

He pulled Rain into his arms. "Finally, some alone time."

She laughed and gave him a quick kiss before pushing him away. "We aren't alone yet. Wait until Emma's gone."

"What?" He took both her hands in his and looked into her eyes. "It's good for her to see a man treating his girlfriend right."

"Hmm..." She stepped closer. "You think you're treating me right?"

He rested his forehead against hers. "Am I?"

She smiled. "So right."

"Okay, we are getting out of your hair." Bekah slung a bag over her shoulder and tugged Emma toward the front door.

"Here, Rain, this is for you." Emma handed her a picture from her coloring book.

"Thank you, Emma. That's so sweet of you." Rain took the page and showed it to Chase.

"It's Belle and the Beast," Emma said. "Like you and Uncle Chase."

"See you tomorrow, squirt." He mussed her hair as she passed.

Bekah and Emma left, and Rain leaned against the counter and set the picture on the surface. "Does your mom live close by?"

"She's got a place in Algiers. Not too far away."

She chewed her bottom lip and fidgeted with her hands as if being alone with him suddenly made her nervous. "Does she live by herself?"

"Yes." What happened to the flirtation and that promise of gratification?

"She never remarried? Or..." She furrowed her brow. "Was she not allowed to remarry? I'm not sure how it works with werewolves."

Ah, it was the girlfriend comment. Werewolf relationships could seem complicated to someone on the outside; he could understand her confusion. He leaned on the counter next to her. "When a werewolf takes a mate, it's for life. Since my dad died, she is allowed to find a new mate, but..." He took her hand, lacing his fingers through hers.

"But?"

"He was her fate-bound. If a werewolf gets the opportunity to mate with their fate-bound, no one else will ever do. That's a bond that can never be broken or replaced."

Something sparked in her eyes. They widened briefly, a look of...recognition...flashing in her gaze before she furrowed her brow. His pulse thrummed. Could she possibly feel the same bond that tied him to her more strongly every day?

Bringing his hand up to her lips, she kissed it. "What is a fate-bound?"

"A fate-bound is your soulmate. The one you're meant to be with forever. It's a feeling we get, deep within our souls, that we can't deny. Our wolves usually recognize it first." He chuckled. "Sometimes it takes our human minds a while to catch up."

"I see." She wrapped her arms around him, resting her head against his chest.

He held his breath, waiting for her to ask the question that had to be burning in her mind. Could he bring himself to tell her she was his if she asked? Would the truth scare her away?

She didn't speak. Instead, she hugged him tighter. Maybe she was afraid of what his answer would be.

He kissed the top of her head, and his tension eased. Maybe after a few more dates. He'd have to tell her eventually, and all he could do was hope she could love him in return. "It's early enough to go out if you want to catch a movie or something."

She inhaled deeply, running her hands up and down his back before leaning away to look at him. "Your sister went out of her way to give us privacy. It would be a shame to waste the opportunity...and I believe you owe me my prize for not being able to break Snow's protection spell."

"I like the way you think." Cupping her cheek in his hand, he ran his thumb over her velvet-soft skin. She nuzzled into his touch, closing her eyes, letting him pull her close.

She parted her lips slightly and angled her face toward

his. That was all the invitation he needed. Tangling his fingers in her hair, he crushed his mouth to hers. She responded, opening her mouth to let him in, brushing her tongue against his. Heat flashed through his body as she melted into his embrace, wrapping her arms around him, holding him tight.

She felt so damn good in his arms, her silky hair tangled between his fingers. Ever since his niece had been born, dating—and women in general—had taken a backseat to responsibility. He'd quit sleeping around the moment he saw what the consequences could be. Making love to Rain wouldn't be sleeping around, though. She was the only woman he wanted to be with for the rest of his life.

Standing in the kitchen, with her curvy body rubbing against his, her lips searing him with kisses, he couldn't deny himself anymore. He wanted this woman. He needed her.

Taking her face in his hands, he kissed her forehead, her cheek, her mouth. He parted his lips to ask if she wanted to join him the bedroom, but the words didn't get a chance to leave his throat before she tugged his shirt over his head and ran her palms down his chest.

"Nipple rings." She licked her lips. "Can I play with them?"

Good God. Who knew something as simple as the aroused look on her face could nearly bring him to his knees. "They're all yours."

She danced her fingers across his skin, taking each ring between her thumb and forefinger and tugging gently. Electricity shot from his nipples to his dick, hardening him even more.

"Does it hurt when I pull on them?" She tugged again, watching his face intently.

"No." Damn. Breathless already? "It feels good."

She grinned. "Really?" A wickedly mischievous look flashed in her dark-gray eyes, and she lowered her head to his chest and flicked out her tongue. Warm moisture bathed his right nipple, and he couldn't help but groan.

Biting her bottom lip in that oh so sexy way of hers, she glanced up at him before moving to his left nipple. She lifted the ring with her tongue, then sucked it into her mouth.

His breath caught in his throat, his entire body humming with desire. If she could get him this turned on by taking his shirt off, he was in for a wild ride.

She released his nipple and glided her tongue up his chest before straightening. "You're so sexy, Chase. Your tattoos and piercings... Your body alone is a ten, but then add in your personality, and..." She grinned. "You're a nice guy wrapped in a bad boy package. The best of both worlds."

His chest tightened. She knew everything about his past, yet she still found him attractive. How did he get so lucky? "I wasn't always a nice guy."

"But you are now." She focused on his tattoos, running her hands up and down his arms, tracing the lines on the drawings. "Our pasts don't define us. Who we are now is all that matters." She looked into his eyes, holding his gaze, waiting for confirmation.

"I agree."

She traced a finger up his arm, indicating his tattoos. "Do they all have meaning?"

"Some do; some don't." He held his arms in front of him and looked at the ink. Full-color drawings ranging from traditional flash art to custom-made designs joined together to create intricate sleeves on both arms. "A buddy of mine is a tattoo artist. When he was starting up, I let him practice on me."

Her gaze traveled up and down his arms as she traced her fingers along the art. "That's nice of you."

He shrugged. "He needed a canvas; I like ink. We take care of our own." Running his hands over her hips, he toyed with the hem of her shirt. "My turn." He tugged her shirt over her head and tossed it on the table before stepping back to admire her.

A lacey, emerald-green bra wrapped around her full breasts, accentuating her slender waist. His fingers twitched with the urge to touch her, so he lifted his hands slowly and reached for her. She inhaled deeply as he ran a finger over the top of her breast, tracing the contour of her bra. Goose bumps rose on her skin.

"You, Rain, are the epitome of sexy. A beautiful soul wrapped in an equally beautiful package."

The muscles in her throat worked as she swallowed. Then, she straightened her spine and unhooked her bra, letting it fall to the floor.

Her perfect breasts beckoned him to taste them, so he cupped them both in his hands, leaned down, and took her nipple into his mouth. She gasped and clutched the edge of the countertop, and he moved to the other breast, circling his tongue around her nipple, hardening it into a perfect, pink pearl before sucking it between his teeth.

A high-pitched mewling sound escape her throat, and he paused. Straightening, he moved his hands to her shoulders and looked into her eyes. "Do you want to stop?"

"No. Goddess, no. It's..." She lowered her gaze before

blinking up at him. "It's been a long time since anyone has touched me like this."

He pulled her close, and the feel of her soft, bare skin pressed to his nearly crumbled him. If the intensity of his emotions was any indication of what was to come, he might not survive making love to Rain. He hadn't known it was possible to *feel* this much. "It's been a long time since I've touched anyone like this. We'll take it slow."

She nodded and nuzzled into his chest.

He stood in the kitchen, holding her, letting the idea of what they were about to do sink in. This would be so much more than sex for him, but he only wanted it if she did too. "Do you want to move to the bedroom?"

She paused, going utterly still for a heartbeat or two before looking up at him. "I do."

He held her gaze, giving her ample opportunity to change her mind. "Are you sure?"

"I've wanted you since the moment I met you. Take me to bed."

"Yes, ma'am." He scooped her into his arms and carried her out of the kitchen. "This is what's called a shotgun house." He stepped into his sister's bedroom. "If you open all the doors, you could shoot a shotgun from the front door, and it would go all the way out the back door."

"Interesting."

"Problem is, we have to go through Bekah and Emma's room to get to mine. Not much privacy." He opened the door to his bedroom and carried her inside.

She grinned. "I guess you don't get a lot of action then."

He chuckled. "Not since Emma was born."

"Your sister taking her to your mom's was quite a gesture then."

He lowered her feet to the floor and kissed her before stepping toward his dresser. "She knows how I feel about you." He took a condom from the drawer and tossed it on the nightstand.

Rain sat on the bed and ran her hands over the comforter. "How do you feel about me?"

He looked at the beautiful woman on his bed, her breasts rising and falling with each breath she took, and he ached with emotion. The words nearly spilled from his lips, but he bit them back. It was too soon to tell her how strongly he felt. He stood in front of her and rested his hands on her shoulders. "You are the most amazing woman I've ever met."

"You're pretty amazing, yourself." She kissed his stomach, trailing her tongue down, past his navel, to his jeans. His stomach tensed, a fresh flood of desire rushing to his groin, and he tightened his grip on her shoulders.

Moving her hands to his hips, she traced a finger along the waistband of his pants. "I believe I'm supposed to decide if there's anything little about the werewolf I'm about to make love to."

"Be my guest."

She popped the button on his jeans and slid the zipper down. Pushing his pants to the floor, she stared at the bulge in his underwear, her pupils dilating with desire. "So far so good."

He couldn't take it anymore. Kicking his jeans aside, he tugged her to her feet. His dick ached to fill her. His wolf begged to claim her. Why the hell had he told her they'd take it slow?

She ran her hands over his body, and every muscle he

had tightened with need. As she glided her palm over his underwear and gripped his dick through the fabric, he closed his eyes and let out his breath in a slow hiss.

"Take these off." She released her hold and stepped back, her gaze locking on his crotch.

He obeyed, dropping his underwear to the floor. Her eyes widened, and she wrapped her silky fingers around his cock and touched her lips to his ear. "Definitely nothing little about this werewolf." She gave him a stroke, and his entire body shuddered.

Holy hell, he had to have this woman. He took her in his arms and kissed her as if she were the water to his insatiable thirst. The air to his lungs.

She released her hold on his dick to grip his shoulders, tugging him on top of her as she fell to the bed. He moved against her, but the coarse fabric of her jeans wasn't the sensation he needed to feel.

Rolling to his side, he continued exploring her mouth with his tongue as he unbuttoned her jeans. Rising onto his knees, he tore his lips from hers to work her clothing over her hips and toss the remaining garments onto the floor.

The woman of his dreams lay in his bed, gloriously naked and reaching for him. "Make love to me, Chase. I need you."

He lay beside her and kissed her, trailing his lips down her neck, nipping at her collarbone, reveling in her intoxicatingly feminine scent. She smelled like a meadow, with a warm, cinnamony undercurrent that was all Rain.

Her breath hitched as he glided his hand down her stomach, and when he stroked her soft folds, she let out a satisfied "*Mmm.*" He slipped a finger inside her, and she moaned. She was tight and wet, and he couldn't hold back any longer.

Grabbing the condom from the nightstand, he tossed the wrapper aside and rolled the rubber down his shaft. She watched him as he moved on top of her and propped himself on his hands, her gaze never straying from his as he settled his hips between her legs and pressed himself against her opening.

Her eyes bore into his soul as he filled her, became one with her, and a deep shudder ran through his entire body. He lowered his chest to hers and held still, memorizing the way she felt wrapped around him, squeezing him. She held his body, heart, and soul in her arms.

He pulled out until only his tip remained inside her, and he roamed his lips over her shoulder, up her neck to find her mouth. Sliding back in slowly, he reveled in the way she gripped his back, the soft moans vibrating from her throat. He took his time making love to her, cherishing her.

He had to move slowly or the overwhelming emotions of joining with his fate-bound, giving himself to his soulmate, would've ended this way too soon. If he could have paused time and made this moment last forever, he would have. The tremor in his soul told him his wolf agreed.

"Oh, Chase. This feels so good." The breathless sound of his name on her lips thrilled him, and he couldn't help but increase his rhythm. She arched her back to take him deeper as he thrusted harder, his need growing stronger.

She hooked her legs behind his thighs and gripped his ass, guiding him faster and harder until she tossed her head back and let out the most beautiful moan he'd ever heard. She quivered around him, invoking her goddess and his name in the same breath.

He let go, giving himself to her. His orgasm exploded through his entire body as he pumped his hips, wave after wave of searing ecstasy burning through his veins. No woman had ever felt so good, so perfect in his arms.

As his climax subsided, he rose onto his elbows to look at his fate-bound. She *would* be his mate. She had to be. His wolf had claimed her, and now it felt as if an unbreakable cord ran from his heart to hers.

Her brow furrowed. Did she feel the strange connection too? Taking his face in her hands, she looked at him with a fierceness in her eyes. "You are mine."

She had no idea…

CHAPTER THIRTEEN

A JEALOUS RAGE BOILED INSIDE ISAAC AS HE TRUDGED away from the werewolf's house. He ground his teeth as thoughts of *his* Rain spending the night with that creature plowed through his mind, digging up long-buried emotions he'd rather not remember.

He'd needed to get a glimpse of her, to see her with his own eyes. Could he possibly care for the woman after what she'd done to him?

Apparently, he could because the need to possess her gripped his chest, tightening his lungs until he couldn't breathe. Ducking into the shadows, he leaned against a wall and pressed a hand to his heart. The sluggish muscle beat lightly against his breast, when it should have been pounding.

Why hadn't he stuck to the plan? A week in the swamp would have been enough time to recover and implement his scheme. But he'd had to see her. *Idiot.*

After the energy he'd expended to satisfy his whim, he'd be forced to drain someone. He couldn't stand to spend another week in the putrid swamp when he was this close to getting his revenge.

His spine cracked as he straightened and pushed from the wall. Closing his eyes, he shut out the world, ignoring his senses and focusing on his tulpa. A mass of static energy buzzed before him, pricking at his skin as the entity took shape.

Peeling his heavy lids open, he gazed at his greatest creation. *Find me a witch. A beautiful one.* If Rain could give herself to another man, Isaac would take another woman.

The tulpa darted ahead of him, slinking through the shadows as it made its way toward Frenchman Street and its eclectic live music venues. He knew of one club in particular that drew a large supernatural crowd—a prime hunting ground for his next taste of life.

Isaac followed his creation, his dirty clothes and the smell of swamp that lingered on his skin causing people to keep a wide berth around him. A woman looked at him with sympathy and muttered something about too many homeless people, and a sinking sensation formed in his stomach. Rain would be repulsed to see him in this condition.

A groan rumbled in his throat. Why did he care?

Dragging his mind back to the mission, he focused on the entity, sending it his thoughts and connecting on a telepathic level. Though the vision was hazy, as if looking through smoke, Isaac could see with the tulpa's eyes. The shadow figure would need a face—a handsome man, tall and strong. Isaac's lip split as he smiled, and coppery blood trickled between his teeth. He found one who would do.

The man leaned against a wall and fiddled with a

matchbook, attempting to light a cigarette, while his friend tossed a beer can into the trash. The tulpa moved like lightening, zipping through the darkness to rest a shadowy hand against its prey's cheek. The man's face fell slack. His shoulders drooped, and his friend barely caught him by the arm before he crumpled to the ground.

"What the hell? Did you see that?"

The man moaned in response.

The tulpa continued toward the club, its form wavering, rolling in on itself until it replicated the man's appearance. Isaac followed, curling his cracked lip at the man as his friend tried to drag him to his feet. The temptation to stop and finish him off gave Isaac pause. If he could take on the bastard's good looks by draining him like his tulpa could, he might have done it.

Instead, he ducked into the alley behind the club and cleared his mind. Through the smoky haze of the tulpa's vision, he searched the room for a beautiful witch to replace his Rain. Though muffled through the entity's senses, the music pulsed and vibrated as bodies writhed on the dancefloor. The tulpa slinked into the crowd, running its hand along the arms of its potential conquests, searching their skin for the magical electricity of a witch.

Through the tulpa's gaze, Isaac spotted dark curls bobbing across the dancefloor, and his throat tightened. He stumbled up the alley toward the door, the excitement that his Rain had left the werewolf driving him forward.

The woman turned, and he halted, the exertion sucking the air from his lungs. Even through the haze, her dark-brown eyes were unremarkable. While the woman held a certain attractiveness, she wasn't Rain.

How dare she have the audacity to resemble his woman? He urged the tulpa forward, and as it stroked her arm, her magical signature danced across the entity's borrowed skin.

The tulpa put a hand on her hip, moving its own in time with the music, and desire sparked in the woman's eyes as she ran a hand up the entity's shoulder. Isaac's jaw clenched. Rain had once looked at him that way.

Bring her to me. Isaac groaned and dissolved the connection, allowing the tulpa to do what was necessary to lead the woman to her doom. There would be no enjoyment in this victim. She deserved her fate for stirring these unwelcome emotions in his soul.

A giggle echoed from the alley entrance, and the woman appeared, her arms draped around the tulpa's shoulders. "Where are we going?" She buried her face in the entity's neck, and from this view, she looked so much like Rain, Isaac's heart missed a beat.

He closed his eyes and focused on the feel of her body pressed against the tulpa. The sensation felt distant, more like a memory, and when her nose glided along the entity's neck as she lifted her head, visions of Rain swam behind Isaac's eyes.

His knuckles cracked as he clenched his fists, and pain shot through his temple. Between his fatigue and the anger rolling through his system, his knees buckled beneath his weight. He leaned against the wall and scowled as the tulpa coaxed the woman deeper into the alley.

"Let's go back to the club." The first hint of fear raised her voice an octave as she tried to wiggle from the entity's embrace.

The tulpa tightened its grip and lifted her from the ground.

"What are you doing?" Panic laced her words as the tulpa carried her toward him. "Put me down!"

As she sucked in a breath to scream, Isaac took her face in his hands and gazed into her dark-brown eyes. Her life energy flowed through his fingers, spiraling up his arms to fill his body.

The woman froze, the frantic rhythm of her heart pumping her lifeforce into his veins. She clawed at his hands, but her strength faded quickly, her breathing growing shallow until a whisper left her lips. "Why?"

"Why, indeed?" Isaac's spine straightened as her energy spiraled through his body, mending his splitting bones, repairing his deteriorating muscles. Her lifeforce was strong, but unlike his Rain, her magic was weak.

The witch's skin shriveled on her bones, her eyes growing distant before the light in them extinguished. Shoving the empty body into his tulpa's arms, Isaac rolled his shoulders and cracked his neck.

"What a waste." Once again, he'd let his emotions rule, and he'd ruined his shot at draining a powerful witch. This one could barely cast a clarity spell, much less harness the amount of magic he'd need to defeat a werewolf.

He hadn't planned on leaving a trail of bodies in his wake, but he'd have to find someone stronger. Someone whose magic was worthy.

Making use of his temporary strength, he lifted the body from the tulpa's arms and tossed it into the dumpster. With any luck, he'd have Rain in his grasp before the rest of the witches caught on to his plan.

Dead or alive, she would be his again. Soon.

CHAPTER FOURTEEN

Rain woke with a strange sense of calm. Of security. She lay on her side, her back cradled into Chase's front, his arms wrapped tightly around her. A ceiling fan whirred from above, sending a cooling breeze onto the sheets, but the warmth of her werewolf kept the chill away.

Her werewolf.

What had come over her last night to claim him like she did? To tell him he was hers, as if he had no choice in the matter? Her pulse quickened, the flutter of a thousand butterflies taking flight like they had when he hadn't denied she was his girlfriend.

Everything about this moment felt right. Her lips curved into a smile. She could see herself spending forever with this man. This felt...real. So different from the way she'd felt with Isaac.

She'd been so desperate for Isaac's attention. Always worrying if he wanted her. Never feeling like she was enough.

With Chase, she didn't worry. He wore his emotions

openly. In the way he looked at her. How he touched her. She'd grown up since her battle with her ex, and she'd never stoop to using a spell to harm someone again.

But she *had* harmed Isaac. She'd killed him.

Her stomach sank. Would Chase feel the same about her if he knew what she'd done? She had two choices: either tell him the truth now before she got in too deep or keep her mouth shut and pray that he never found out.

Rolling onto her other side, she lay face to face with him.

Her movement roused him from sleep, and he opened his eyes and smiled. "Good morning, beautiful. How did you sleep?"

"Good." The best sleep of her life. "I need to tell you something."

"Hmm…" He rolled on top of her and nuzzled into her neck, trailing his lips up to her earlobe and raising goose bumps on her arms. "Is it that you think your mind is playing tricks on you? That there's no way the sex last night was that amazing and you need to do it again, just to be sure?"

He kissed his way down her throat and circled his tongue around the dip in the center of her collar bone. "If that's what you need, I'm happy to oblige."

She could have lain there all day letting Chase cover her body in kisses. The softness of his lips followed by the tickle of his beard on her skin. The warmth of his tongue on her breast as he sucked her nipple into his mouth. Her will almost crumbled. "You might not want to after what I need to tell you."

He paused and looked at her. "That sounds serious."

As she opened her mouth to spill her awful truth, his

phone rang from somewhere on the floor. He ignored it, focusing instead on her. "Is something wrong?"

She couldn't force the confession over the lump in her throat. "Aren't you going to answer your phone?"

"I suppose I should." He sighed and rolled off her, reaching for his jeans and digging through the pockets until he retrieved the phone. It had stopped ringing, but his sister's name lit up the screen as a missed call. "Why the hell is Bekah calling this early in the morning?" He sat up, furrowing his brow at the phone. "I better call her back." He ran his fingers down Rain's cheek and smiled his heart-melting smile. "Give me a sec."

She nodded as he pressed the button to return his sister's call.

"You rang?" He paused and listened, his grin falling into a scowl as his sister spoke. "They don't know what's wrong?"

Another pause, and he clutched Rain's hand in his. "Do you know where Tommy is? Surely he'd be willing to see you again to heal his daughter."

His shoulders drooped. "No. I suppose you're right. Bastard." He looked at Rain, and the brightness returned to his eyes. "I think I know another witch who can help. Hang tight. I'll be there as soon as I can."

Chase stood and gathered their clothes. "I'm sorry, *cher*, we're going to have to finish our conversation later. Emma's in the hospital."

Rain's heart thrummed in her chest as the pieces of the conversation began clicking into place. "What's wrong with her?"

He laid her clothes on the bed and put on his jeans. "They don't know. High fever. Vomiting. She's dehydrated and barely conscious."

Her throat tightened. "You mentioned Tommy...her father?"

"Yeah. Let me get your shirt." He paced into the kitchen and returned with the rest of her clothes.

Rain put on her pants and turned her shirt right side out. "How could her father heal her? Is he..." A sickening feeling swirled in her stomach, creeping its way up to her throat. "Is he a witch?"

Chase pulled his shirt over his head. "Yeah, but Bekah hasn't heard from him since he left her. He has decent healing abilities, but maybe Snow can make one of her potions, like the one you gave me?"

She sank onto the edge of the bed. *No, no, no.* This couldn't be happening. "Emma's half-witch?"

"Yeah, but..." His eyes widened. "Your...No, it wasn't your curse."

"It was, Chase. It is." She yanked her shirt down over her head and shoved her feet into her shoes. "She colored that picture for me. *Beauty and the Beast*, remember? She gave it to me...in kindness. She was kind to me, and now she's suffering for it."

He dropped his arms to his sides. "But she's a kid."

"So? She's a witch. That's what matters." She stood and paced to the living room. This was her fault. She'd let her guard down. Gotten close. And now a sweet little girl was suffering because she'd been careless with her curse.

"Rain, wait." Chase followed her. "This is not your fault."

She whirled around to face him. "No? Then whose fault is it? It's *my* curse. My burden."

"It's my fault." He caught her hand. "I'm to blame. I never told you her dad was a witch."

"Why didn't you?"

He squeezed her hand and let it go, a pained expression puckering his brow. "I don't know. It never crossed my mind. When I told you she was half-werewolf, I guess I assumed...I don't know." He let out a hard breath. "I'm sorry. I...this is one hundred percent my fault."

"No. It's mine. I've lived with this curse for seven years; I should know better. I assumed she was half-human when I should have asked." She was stupid and irresponsible, and now poor Emma had to pay the price.

"Look, we can argue over whose fault it is later. Do you think Snow will make a healing potion?"

She swallowed the sour taste from her mouth. "You'll have to ask her yourself. She can't do it for me."

Confusion clouded his eyes. "She did it for you when I was sick."

"She did that on her own. We've found loopholes... ways to get around the curse. I told her you were sick, but I didn't ask for her help. She made the potion on her own and made it very clear when she gave it to me that she did it for you, not for me."

He grabbed his keys from the counter and opened the door. "I'll ask her then. We'll take care of Emma. Come on."

She followed him outside to his bike. "My car is parked down the road." She texted him Snow's number. "You'll have to call Snow and ask her to meet us at the bakery."

"Okay." He fished his phone from his pocket, and Rain hurried to her car.

She started the engine and headed to the bakery before Chase finished his phone call and mounted his bike. What had she been thinking getting that close to him and his family? She'd been concerned about *him* having witch blood somewhere along the lines, but the thought that his niece might had never even crossed her mind.

Selfish. That was what she'd been. Only thinking of herself and her desires for Chase. So much for learning to lead a selfless life. This was why she didn't get close to people.

Parking in the alley behind the building, she shook her head as she climbed out of the car and slammed the door. Seven years. After the initial shock and the realization of how swiftly her curse worked, she'd spent the past seven years avoiding friendships like they were...well, a curse.

And then Chase came along with his hot body and tender touch, and her brain checked out, letting her hormones take over.

No more.

Her hands trembled as she fumbled with the lock and let herself in. The shop didn't open for another four hours, but she heated the ovens and took the dough and batter from the fridge to prepare the day's offerings.

Snow and Chase would handle the potion, and as much as Rain wanted to go to the hospital to comfort Emma, she couldn't. She could never see the little girl again. It wasn't worth the risk. How could she explain to a six-year-old that she was suffering because she'd done something nice for a cursed witch?

She couldn't, and the only way to make certain she wasn't a threat to Emma was to stop seeing Chase. Her heart wrenched at the thought of never feeling his strong arms wrapped around her again. But this was the way it had to be. She never should have tried to be with him in the first place.

A knock sounded on the front door, and she shuffled into the storefront to let Chase in. Snow wouldn't be far behind. She opened the door and stepped aside for him to enter, shutting it when he crossed the threshold.

He faced her, concern furrowing his dark brow. "We're going to fix this."

She wrung her hands and nodded, biting her bottom lip to hold back the tears. Thankfully, Snow stepped through door, saving her from having to answer.

She strutted past them toward the kitchen, waving a hand for them to follow her. "Give me ten minutes and I'll whip something up. What are her symptoms again?"

"Fever, vomiting, dehydration, but they've got her hooked up to an IV."

Snow grimaced. "Sounds like what happened to me that time I made a cake for your birthday."

The first tear rolled down her cheek. "I know."

Chase cupped her face in his hand, wiping the tear away with his thumb. "Hey, look at me." He stooped to catch her gaze. "I am taking full responsibility for this. You didn't know, so it's not your fault."

"It doesn't matter. I should have asked. I should have made sure."

Snow cleared her throat and busied herself with the potion, mixing eucalyptus with mango leaves and other healing herbs before reciting the spell and bottling the mixture. "Here you go." She handed it to Chase. "Don't expect it to work as fast as it did on you, though. If she hasn't come into her werewolf self-healing abilities yet, it's going to take at least a day for the full effect."

Chase pocketed the potion and took Rain's hand. "We better get this to Emma." He stepped toward the storefront, but Rain didn't budge. "Emma will want to see you."

"She can't. I'm too dangerous. It's best if she never sees me again."

He pressed his lips into a line and let out a sigh. "We'll figure something out. We can coach her on how to act around you so it doesn't happen again. We'll make a game out of it. She likes games."

Her throat tightened. "No. *We* won't do anything. It's best if you never see me again either."

The pain in his eyes tore at her heart. "Don't say that. I belong to you, remember? You told me so last night." He smiled weakly.

"I know what I said, but that was before…" She sighed. "I was careless, and a little girl is hurt because of it. She lives with you. She's family. I'm just a dud witch with a curse to keep me alone for the rest of my life."

"Rain." He reached for her, but she backed away.

"I'm sorry, Chase. Go to Emma. She needs you."

Snow glared at her with a look that said she'd be hearing from her later. "I'll go with you, Chase." She brushed past Rain and stomped out of the kitchen.

He pulled his keys from his pocket. "I'm going to find a way to break your curse. This isn't over."

She sucked in a shaky breath. "I'm afraid it is."

He shook his head and followed Snow out of the bakery.

———

Chase mounted his bike and slammed his helmet onto his head. He'd had a taste of his fate-bound mate, and he'd be damned if he would let some curse stand between them.

Snow opened her car door. "What hospital? I'll meet you there."

"Tulane."

She nodded and climbed into her Mazda. Chase revved his engine and peeled away from the store, leaving a black mark on the ground where his tire had spun. Childish? Yeah. But he was losing his fate-bound. He wasn't thinking straight.

His pulse thrummed in his ears as he wove through traffic on Basin Street and turned into the hospital parking lot. He'd help his niece. As soon as her condition stabilized, he'd go back to Rain and convince her they were meant to be together.

Why hadn't he thought to mention the fact that his niece was half-witch? He didn't care if he got hurt or sick. Nothing short of death could keep him away from the woman he loved, but he'd only been thinking about himself. He hadn't considered the effects his fate-bound could have on others. *Who's the asshole now?* He paced across the parking garage and jabbed the button for the elevator.

"Chase, wait up." Snow trotted across the pavement and stood next to him. "What did your niece do for Rain?"

"She gave her a picture she colored of *Beauty and the Beast*. Said it was Rain and me."

Snow smiled. "Aw, that's so sweet."

And she'd made their relationship official when he hadn't had the balls to bring it up. He'd always be grateful to his niece for that. "Sweet enough to land her in the hospital, apparently."

Her smile faded. "It wasn't *that* big of a kindness. I'm sure she'd recover fine on her own, but the potion will speed it up."

He slipped his hand into his pocket and toyed with the vial. "Thanks for this."

"My pleasure."

The elevator dinged, and the doors *whooshed* open, sending a gust of chilled air into his face. They rode the contraption to the third floor and paced down the hall to room 3C.

Emma lay in the bed, looking tiny and helpless, her dark hair matted to her forehead, her skin taking on an ashen pallor. Bekah sat in a chair next to her, holding her hand and softly singing "Belle" from *Beauty and the Beast*, Emma's favorite song. Chase had watched the movie with his niece so many times, he was tempted to sing along. Anything to make Emma feel better.

When his sister reached the end of the verse, she looked up at him.

"This is Snow, Rain's sister."

Bekah smiled weakly. "Frozen bubbles?"

"That's me," Snow said.

He took the spell from his pocket. "She made a healing potion. Like the one Rain brought over to me when I was down. It should speed up her recovery." He handed it to Bekah.

She took the vial and gently shook Emma awake. "Here, sweetie, you need to drink this. It will help you feel better."

Emma's eyes fluttered halfway open. Her dry lips stuck together at first, but she peeled them apart and let her mom pour the potion into her mouth.

"I can cool her fever." Snow held up her hands. "I did it for Rain when she was little. It won't hurt her."

Bekah gave her a confused look. "Like you froze the bubbles?"

"I won't freeze her. Just cool her down a little."

Chase stepped toward the bed. "You can trust her." He never imagined that phrase would pass from his lips when speaking about a witch, but he meant every damn word of it.

Bekah nodded, and Snow pressed her hands against Emma's forehead. She whispered something that rhymed —a spell, he assumed—and slid her palms down his niece's arms before resting them on her chest, her stomach, her legs. She repeated the movements three times and touched Emma's forehead with the back of her hand. "Should be 98.6 now. You can call in a nurse to take her temperature if you want."

Bekah placed her palms against Emma's cheeks. "Incredible. You've been so kind. Thank you."

"I'm glad I could help."

Chase shoved his hands into his pockets. "Speaking of kindness…" He nodded to Emma. "She's sick because of me."

Bekah furrowed her brow. "Full werewolves don't get viruses. She didn't catch this from you."

"She's sick because she was kind to Rain." He explained the curse, making sure to put all the blame on himself for not telling Rain that Emma was half-witch. "She never would have come over to babysit if she'd known."

"She feels terrible," Snow added. "My sister is very conscious about her curse. She won't let it happen again."

"I see." Bekah lowered her gaze and stared at her daughter. "It doesn't make sense." She motioned for Chase to move closer and whispered in his ear, "Fate wouldn't make you choose between your family and your soulmate would it?"

He tried to respond, but he couldn't get enough air into his lungs. Choose between his fate-bound and his family? It was an impossible decision, but it seemed he'd be forced to make it.

When he didn't answer, Bekah straightened her spine. "I'm sorry to say this, but as long as she's cursed, she can't be around Emma."

"I know."

"Emma is family, and she's pack. She's not going to stay home all the time because Rain is around."

He held her gaze. He knew exactly what his sister was saying. Family and the pack came first. Rain would have to be the one staying home, missing out on pack gatherings. Who knew how many other weres had witch blood flowing through their veins? He'd be putting his pack in danger by taking Rain as his mate.

Sharp pain flashed through his heart, and he placed a hand against his chest to rub it away. He looked at Snow. "Isn't there a way to break the curse?"

Snow's eyes tightened. "She hasn't talked to you about that?"

"No." If she had, he'd be doing everything in his power to break the damn thing.

"She needs…" Snow inhaled deeply, pressing her lips into a hard line. "She needs to commit an ultimate act of selflessness."

His head spun. Could she be any vaguer? "What does that mean? She needs to give her life to save someone?"

"No. If she gave up her life, that would defeat the purpose of breaking the curse, don't you think?" She laced her fingers together and gave him a strange look. Was it pity? Hope? She looked like she wanted to say something, and if she didn't spit it out, his head might explode.

"What then?" he said through clenched teeth. "What does she have to do?"

Snow deflated. "I don't know. She's become the most selfless person I know. She's reined in her temper. She gives, volunteers. Nothing has worked so far, but…" Her expression turned pained.

"But what?"

"You need to talk to her about it. Maybe the two of you can figure it out together."

"Uncle Chase?" Emma's voice sounded tiny. "Where's Rain?"

With two purposeful strides, he moved to the bedside and brushed the hair from his niece's face. The color was already returning to her cheeks, and she managed a weak smile. "She couldn't make it, squirt, but Snow is here."

"Hi, Emma." Snow waved from the foot of the bed.

Emma's smile widened. "When Rain becomes my aunt, will you be my aunt too?"

"Emma…" her mother chided. "Grown-up relationships are complicated."

She huffed. "Rain is going to be Uncle Chase's mate, Momma, and then she'll be my aunt."

A lump the size of a cantaloupe wedged into his throat. He could only hope. But as long as she was cursed, he didn't see how…

Snow suppressed a smile. "What makes you say that?"

"They love each other."

Warmth spread through his body. He obviously loved Rain. His wolf had made up his mind the moment he met her. The thought that she might already love him too sent his heart racing. Sometimes kids were more perceptive than adults.

Snow laughed. "What makes you say *that?*"

Emma sighed and rolled her eyes. "A girl just knows these things."

Snow arched an eyebrow at Chase. "A girl does, doesn't she?"

He raked a hand through his hair. A guy knew too. Fate would not send him a mate he couldn't be with. He had to figure out a way to break the curse. He pinched Emma's cheek. "How you feeling, squirt?"

"Better. The medicine tasted like bubblegum."

He looked at Snow. "Did you make the same potion you gave me? Mine tasted like honey."

"It tastes like whatever you need it to taste like. Does whatever it needs to do. That's how magic works."

That was how he worked too. He would do whatever he needed to do to keep his family and his pack safe *and* save the woman he loved from a curse. "What will you tell the doctors when she mysteriously recovers?"

Bekah shrugged. "They have no idea what's wrong with her. I doubt it's the first mystery illness they've encountered."

"I'm going to head to the bakery and see if I can talk some sense into my sister." Snow patted Emma's leg. "Take care of yourself, little one."

"I'll be there shortly." Chase nodded at Snow. "Thanks for your help."

He stayed at the hospital for a few more hours to make sure Emma's condition improved before heading to the parking garage. Hopefully Snow would have calmed Rain down by the time he got to the bakery. Seeing so much pain in her eyes had torn him to pieces.

CHAPTER FIFTEEN

RAIN SLIPPED HER HANDS INTO A PAIR OF OVEN MITTS and pulled a tray of fresh-baked clarity cookies from the oven. Setting it on the counter, she dropped the mitts in a drawer and stared at the plain, beige treats. If she were to eat one now, before they were frosted, she could focus the effects on anything she wanted.

She chewed on her lip. Sliding a spatula beneath a warm cookie, she lifted it from the platter. Her breathing grew shallow as she gazed at the spellbound treat, and she let it fall back to the tray. *Don't be an idiot, Rain.*

She'd made the right decision about Chase; she didn't need a cookie to confirm it. Putting his family and his pack in danger wasn't a risk she wanted to take. No matter how much her heart ached to be with him, she couldn't. Even if he figured out a way to balance his time between her and his pack, she couldn't ask him to make that sacrifice.

Of course, if he gave her two drops of his blood, her curse would be broken and he wouldn't have to divide his time. But after everything he'd been through...asking him to give her a sacred part of himself, to break his pack laws and risk who-knew-what kind of punishment...she couldn't do that to him. What good would it be to have her curse broken but lose the trust of the man who'd broken it?

The door chimed, signaling a customer, and Snow's heels clicked across the tiles as she entered the kitchen. "Ingrid is here. She wants the rent."

"She told me she was coming for it tomorrow." Rain rolled her eyes. Leave it to Ingrid to insist on getting paid early. Though, the check was already late, so she couldn't blame her. "I'll bring it out to her. Can you take care of these cookies?"

"Sure thing."

Rain snatched the rent check from a drawer and padded into the storefront, but she stopped short at the sight of the person standing by the window. To the naked eye, the woman appeared to be Ingrid. She had the same red hair and slim build, but her aura was off.

Really off.

All witches' auras glowed a shade of magenta. Some leaned more toward deep purple, while others could be light pink depending on the level of their power, and Ingrid's aura usually had a dark, rosy radiance. This woman's aura didn't glow at all. Instead, a dull gray, almost mist-like form hovered around her body.

"Ingrid?"

Her landlord turned around. "I'm here for the rent check." She looked like Ingrid, but her voice...her expression...wasn't quite right.

Rain forced a smile. "How was your trip? Did you get home today?"

"I'm here for the rent check." She blinked rapidly, plastering a fake smile on her face. She never smiled at her.

Rain's pulse thrummed. This wasn't the Ingrid she knew. "You told me where you went, but I can't remember. Was it Cancun?"

"I'm here for the rent check." *Blink. Blink. Blink.*

A chill crept up her spine to pool at the top of her head. What if this wasn't Ingrid at all? Could demons shapeshift? Chase had mentioned they hadn't found the shadow he'd seen by the river. Maybe it had been hiding, gathering its energy so it could catch Rain alone and...what? Collect a rent check? It didn't make sense. If whatever had taken on Ingrid's form wanted Rain dead, it would have killed her by now.

Unless this really was Ingrid, and the demon possessed her, using her until her magic and energy were drained before moving on to the next host. And since Rain's magic was bound, the demon didn't deem her a potential target.

But Snow would be...

She shoved the check into her pocket. Whether or not this was really Ingrid's body, the entity in control was not her landlord. "I'll bring the money by tomorrow. It's locked in the timed safe, and I can't open it again until morning."

Ingrid stared at her blankly as if she only knew how to speak the single sentence.

Dread trickled from the base of Rain's skull down the length of her spine. "Will that be okay, Ingrid?"

She opened her mouth, and her lips trembled as she fought to form an *O* shape. "Okay." Her scratchy voice sounded forced. Not at all like Ingrid. She nodded and shuffled out the door.

Ingrid didn't shuffle; she always walked with purpose.

Rain watched as she made her way down the sidewalk and disappeared from view.

What the hell was going on?

An image of the dead witch flashed in her mind. Could Isaac have summoned a demon and sent it after Rain? Not unless he'd summoned it from the grave. *Stop being ridiculous.* Seeing that body in the morgue was affecting her more than she'd thought. Isaac wasn't the only energy vampire to ever exist, and if he were alive, he wouldn't send a demon after Rain.

He'd want to kill her himself.

Rain yanked her phone from her pocket and dialed Ingrid's number. It rang five times before going to voicemail. She hung up without leaving a message.

What if this was an effect from her curse? Could Ingrid be deliriously ill because of her? No, she hadn't shown her kindness. She hadn't spoken to her in a week.

Rain dialed her number again. No answer.

Snow carried the tray of cookies from the kitchen and put them in the display case. "Rent's all paid?"

"Did Ingrid seem...off to you?"

"She wasn't her usual cheerful self." Snow winked. "She told me she was here for the rent check, so I came to find you. That's all she said to me. Is something wrong?"

What if she were dead? Rain couldn't live with herself knowing she'd been the last person to see Ingrid. Knowing she could have—should have—done something to help her.

"Her aura was off. I'm going to go check on her." She grabbed her keys and headed out the back door. A chill ran through her body as she climbed into her car and drove to Ingrid's house, a sure sign something was awry. A cyclist darted out on Esplanade, and Rain slammed her brakes to avoid a crash. She needed to calm down, but the closer she got to Ingrid's house the more thoughts swirled through her mind.

Focusing on the scenery, she took in the nineteenth-century mansions painted in shades of peach, lavender, and blue. White columns led up to second-story galleries, where colorful flags and plants adorned the buildings. Giant oaks towered from the neutral ground, the grassy median separating the opposing flow of traffic, and created a canopy over the street.

She accelerated, and the mansions gave way to smaller, more modest houses. Hanging a left on North Miro, she navigated through the neighborhood and found her landlord's home. Ingrid's car sat in the short driveway, and all the shutters were drawn.

Parking on the curb, she darted up the front steps and knocked on the door. "Ingrid?" Her hands trembled, so she clenched them into fists as the lock disengaged and Ingrid opened the door.

Ingrid squinted as she peered between the door and the jamb. "Rain? What are you doing here?"

"Are you okay?" Did she not remember coming to the bakery at all?

She opened the door wider. Her disheveled hair hung tangled over her shoulder, and indentions from a pillow marred one side of her face. Though her purple button-up had appeared freshly-ironed when she'd arrived at the shop, creases now zigzagged across it as if she'd lain in the same position for hours. "I've felt better. I must be coming down with the flu."

Rain's throat thickened. "Does your entire body ache? Like you've had the life drained out of you?"

Ingrid rolled her head from side to side, stretching her neck. "Yeah. Is something going around?"

That was the same way Rain had felt after Isaac stole her energy, but she'd always awoken coherent. The way Ingrid had acted that afternoon had seemed like it wasn't her. "Any other symptoms?"

She narrowed her eyes. "Not that it's any of your business, but I might be having hallucinations too. I thought I saw a shadow."

Rain clutched the doorframe. "A shadow?"

"Yeah. I was lying on the couch, and I heard a shuffling sound. Then this shadow appeared in front of me, and it touched my face. I must have been dreaming. I woke up when you knocked on the door, and now I feel like shit."

Rain tugged the crumpled check from her pocket and tried to keep a neutral expression. "Here's the rent. I'm sorry I woke you. I hope you feel better soon."

"Thanks." Ingrid took the money and shut the door as Rain darted to her car.

Collapsing into the driver's seat, she leaned her head against the headrest to stop the spinning sensation. Someone drained Ingrid's energy and then took on her form. It was the only explanation. She let out a slow breath and started the engine.

Rain drove to the bakery and double-checked the locks on all the doors and windows. As long as they remained engaged, Snow's charm would keep evil out of her space. If the demon decided to come back for her, it wouldn't be able to get inside unless she let it in.

She hung a sign in the door that read *please ring bell for entry* and shuffled behind the counter. Keeping the door locked wasn't the best for business, but at least she could check out the customers' auras before she invited them in.

Snow glanced at the sign and gave her a quizzical look. "We're screening customers now?"

"Ingrid wasn't okay. Something drained her energy."

Snow's mouth dropped open. "Isaac?"

Rain shook her head. "Isaac didn't do it, nor any other witch. Ingrid said she saw a shadow right before she passed out. Whatever came to the bakery wasn't our landlord; it was a shapeshifter."

Snow's shoulders relaxed as she let out her breath. "Didn't you and Chase see a shadow by the river last week?"

"He assumed it was a demon targeting him, but it sounds like it's targeting witches."

"Why would a demon be hunting witches?"

"I don't know, but it seems more probable than possible at this point, don't you think? *Something* is draining witches' energy."

Snow nodded. "I hate to say it, but I'd rather it be a demon on the loose than to think Isaac has returned from the grave."

She let out a slow breath. "*I* hate to say it, but I agree."

Snow's brow knit. "Why did it come here? Are we its next targets?"

"That's what I thought at first, but if it drained Ingrid's life force, it probably got a glimpse into her mind. And knowing Ingrid, she was thinking about getting the money, convincing herself she wasn't showing kindness by not evicting me immediately."

"So it took some of Ingrid's energy, took on her form, and showed up here because that was what she'd been thinking about?"

Rain bit her lip. "It makes sense, doesn't it?"

"I guess so." She nodded, the wariness in her eyes making way for resolve.

"And it didn't bother attacking us because it had plenty of Ingrid's energy running through its veins."

"Do demons have veins?"

Rain straightened her spine. "It doesn't matter. Demons are nasty creatures, hell-bent on causing death and destruction. We aren't targets any more than any other witches. And we're Connollys."

Snow put her hands on her hips. "That's right. We can take care of ourselves. No demon is getting past my charm." She leaned against the counter. "But you should probably tell Chase. Fighting demons is what werewolves do."

Her sister had a point, but to talk to him after everything that had happened? "I can't. You call him."

Snow crossed her arms. "You're the one who talked to Ingrid. It's your theory. Besides, I *know* he'd want to hear it from you."

Pressing her lips together, Rain closed her eyes for a long blink. As much as she ached to hear his deep velvet voice, she couldn't do it. Instead, she dialed the number for O'Malley's Pub and asked for Luke. Cool relief flooded her veins when he picked up the phone. She explained what happened with her landlord and her theory that the shadow demon had taken on her form.

"You're sure it came to the bakery because of Ingrid's thoughts? Someone didn't send it after you?" Concern emanated from Luke's voice.

Thoughts of Isaac raced through her mind, but she pushed them aside. "I don't have any living enemies. I don't believe it was targeting me."

"Okay. Let me talk to Chase."

Rain swallowed. "He's not here. We're...not talking at the moment."

Silence hung on the other end, stretching out until she thought the call had dropped. Finally, Luke responded. "I see. I can send someone else over to stand guard."

"That's not necessary. My sister is here, and the doors are locked. Please don't send anyone over."

Luke paused again. "If you insist. Chase will be informed, though."

"I understand." Hearing the news from his alpha rather than her would feel like betrayal. What had she been thinking calling Luke instead of Chase? Her mixed-up emotions had gotten the better of her. Maybe she should have eaten that clarity cookie after all.

"Thank you for the information."

She pressed *end* and looked at her sister. "I'm sure we're fine."

Snow furrowed her brow. "You don't think Isaac could have summoned the demon? I mean...you never actually saw him die."

She wrapped her arms around her middle, holding herself together. "There's no way he survived." He couldn't have. Even if he had, seven years had passed and he hadn't come for her yet. Why would he start now?

Snow nodded. "I believe you. Between your aura-reading ability and my magic, we'll be fine." She drummed her nails on the countertop. "So...can we talk about Chase now?"

Chase strode into the hospital parking garage, heading for

his bike, when a dark, human-like figure sprang from behind a pickup truck and darted around the corner.

"Shit." He picked up the pace, following the shadow, and stopped to peer around the corner. The figure stood at the garage exit, and it whirled to face him, cocking its featureless head before inching away from the building.

The semi-translucent figure was nearly solid black, but as it regarded Chase, its face seemed to morph, taking on liquid-looking features that smoothed into nothingness as quickly as they formed.

At midday, the sun had risen plenty high enough to chase away the darkness, and demons only came out at night. There was no mistaking this was the same shadow Chase had seen twice before, but if it wasn't a demon... what the hell was it?

It took two cautious steps backward before turning and running down the street.

"Goddammit." Chase took off after the creature. Mending his relationship with Rain would have to wait.

The figure jetted around a corner, sticking to the fence line as it ran, stopping every now and then to look back at Chase...almost as if to make sure he followed. Chase texted Luke and James, sharing his location and asking for backup. They'd call it his imagination if he claimed to see a demon out in the daytime.

He tracked the creature out of the Central Business District and into a dense patch of trees in City Park. Leaves crunched as boots pounded the ground behind him, and he looked over his shoulder to find Luke and James making their way toward him.

"What's going on?" Luke caught up first, followed by James.

"The shadow. It's out in the daytime."

"What the hell?" Luke scanned the trees. "Rain said it was a demon."

Chase froze. "When did you talk to Rain?"

Luke jerked his head, indicating they needed to walk and talk. "She called me half an hour ago. Said the demon attacked her friend and took on her form. I've heard of demons who can shape-shift, so I assumed she meant it happened last night."

"Goddammit, Rain. She was with me last night." He clenched his jaw to stop himself from asking permission to leave the hunt. His duty came first, but if his woman was in trouble...

"She's fine," Luke said, as if reading his mind. "You can go back to her as soon as we're done here." Thankfully, he didn't ask what happened between them. The fact that Luke believed in her safety eased his fears. His best friend wouldn't leave his fate-bound unprotected if she were in danger.

James squinted at the sky. "Can demons handle sunlight?"

"Not that I'm aware of." Hell, the first time Chase had seen a demon was a few months ago when a crazy halfling tried to build an army to take over the city. The werewolves had crushed his plans within a few weeks' time. They could take out one daylight-proof shadow demon. *If* that was all they were dealing with.

Luke turned in a circle, scanning the perimeter. "Weekday afternoon. Park's deserted. Humans rarely come this far out anyway. Duck into the trees before you shift. Vanquish it and get out."

Chase nodded, and they moved deeper into the thicket before shifting into their wolf forms. As Chase's beast took control, his first instinct was to run to Rain and make things right with her. He fought it, using his human thoughts to remain in control. One demon wouldn't be hard to kill. Then he could win back his woman.

The shadow moved from behind a tree. It barreled toward James, plowing into him and knocking him from his feet. James grunted as he hit the ground, but he sprang up, ready to attack. The creature tried to get Chase from behind, but he spun around, swiping his massive claws across the shadow's chest. His paw passed straight through the entity as if it didn't exist.

What the hell?

The thing stood there, tilting its head, its features wavering as if trying to take on a face-like form.

Luke and James fanned out around the entity until they all encircled it. Chase rocked back on his haunches, energy coiling in his legs, and sprang for the fiend.

No impact. His body propelled through the shadow; the surprise of not making contact threw him off-balance, and he tumbled into a tree, hitting the trunk with a *thud*. He scrambled to his feet and inhaled deeply. If this creature were a demon, the distinct scent of rotting garbage would have assaulted his senses. Instead, he smelled grass, earth, and trees. Nothing to indicate this creature had ascended from hell.

He growled low in his throat, and the wolves converged, stalking the...whatever it was...as it stepped backward in retreat. How the hell could they kill something they couldn't touch?

The entity took a few more slow steps backward before it stopped and dissolved into nothing. Chase scanned the area, but not a trace of the shadow remained. His friends split up, searching through the trees.

Nothing.

Luke shifted to human form, and Chase and James followed their alpha's lead. "Christ! What the hell was that?"

Chase shook his head. "I have no idea, but I'll see if I can get more information from Rain." His chest tightened. If she would even talk to him.

Isaac opened his eyes as his tulpa reformed before him. Perhaps draining a werewolf would be a better option for his next move. The healing abilities he'd gain might give him enough strength to create the spell he needed with his own magic. His body had burned through most of his last victim's lifeforce in less than twenty-four hours.

Using a tree for support, he pushed to his feet. The rough bark cut into his hand, tearing the paper-thin skin as he clutched the trunk. His back was stuck in a hunched position, and his spine snapped and cracked with splitting pain as he forced himself upright.

Werewolves were too strong, and they were on high alert since he'd allowed his tulpa to play with them. He'd drain a witch. Use her power to cast his spell, and then it would be his turn to play with the werewolves. First, he'd finish what he started with the one trying to claim his Rain. With his rival dead and his magic restored, he might stick around to punish the rest of the pack.

CHAPTER SIXTEEN

"YOU NEED HIM, RAIN. EVEN IF YOU DON'T HAVE feelings for the guy, he's the key to breaking your curse."

Rain eyed her sister. The more she thought about it, the more she agreed with Snow; she did need Chase. Not to break her curse, though that would be a nice bonus. She needed him because life without him would be unbearable. If he thought they could make it work, who was she to tell him no?

"I suppose even seeing him once a week would be better than not at all." She wouldn't be able to go anywhere near his niece, and that thought made her heart ache. She loved the little girl, but seeing her wouldn't be worth the risk. And the other werewolves... Chase would have to talk to them. Explain her curse. Her throat thickened. How could he possibly think *she* was worth the risk?

"The blue moon is getting close." Snow wiped her hands on a towel and dropped it in the laundry bin. "But seriously, sis. You dig the guy. You get heart eyes every time you mention his name." Her heels clicked on the tile as she strode to the cash register. "I'm taking my pay for the day and heading home. He's coming over to talk to you. Please don't be an idiot."

"Thanks."

Snow left through the back door, and Rain shuffled across the store to check the lock on the front door. Glancing through the window, she scanned the street. No sign of Chase. Would he even show up? Snow had said Emma already felt better by the time she'd left the hospital. Maybe Chase had stayed there all day. Or maybe he'd had to work. Dozens of reasons could have kept him away. This didn't mean he'd given up on her.

It wouldn't hurt to send him a text to see how Emma was doing. Glancing through the window one more time, she sighed and padded to the counter. Climbing onto a stool, she tugged her phone from her pocket and typed a message to Chase. *How is Emma?*

Seconds stretched into painful minutes without a reply. Maybe he'd decided she was right. That her curse was too dangerous.

The phone buzzed, and his response lit up the screen. *Fine.*

Her stomach sank. Fine. A four-letter word loaded with so many meanings. The user rarely meant its literal definition. In this case, fine most likely meant final. It meant, "Emma is good, but I don't care enough about you to elaborate. You're only worth one word, so leave me alone."

The phone buzzed again. *Look up.*

She lifted her gaze to the window. Chase stood on the sidewalk outside, his phone in his hand. Her mouth fell open as she sucked in a breath. Maybe he did mean fine literally.

When she didn't move from her stool, he scrunched his brow and typed something into his phone.

Her screen lit up. *Can I come in? I'd like to talk to you.*

She smiled and slipped off her stool, forcing herself to stroll to the entry when she really wanted to run. Unlocking the door, she opened it and stepped aside so he could enter. His warm, musky scent filled her senses, lightening her head. She locked the door and turned to face him, and the sadness in his eyes crumbled her.

She wrapped her arms around him, burying her face in his neck. "I'm sorry."

The scent of soap lingered on his skin, and his hair was damp as if he'd showered shortly before arriving. "Rain." He held her tight. "We can work this out. I'm not letting you go so easily."

She leaned back and placed her hands on either side of his face. As she looked into his hazel eyes, she saw the rest of her life reflected in his tender gaze. "You don't have to let me go."

The worry lines in his forehead smoothed as the tension drained from his body. His lips curved into a tiny smile, and she couldn't resist. She took his mouth with hers, brushing her tongue to his. He tasted like peppermint toothpaste, and a deep rumble vibrated from his chest to his throat.

With his hands in her hair, he cradled her head and kissed her as if he were drinking in her essence. Held her as if she were the most precious thing in the world. He pulled back, searching her eyes as he grazed his fingers across her cheeks, running his thumb over her lips. "Luke told me you saw the demon. Are you sure you're okay?"

"I'm fine. We kept the doors locked all day. As long as Snow's charm is intact, nothing can get in."

He nodded, looking her hard in the eyes. "Next time, call me. I have a vested interested in your safety, and it goes far beyond wedding cake."

She took his hands, lacing her fingers through his. "I will. Emma's doing better?"

"She's almost fully recovered. They're keeping her overnight for observation, but she's going to be fine."

She swallowed the guilt that tightened her throat. "That's good. Did you tell her it was my fault?"

"Bekah knows what happened. Emma doesn't, but…" His eyes tightened in a pained expression. "My sister doesn't want you around her until we can figure out a way to break the curse."

"That's understandable." She chewed the inside of her cheek and dropped her gaze to the floor. It was a fitting reaction for Bekah to have, but the appropriateness didn't lesson the blow. "Being with me will make your life complicated. Your pack might not even accept me."

"They'll accept you." He hooked his finger under her chin, raising her gaze to meet his. "And I'll deal with the complications as they come."

"Are you sure it's worth it?"

"I've never been more sure of anything in my life. I love you."

His words hit her like a can of biscuits popping open in her chest. She couldn't get her breath to flow in nor out as the sensation expanded, spreading through her body.

Chase loved her.

A mix of warm elation and frigid fear swirled through her core, making her pulse race. How could something make her feel so incredibly happy and freeze her in terror at the same time?

She loved him too. There was no other way to describe

her feelings for this man, but love could make people do terrible things. If she had truly been in love with Isaac and not under a spell…

But it wasn't like that with Chase. She felt real, raw, reciprocated emotions, and he deserved to know the entire truth about her past. The whole, horrible story. She shook her head. "Chase…"

"It's okay." He ran his fingers through her hair, tucking a curl behind her ear. "I know it's too soon, and you don't have to say it back. But you need to know…I'm not going anywhere."

The emotion…the passion in his eyes made tears well in her own, but she blinked them back. She had to be strong; she couldn't lie to him anymore. "It's not that." She doubled-checked the lock on the front door. "Come to my room. You might want to take those words back after you hear what I have to tell you."

He gave her a quizzical look and followed her through the kitchen into her make-shift bedroom. She grabbed her robe from the chair and motioned to the seat. "You might want to sit down for this."

He flashed his signature cocky grin, trying to lighten the mood. "Come on…it can't be that bad."

She raised her eyebrows, giving him her best *you'd be surprised* look without saying the words. No amount of banter could lighten the weight she was about to throw at him. Turning her back to him, she hung the robe on the tri-fold partition that separated the closet area from the rest of her bedroom. When she turned around, he sat in the chair and fisted his hands on his legs.

Rain lowered herself onto the edge of the bed, and her knee bumped his. "Sorry it's so cramped in here."

He lifted a leg, positioning it between her knees and

resting his hands on her thighs. "Nothing to apologize for."

Her heart thrummed, her throat tightening and threatening to choke the words she needed to say, but she had to say them. She took a deep breath and blew it out hard. There was no easy way to put this. No way to lessen the blow. "I lied to you about my curse."

He straightened his spine, returning his hands to his own lap.

Crap. That wasn't how she wanted to start. "I didn't actually lie. I...let you believe a lie."

He arched an eyebrow. "And that's better?"

"No. It's...okay. Here's the truth. Isaac didn't put the curse on me. The national witches' council did."

Confusion clouded his eyes. "Why would they do that?"

She lowered her gaze to her lap. "Because of what I did to him. To Isaac." Tears collected on her lower lids. She tried to blink them back, but a single traitor escaped, dripping onto her jeans, darkening the fabric.

"Hey." Chase gripped her hands. "I'm not proud of everything I've done in the past. Whatever it is, we'll get through it."

His touch gave her the strength to continue. "When I confronted him about the cheating and the energy stealing, I cast a spell on him. A terrible spell that wasn't supposed to kill him...but I'm afraid it did. I broke the most sacred of all rules: harm no one."

He squeezed her hand, urging her to go on.

"I don't know if I was in love with Isaac or not. I know I was obsessed. Desperate for his approval. For his attention. My entire life revolved around him, and I thought that was what love felt like. But since I met you, I'm not sure, because I'm not obsessed with you."

She looked into his eyes, waiting for a reaction, but he kept his expression neutral. Neither of them moved, and for a moment nothing but the sound of her trembling breath filled her ears. "The way I feel about you is completely different. With you, I feel safe. I never worry if I have your approval because you show me every day that I do. Maybe it's because I'm older now and mature enough to not be so desperately dependent on a man. I don't know. I'm getting off track."

"I've got all night. Take your time."

She nodded. "When I found out he was cheating and stealing my energy, I went into a fit of rage. I cast a spell, thinking I'd stop him from being with the other woman by making her reject him. It was a spell meant to hinder free will, and that in itself is worthy of my punishment. But what happened was way worse than making his girlfriend hate him."

Chase moved to sit on the bed beside her and wrapped his arm around her shoulders. Supporting her. Giving her strength as she confessed the worst sin she'd ever committed.

"I wrote the spell so that the thing he loved the most would reject him forever, but the thing he loved the most wasn't a person. It was his magic. His power. Since magic resides in the blood, his own blood turned against him. Rather than delivering oxygen and nutrients to his cells to keep him alive and healthy, it stopped flowing like normal. He deteriorated rapidly. The last time I saw him, he looked like he'd aged fifty years. His girlfriend found him and reported me to the council. By the time they arrived to give me my punishment, Isaac had disappeared. His girlfriend too. I assume she took him away, so he could die with some dignity."

Chase kissed the side of her head, leaving his lips pressed against her hair, his body going still. She held her breath, waiting for him to respond. To move. To do something to break the endless silence that felt too much like rejection. Had he changed his mind? Could he take away his love so quickly after giving it to her?

"It was a terrible thing for me to do, and I'm not defending myself. But I honestly think he had me under a spell first. That he had hindered *my* free will. The way I felt about him wasn't natural. I see that now. Now that I know what real love feels like."

Aside from the subtle rise and fall of his chest, he sat motionless. What was he thinking?

"If you want to leave, I understand. You can walk out, and I'll never bother you again. I'll be devastated, but I won't try to hurt you. Not that I could, since my powers are bound, but you know what I mean." She was babbling. She needed to shut up before she dug this pit any deeper. "Please say something."

He inhaled deeply, finishing the kiss as if he'd simply pressed pause while she explained. Then he slid off the bed and knelt in front of her, taking both her hands in his. "I love you. I will never walk out on you."

"I killed a man, Chase. I killed a man because he was cheating on me."

"He was also draining your energy. You saw the woman in the morgue; he could have done that to you. I don't buy for a minute that you are capable of hurting someone on your own. I think you were under a spell too. It makes sense. He wanted to steal your magic, so he had to keep you close."

Another tear rolled down her cheek. "What if I wasn't? What if I *am* capable of hurting people?"

He wiped the moisture from her cheek with his thumb. "You're the kindest, sweetest woman I know. Your past doesn't define you. I am in love with the woman you are today. And the Rain that's sitting here in front of me would never hurt anyone."

She looked at the man kneeling before her, and her chest ached with the amount of love he'd filled her with. He accepted her—sordid past, curse and all—and he loved her.

He sidled closer, spreading her knees apart so his body fit between them. "Who knows? Maybe falling in love will be the selfless act that breaks your curse."

She laughed. "As much as this feels like a fairy tale, I don't think true love's kiss is going to fix my problems."

A sly grin curved his lips. "It won't hurt to try."

"No, I suppose it won't." She took his face in her hands, running her fingers through his beard, and pressed her lips to his. The warmth and gentleness of the kiss loosened the tension in her muscles. He ran his hands up her legs, gripping her hips as his tongue brushed hers. His beard tickled her chin, and the softness of his lips sent buzzing energy zipping through her veins.

He moved his hands to the small of her back, holding her close as he deepened the kiss, and she got lost in the moment. In the man. They could make this relationship work. He believed they could, and now, so did she.

Pulling away, she rested her hands on his shoulders. "Still cursed."

He shrugged. "It was worth a shot." He rose from the ground and settled onto the bed next to her. "Seriously, though. I will do whatever it takes to help you break this curse. Just name it."

Her brow furrowed. Not if he knew what he'd actually have to do. And she certainly couldn't ask him now—when she'd confessed to murder.

The heat from his body so close to hers warmed her from the outside, but the fact that he forgave her for her past chased away the chilling guilt she'd been carrying in her chest since she first told him about her curse.

She couldn't ask him for his blood. What if he gave it to her and then he ended up in werewolf prison for the rest of his life? Or worse? She'd lived with the curse for seven years, and she could continue to bear it. She had to. "I know something you can do for me. It won't break the curse, but I think you might enjoy it." Leaning toward him, she glided her hand up his thigh, stopping half an inch shy from reaching his hip.

He closed the distance between them, lightly grazing his lips over hers. "Are we good now? Can I still call you mine?"

His breath against her skin raised goose bumps on her arms. "Yes, Chase. I'm yours."

He kissed her, tangling his fingers in her hair as he traced his lips down her neck, across her collar bone, and up the other side, leaving a trail of tingling magic on her skin, lighting her soul on fire.

She wanted to give him everything. To show him the love she felt for him before she said the words. Tugging his shirt over his head, she ran her hands over his firm chest and pushed him onto his back.

He grinned, pulling her down with him as he moved to the center of the bed. She showered his face and neck in kisses, allowing his masculine scent to intoxicate her, reveling in the hungry sounds he made in the back of his throat.

With one more deep inhale, she sat up, straddling his hips and running her palms up his stomach. On his left arm, the tattoo sleeve ended at his shoulder, but on the right side, it spilled over onto his chest. A series of roses surrounding an intricate compass occupied most of his right pec.

She traced the design with her fingers. "Does this one have a meaning?"

He placed his hand on hers, holding her palm against his chest. "I was lost for most of my childhood. Being in the pack helped me find my way."

She moved her hand to admire the drawing, following a trail of interwoven vines over his shoulder where they created a frame around another tattoo—a wolf head designed from a fleur-de-lis. "Is that why it's connected to your pack crest?"

"It is." He watched her with a heavy gaze as she ran her fingers over his tattoos. They were all beautiful. Intricate. Even without the ink, Chase had a body sculpted like a god. The gorgeous tattoos tipped his sexiness meter over the edge.

"Your friend is a talented artist." She used her thumbs to toy with his nipple rings.

He sucked in a breath. "He is."

She lowered her mouth to his chest, circling his nipple with her tongue before sucking the ring into her mouth. The sharp, metallic taste of the jewelry mixed with the slight saltiness of his skin, and his chest vibrated as he let out an aroused, *"Mmm."*

He caressed her shoulders. "You found my weakness on the first try."

She moved to his other nipple, sucking it harder as she tugged the other ring with her fingers. Another moan vibrated in his chest, sending her heart into a sprint. She loved that she could do this to him. Make him feel this way so easily. The pleasure it brought her to arouse him was palpable. This man was made for her.

She sat up and pulled her shirt over her head before unhooking her bra and tossing them to the floor. Lying on top of him, skin to skin, the tingle of his magic and the warmth of his body was almost too much to bear. "I'm sure there are other places you'd like to feel my mouth, aren't there?" As she glided her tongue down his chest, she slipped her hand between their bodies to rub him through his jeans.

His response came out more growl than words.

"I'll take that as a yes." She moved down his body, kissing, licking, and nipping her way to his navel. His stomach contracted as she reached the waist band of his jeans and undid the button.

He rose onto his elbows and watched as she slowly pulled the zipper down, the teeth coming apart one by one to reveal his dark-gray boxer-briefs. "You do that any more slowly, and I might explode."

She yanked the zipper the rest of the way down and slipped her hand beneath his underwear to grip his dick. "There will plenty of explosions tonight, wolf man. Be patient."

He grunted, his head falling back onto the pillow as she tugged off his clothes and dropped them on the floor. He had a sleek, powerful build, defined muscles rolling through his entire body, radiating a raw, primal strength. She sat back to appreciate his gorgeous perfection, her gaze traveling from his hooded, hazel eyes, down the length of him. He was thick and hard, and as a bead of moisture gathered on his tip, her mouth watered to taste him.

Taking his dick in her hand, she dipped her head and circled her tongue around the tip. He sucked in a sharp breath through his teeth and fisted the sheets in his hands. Her own stomach tightened, a giddy sensation bubbling up to her throat, escaping as a giggle.

"Something funny?" He rose onto his elbows again, arching a brow over his passion-drunk eyes.

"I like the way you react when I touch you." She held his gaze as she ran her tongue from base to tip."

His eyelids fluttered. "I like the way you touching me feels."

"Good." She took him into her mouth, and he let out his breath in a hiss. The weight of his gaze settled on her as she sucked him, and she took him in as deep as she could before sliding up until only the tip remained in her mouth. The taste of him made her heart sprint, and she wanted…needed…to take him all the way. She moved her mouth down and back up again, caressing his shaft with her tongue, and he moved his hips in unison with her strokes.

His hand on her shoulder slowed her rhythm, and when he stilled her head with his other hand, she released her hold. He sat up, pulling her into his lap, taking her mouth in a kiss. Gliding a hand up her back, he flipped her around, tossing her onto the bed, covering her body with his.

His strength amazed her. That he could pick her up as if she weighed nothing and put her right where he wanted made her stomach flutter. This was a man who was used to getting what he wanted. Good thing they both wanted the same thing.

He sat back on his heels and removed the rest of her clothes, his pupils dilating with desire as he caressed her with his gaze. He kissed her stomach, massaging her inner thighs as his lips neared her sensitive center. Her core tightened, anticipation building, coiling in her stomach. She arched her back, silently begging him to taste her.

His chuckle sent a puff of warm air across her clit, just enough sensation to force a whimper from her throat. He rested his cheek against her inner thigh, his beard tickling the delicate skin. "You are so sexy, Rain."

Her name on his lips. His breath teasing across her folds. It was enough to drive her insane. "Please, Chase."

"Tell me what you need."

"I..." Her voice came out in a breathy whisper. "I need you to touch me."

He slipped a finger inside her, and she gasped. "Like this?"

"*Mmm*...taste me. Please. I want to feel your tongue."

He moved his lips closer, a scant centimeter away from their destination. She could almost feel the smile playing on his lips as he made her wait, sweetening the reward. She'd take back everything she'd said about delayed gratification if he would just lick her.

The warmth of his tongue moved across her center, and she held her breath. When he reached her sensitive nub, the air left her lungs in a gush as tingling electricity shot through her core. His satisfaction vibrated across his lips, shooting another electric burst through her body, lighting every nerve on fire.

He knew where to touch, exactly how to move his tongue to drive her wild. He seemed to know his way around her body as if they'd made love a thousand times.

When he slipped a second finger inside her, she couldn't hold back anymore.

Cresting like a wave, her climax crashed into her, tumbling through her core, surging through her limbs. She cried out, arching her back as he continued to caress her, enchanting her senses until they were the only two people left in the world. Softly, slowly, he eased her down, gliding his tongue across her one more time before moving to lie beside her.

She rolled to her side, draping her top leg over his and taking his length in her hand. "You are the most amazing man I've ever met." She nuzzled closer, kissing him gently before catching his lower lip between her teeth.

He rolled to his back, pulling her on top of him, his lip slipping from her grip. "You're pretty amazing yourself."

She straddled him, sitting on his thighs and stroking him. "You didn't happen to bring a condom, did you?"

He closed his eyes. "No."

She spread the moisture beading on his tip over his shaft, allowing her hand to glide up and down with ease. She needed him inside her. Making love. Becoming one. He knew her so well, but she wanted him to know all of her. Body, mind, and soul. "I'm on birth control."

He opened his eyes and pinned her with a heated gaze. "Werewolves are immune to disease."

Her stomach fluttered, her pulse quickening with longing. "Sounds like we're good to go then."

His mouth tugged into a sexy grin. "I suppose we are."

Rising onto her knees, she guided him to her entrance, gasping as he filled her, his girth stretching her to a pleasurable ache. With her hands on his chest, she moved her hips, sliding up and down his length, each stroke shooting tingling energy to her womb.

He held her gaze, the look in his eyes so full of passion and love that she thought her heart might burst. Leaning forward, she rested her chest against his and kissed him, putting all of her emotions into the kiss, willing him to understand how much he meant to her.

He moaned into her mouth, and gripping her hips, he drove himself deeper inside her. She held still, allowing him to take her, giving herself to him as the overwhelming sensations of ecstasy drove her over the edge.

Her orgasm ripped through her body, shattering her soul into a thousand pieces that only Chase could put back together. He moved faster, his breath coming in short pants until he found his own release, and he held her tight, a low moan shuddering in his chest as he spasmed inside her.

Relaxing his grip, he glided his hands up and down her sweat-slickened back. She nuzzled into his neck, letting his intoxicatingly masculine scent fill her senses, relaxing her into a state of semi-slumber.

He was *her* wolf.

She blinked, lifting her head to look at him. Where had that thought come from? Though she'd always been aware of the duality of his being—even seeing him shift into his wolf form—she'd never thought of him as anything more than a man. But something about the intimacy they shared...the fact that she had finally given her whole self to him...created a strange bond she hadn't felt before. Deep. Primal. It was nothing scary or obsessive. It was rather...comforting. Something about being here with Chase lying in her bed...it finally felt like home.

He tucked a strand of hair behind her ear. "You look confused. What's on your mind, *cher*?"

Resting her weight on her right elbow, she placed her left hand over his heart. "I'm in love with you."

He smiled and took her hand, bringing her fingers to his lips. "You just made me the happiest man alive."

"And your wolf?"

He gave her a curious look. "That part of me has wanted you since the moment I saw you. The rest of me had to get over some misplaced anger issues first, but I'm all yours now. One hundred percent. I love you."

"I love you too." Her smile widened, and she moved to lie on her side, snuggling next to him and resting her head on his chest. "I like the way that sounds."

"So do I. You're way better than a goat."

She laughed. "You're not going to let me forget I said that, are you?"

"Not a chance."

She traced her fingers along the cuts of his muscles, and he let out a contented sigh. She loved Chase, and he loved her. Did that mean she was his fate-bound? When he'd talked about them, he'd made it sound like a werewolf could fall in love with someone who wasn't his fate-bound. If that were the case, what would happen if he met his fate-bound later? Would he stop loving her to be with the other woman? If Rain married him...if she was his mate... would he even be allowed to leave her?

A sickening feeling formed in her stomach as her mind spun with questions. If she was his fate-bound, none of them mattered, but...wouldn't he have told her if she was? She could ask him, but what would she do if the answer was no? She'd rather not know in that case. He loved her, and that was the important thing. She'd deal with the fate-bound issue when and if it ever came up.

His stomach vibrated as a deep growl rumbled from inside him.

She lifted her head. "I guess we missed dinner."

He chuckled. "And breakfast and lunch. I've been a little distracted today." He kissed the top of her head. "You wouldn't happen to have food other than cake in the kitchen, would you?"

She rose onto her elbow. "I do live here, you know. Of course I have food. No meat, but I can make a killer cucumber and avocado sandwich."

He wrinkled his nose.

She rolled her eyes. "Try it. I'll add extra cheese so it won't taste too healthy." Before he had a chance to protest, she rolled out of bed and put on her robe, cinching it at the waist. "You stay where you are. I'll be right back." She let her gaze wander over his magnificent body before turning and scurrying out the door. With Chase in her bed, she'd be back again and again. *What a man.* She grinned. Not gay, nor about to be married like she'd first thought. Lucky her.

Rain wasn't the type of woman who normally pranced, but she felt so damn giddy, she couldn't help herself. Happiness bubbled in her chest, its effervescence lightening her steps.

As she pranced into the kitchen and flipped on the light, her happy little heart got stuck in her throat. A man —or what was left of one—stood in the center of the room, toying with something in his hands.

Rain froze. Instinct told her to run or to call for Chase, but an icy flush of dread glued her to the spot, cutting off her ability to speak.

Ashen skin hung loose on the man's bones, giving him the appearance of having recently crawled out of the grave. His aura, once dark-purple and sparkling with magic, had turned a murky shade of brownish-black, illness dampening even the bluish glow of life. Though his dark eyes had dulled to a death-like state, they were unmistakable.

She clutched her robe together at her neck and forced out a whisper. "Isaac."

"Good evening, Rain." His voice came out as a croak, and his lips cracked as they peeled into a smile, revealing his rotted teeth.

Her stomach tumbled to her feet. Her heart pounded against her ribs. This couldn't be real. Isaac was dead.

"I think you've met my tulpa." He gestured to a darkened corner, and a figure emerged from the shadows. Though human-like in form, its featureless face made it look more like a nightmare than a person.

Her mind reeled, thoughts spinning through her head like a tornado. She blinked, cutting her gaze from the shadow to her ex-boyfriend. "You…made a tulpa?"

"I couldn't have done it without your help."

"That's not possible." Finally able to move her feet, she took a step back.

He sneered, the skin around his mouth cracking farther until a blackish goo oozed from the wounds. "It wasn't possible for *you*. The spell I had on you made sure you thought of little other than me. I, on the other hand, have had seven years of using nothing but my mind."

She shook her head, trying to bring herself up to speed with the situation. She'd been right about his spell, but she hadn't killed him. Now he stood in her kitchen, with a monster he'd created from his imagination, while Chase lay in her bedroom.

The blood drained from her head, making the room spin. *Chase.* Oh, goddess, she couldn't let Isaac get to Chase. If she stayed quiet, maybe Isaac wouldn't realize he was here. She could deal with her ex if he thought she was alone. She took another step back, and her body betrayed her, involuntarily glancing down the hall toward her bedroom. Faster than humanly possible, the tulpa swiped a knife from the block and pressed it to her windpipe.

"No yelling for your boyfriend." Isaac shuffled toward her. "I've got plans for him too."

She swallowed, and the edge of the blade scraped against her throat. The entity's hand held the back of her head, and she leaned into it, willing herself to pass through it. The tulpa only existed in Isaac's imagination. She closed her eyes and breathed as deeply as the cold steel against her trachea allowed. *It's not real. I can pass through it because it doesn't exist.* But the sharp metal pressing into her throat insisted on its reality. She opened her eyes. "How did you get in here? Snow set up a ring of protection."

Isaac held her broken totem between his thumb and forefinger and nodded toward his creation. Rain shifted her gaze to the shadow, and its faced morphed into a wavering, watery resemblance of her landlord.

She focused on the tulpa's aura—the same dull-gray she'd seen surrounding the thing posing as Ingrid. "You're the demon."

Isaac scoffed. "You've called me worse, love."

"You set this up. You sent your tulpa here to break the circle of protection so you could get inside my home." As her voice grew louder, the tulpa pressed the knife harder against her skin to silence her.

She clawed at the arm holding the knife, and her

hands passed through it as if it were made of nothing. It moved its free hand to the side of her face. Though its touch felt cold, it was too solid to be a figment of Isaac's imagination. She couldn't convince her mind otherwise.

"Smart girl. But be quiet. I don't want to alert your werewolf boyfriend to my presence. I'm not strong enough to fight him yet."

Her stomach turned at the thought of him going after the man she loved. She had to protect Chase. "How did you find me?"

He clutched the edge of a countertop, and something thick and black oozed from a moss-covered wound on his wrist. "Surely, you've heard about the Miami witch that turned up dead in New Orleans? The one that was missing an eye?"

She cringed. "She had the gift of sight?"

"Eye, she did." He attempted a laugh that turned into a muffled cough. "Get it? Aye like yes, but also eye?"

Rain hardened her gaze. How had she found his sense of humor delightful at one time? Oh, right, because he'd had her under a spell. "Who was she?"

His eyes brightened. "You'll be happy to hear that was Giselle."

"Your girlfriend?"

He let out a wistful sigh. "I never had to put her under a spell. She liked me as I was…until you did *this* to me. She stuck around for a little while, until she figured out I wasn't going to recover."

"So you killed her?"

"I needed to drain someone to gain enough energy to make the journey to find you, my love." He shrugged. "She didn't have the sense to run away from Miami like you did. I took her life for her betrayal."

Rain narrowed her eyes. "And now it's my turn?"

A look of regret flashed in his eyes before he scowled. "You owe me more than your life. I'm going to make you suffer. Good night, sweet Rain."

The tulpa dropped the knife onto the counter and gripped the sides of her head. She struggled to free herself from its clutches as a dull ache spread across her scalp and her vision tunneled until two pinpricks of light remained.

Then darkness.

CHAPTER SEVENTEEN

CHASE PUT ON HIS UNDERWEAR AND SAT ON THE edge of the bed. How long did it take to make a cucumber and avocado sandwich? Maybe she had a garden out back, and she had to pick the vegetables first.

No, he'd been around back, and this building didn't have a courtyard like so many other French Quarter structures did. The only thing behind Rain's bakery was a dumpster that desperately needed emptying, based on the faint rotting smell creeping into his senses. Something wasn't right.

As he reached for his pants, she stepped through the doorway, grinning and holding a cookie in her hand.

"I was starting to worry about you, *cher*. Did you bake that from scratch?"

Her grin widened, and she shuffled toward him, offering him the treat.

He took it and held it up to his nose for a sniff. Chocolate chip. "What happened to the sandwich? I don't think a cookie is going to hold me 'til morning."

She sighed and tilted her head.

He started to ask if she'd put a spell on it but thought better of it. That would've been a dick move, especially since they'd just declared their love for each other.

Lifting the cookie to his lips, he took a bite, and she watched him intently as he chewed and swallowed. He looked at her, and she nodded, encouraging him to finish. She was normally more talkative, but if she wanted him to eat the whole damn cookie, he'd eat it for her.

Finishing the last bite, he licked his fingers for emphasis. "Delicious as expected, though I was planning on having you for dessert."

She giggled.

"How about that sandwich? I need some sustenance for all the things I have planned for you tonight."

She turned on her heel and darted out the door.

What kind of game was the woman playing? He stood and peeked out the door, but she'd disappeared around a corner. As he stepped into the hall, a wave of fatigue crashed into him, spreading from his core to his limbs. His mouth went dry, and his head spun as his muscles contracted with searing pain. "What the hell?"

He stumbled down the hall into the kitchen, and his heart plummeted to his feet when he found Rain lying on the floor.

"Rain!" He rushed to her side, and dropping to his knees, he put a hand on her chest. It rose and fell steadily with her breaths, but his own breathing became labored and raspy. Rolling her onto her back, he patted her cheek gently. "Rain? *Cher*, are you okay?" *She's lying on the cold kitchen floor. Of course she's not okay, asshole.*

Her skin was clammy to the touch, and her eyelids fluttered as if she were trying to open them.

"Rain?"

She sucked in a sharp breath and opened her eyes. Blinking wildly, she darted her gaze about the room and locked eyes with him. "Chase? Is it really you?" She lifted her hand, slapping him across the face before letting her arm flop to the floor.

A stinging sensation spread from his cheek to his jaw, and he rubbed his face. "It's me. Ow."

"Sorry. I thought you weren't real." She tried to sit up, but her elbows buckled beneath her.

He caught her and scooped her into his arms. Had she always been this heavy? "What's going on? What happened?" He tried to stand, but his knees gave out before he could right himself. Setting Rain on the floor, he sat back on his heels. "What was in that cookie?"

She rubbed her temples. "What cookie?"

"The one you gave me. Wait…why did you think I wasn't real?" His head pounded, and he squeezed his eyes shut, trying to stave off the nausea that threatened to give that cookie a reappearance.

"I didn't give you a cookie." She moved to all fours, rocking slightly before steadying herself.

He scrunched his brow, shaking his head to clear the confusion clouding his mind. Shifting his weight to his feet, he tried to rise, but his knees wobbled. He put a hand on the floor. Why did he feel so weak? "Did you put a spell on me?" The moment the words left his lips, he regretted them.

Rain narrowed her eyes and peered at him through a curtain of her hair. "Seriously? You're really asking me that?"

Clutching a counter for support, he rose to his feet. "I'm sorry. I know you can't cast spells."

"It's not that you know I can't, Chase. It's that you

thought I *would*." She stood and stumbled before catching herself on the wall.

"I don't think that, and I'm sorry I said it. Please explain what's going on. You came into the room and gave me a cookie. Then you ran out, and I found you unconscious on the floor. And I feel…" Ice flushed his veins. "I can't feel my wolf." He grabbed at his chest as if he could physically grab hold of the missing piece of his being. What the hell was happening to him?

Rain squinted, studying him. "Oh, goddess, no. Not you too."

"Me too what?"

With her back against the wall, she covered her face with her hands and slid to the floor. "I need to lie down."

Panic raced through his veins like a freight train. Reaching beneath her arms, he lifted her to his chest and carried her to the bedroom. His dizziness had subsided, leaving behind nothing but weakness in his muscles to indicate anything had happened to him. Weakness…and the absence of his wolf.

He laid her on the bed and sat beside her. "I know you don't feel well, *cher*, but I need you to tell me what happened. To you and to me."

She inhaled deeply, fluttering her eyes open to meet his gaze. "It was Isaac."

"Isaac? I thought he was dead."

"So did I, but he was standing in the kitchen with his tulpa when I got there."

"What the hell is a tulpa?"

"The shadow you've been seeing. It's not a demon. Isaac created it with his mind."

He squeezed his eyes shut and rubbed his forehead, trying to make sense of her words. He knew it wasn't a demon because he'd seen it in the daylight. Aside from the first time he'd encountered it in the swamp, it had only appeared when Rain was near. The damn thing hadn't been targeting him, it had been after his woman.

His spine went rigid, his muscles contracting as he fisted the sheet. How could he have been so stupid? "This tulpa...how did Isaac create it with his mind? Is it some kind of spell? A hologram? What is it?" He shook his head. "That's not important. What happened to you? Are you sick? What can I do?"

"The tulpa used my energy to shape-shift, like it did to my landlord, but I'll regain my strength." She inhaled a shaky breath. "My guess is that it made you think you saw me, so you would think that I..." She lowered her gaze to her stomach.

He clutched her hand. "That you what, Rain? Please tell me what's going on."

"Did you eat the cookie?"

"Yeah."

Tears gathered on her lower lids. "Isaac sent the tulpa, disguised as me, to give you a binding spell."

"A binding spell?"

She blinked up at him, and tears spilled down her cheeks. "He bound your power. Your wolf. You're like me now."

"No." He wouldn't believe it. Shaking his head, he stood and paced the small bedroom. His wolf was half of his soul. Without it, he wasn't himself. He was...nothing.

"Yes, Chase. I can see it in your aura. Or rather...I *can't* see it. Your aura looks mundane, so your power must be bound."

He jabbed his fingers into his hair, pulling it at the roots. "I can't shift? I've lost my strength?"

She nodded.

"I'm useless." He threw his hands into the air. This couldn't be happening.

"No. You're still you, like I'm still me. Your power is there, in your blood."

He stopped and leaned his head against the wall. Leave it to a witch to use someone he loved against him. "How did he find us? How did he know?"

"The witch from the morgue had the gift of sight. He..." She blew out a hard breath. "He killed her and used her gift to find me. To find us."

"Her missing eye." His muscles tensed, a sharp pain shooting through his jaw as he ground his teeth. The bastard would not get away with this. "How can I break the spell? What if I finished the job and killed him myself?"

She pushed into a sitting position and leaned her back against the wall. "Binding spells aren't tied to the caster. They get inside you, stay with you until they're broken."

"What about the coven? Or Snow? Can't someone write an *un*binding spell?"

A pained expression flashed across her features before morphing into sadness. "Unbinding spells are a bitch." She let out a dry laugh. "High-level witches have to write them, and they require months of preparation and ingredients that aren't easy to come by."

He sank onto the bed.

Rain scooted toward him and wrapped her arms around him from behind. "Snow doesn't have that kind of power. Anyway, if they were easy, don't you think I'd have found a way to break my curse by now?"

So...what? He was stuck this way? Was the universe playing some kind of cruel joke on him? Leading him to his fate-bound. Making her a witch of all creatures, and then waiting until he let his guard down to send in another witch to steal his wolf? "How'd he get in? You said no one could break the circle of protection."

"Remember what I told you about my landlord being drained by the shadow? I think it did that to gain the ability to take on her form. When it came into the bakery disguised as Ingrid, it took one of the enchanted totems. Breaking it broke the circle. The magic was tied to the lock, so we didn't notice the spell had stopped working."

"How did it know what to take?"

"I think Isaac can see through the tulpa's eyes. It's a projection of his mind, so wherever the tulpa goes, his vision goes. Isaac would have recognized the spell; it's basic witchcraft. He planned this. Knew you were here."

"And he's coming after me in order to hurt you."

She nodded and pressed her lips to his shoulder. "I'm so sorry. He's here for revenge. He'll go after you and Snow first—the people I love—to make me suffer. Then he'll kill me. The spell I cast on him is tied to me. With me dead, it will be lifted, and his power will return."

"We can't let that happen." No way in hell would he let anything happen to his fate-bound. "But I can't fight him like this. I'm weak."

"So is he. Chase, he's in bad shape. His arm is injured, and he looked like death. He must have drained another witch to get the power to create the binding spell he gave you. With his blood working against him, he doesn't retain power long. He'll need to recover before he strikes again. If we could figure out where he's hiding, we could catch him off-guard. Capture him and force him to remove the spell."

"He's in the swamp." He moved to face her and took her hands in his. "You said his arm was injured?"

"Yes, his wrist was wrapped in blood-soaked moss."

His heart raced. "A snake didn't bite me when I was hunting. I was following the shadow when I slipped into the water. I turned around and bit whatever had hold of my leg. It had to be Isaac. He was draining me."

Her eyes widened. "That's why he bound your power. He knew you were too strong for a fair fight."

"And if he knows anything about werewolf politics, he also knows I'll lose my rank in the pack if anyone finds out I've lost my wolf." Not that rank mattered to him; his position was temporary anyway. But if the guy was out to hurt Rain by hurting the ones she loved...

"But you haven't lost your wolf. He's in you...bound in your blood."

He shook his head. "Doesn't matter. Only shifting wolves can hold rank." How long would Isaac try to stretch this out? Would he try to tear Chase's life apart before moving on to Snow's, saving Rain for last so he could watch her suffer?

"Then we'll fix this without telling the pack. Isaac isn't a threat to them. He's after me and the people I love, and he's probably at his weakest right now. Let me get dressed, and I'll call Snow." She slid off the bed, but as soon as she stood, her knees buckled.

Chase caught her by the waist and guided her to the bed. "You're not going anywhere in your condition. I'll get James and Luke to go with me. Snow and another wolf will stay here with you in case he comes back."

"But if you can't shift..."

He grabbed his shirt and pulled it over his head. "I wouldn't be where I am today if it weren't for the pack. I'm not going to turn my back on them now, but I have to figure out how we can get past the tulpa." He turned his jeans right side out and shoved in his legs. "We've tried to fight it before. It can touch us, but when we try to attack, it's as if the damn thing doesn't exist."

"That's because it doesn't. If you can convince your mind that it's not real, its blows will pass through you too. As long as it doesn't get ahold of a weapon." She rubbed her throat. "That knife was real enough."

He paused, and another flash of anger surged through him. "It had a knife against your throat?" And he'd been lounging in her bed, oblivious to the danger lurking a few feet away. *Asshole.* Fumbling with the button, he cursed at his jeans and yanked up the zipper.

"Don't you think I would have called for help if I'd been able?"

"This guy is dead. I'm going to take care of you, *cher.*"

Rain lay on the pillow, her lids fluttering shut as he spoke, and his heart ached for her. Even with his wolf bound, the overwhelming urge to protect his mate-to-be tore through him. He would do *anything* to keep her safe. "Before you fall asleep, is there a way to kill the tulpa?"

She shook her head. "Isaac would have to imagine it dead."

"If Isaac is dead himself?"

A tiny smile curved her lips. "Bye bye, tulpa."

CHAPTER EIGHTEEN

RAIN WOKE WITH A START, SITTING UP IN BED, HER head spinning as she tried to regain focus. Memories began clicking together like pieces of a puzzle, expanding in her mind like a pressure cooker. "Chase."

"He's out looking for Isaac." Snow sat in the chair next to the bed and leaned her elbows on her knees. "How are you feeling?"

Rain blinked at her sister. The pounding in her head had subsided, and her muscles felt mildly achy. "Better. He told you what happened?" Her robe had come open while she slept, so she tied it shut.

Snow's lips quirked, suppressing a grin. "Not the whole story." She motioned with her head toward Rain's clothes discarded on the floor. "I take it you made up before all this went down?"

Warmth spread through her chest, elation tingling through her limbs. "You could say that. How long have I been out?"

"Chase left as soon as we got here...about twenty minutes ago, so maybe an hour."

She let out a slow breath. "I'm scared."

"For yourself or for Chase?"

"Both." She scooted to the edge of the bed and picked up her clothes. "Isaac is weak, but..."

Snow stood. "I made a new circle of protection, and I hid the totems this time." She nodded to a lumpy dishtowel lying on the table by the window. "And your boyfriend is a big, bad werewolf. He can take out your miserable ex with one swipe of a paw. I'm sure this will all be over soon." She smiled. "And the blue moon is right around the corner..."

Rain cringed inwardly but kept her expression neutral. How could she tell her sister—who had worked so hard on the unbinding spell, who had risked so much by simply moving to New Orleans and working with her—that she didn't plan on asking Chase for his blood?

She pulled her shirt over her head and shoved her legs into her jeans. "Chase said he was going to send a werewolf over to keep watch."

"He sent two. Why don't you come meet them?" Snow gestured toward the store front and stepped into the doorway.

Rain glanced in the mirror and tousled her tangled hair. "I suppose I've looked worse."

Snow rolled her eyes. "You're glowing like a woman in love. Now, come say hello to our guests before they start thinking we're rude."

After slipping on her shoes, Rain followed her sister into the storefront. Macey sat at the small cake tasting table in the corner with a tall, blonde woman. Though their statures were different, they both had bright-green eyes and similar facial features. The taller one's aura glowed the deep orange of a werewolf, while Macey's was a more muted tone.

Rain approached the table. "Hi. I'm sorry for dragging you out here in the middle of the night."

Macey stood and shook her hand. "It's no problem. I work nights, so I'm used to it."

The other woman rose to her feet and offered her hand. "Alexis Gentry. Nice to meet you."

Rain cut her gaze between the two women. Wasn't Macey's last name Carpenter? "You're obviously sisters, so I take it Gentry is your married name?"

She paused, her lip curling as if the idea disgusted her. "No, it's not."

Rain gave her a questioning look. Sisters with different last names? Did that mean they had different fathers? Weren't werewolves supposed to mate for life?

Alexis shrugged. "Long story."

She made a mental note to ask Chase about it later and turned her gaze to Macey. "Since you're here, do you want to talk about your wedding cake? I can show you my portfolio." She shuffled to the cabinet that held her books.

"Are you up for that?" Macey followed. "With everything that's happened…"

"There's a murderous madman on the loose, and people are dying because of me." A sob threatened to bubble from her chest, but she swallowed it down. She would not lose control in front of these women. Taking a heavy album from the shelf, she clutched it in her arms. "It will help keep my mind occupied until Chase comes back."

Macey nodded. "We'll be feeding several hundred people, but I'd like to keep it as simple as possible."

Rain set the portfolio on the table and sank into a

chair. "Simple. Elegant. Big doesn't have to mean elaborate."

"Gentry…" Snow sat on a barstool and tapped a finger against her lips. "Where are you from?"

Alexis cut her gaze to Macey. "All over. Our parents were rogues, and they traveled a lot."

Snow smiled. "We might be related."

Rain's stomach turned. "What?"

"Way, way back…I'd have to look at my notes…one of the Connolly witches married a Gentry werewolf." She hopped off the stool and sashayed around the counter. "I researched our family tree as a gift for our grandmother's eightieth birthday. Coffee?"

Macey looked up from the portfolio. "That would be great."

Rain's throat went dry. "Why didn't you tell me that?"

Snow shrugged and filled the pot with water. "It was a long time ago; you wouldn't have been interested back then. Anyway, I think it was our great-great-grandmother's sister who married the Gentry. We don't have any werewolf in us." She smirked. "Well, *I* don't have any werewolf in me. You, on the other hand, occasionally do."

Heat crept up Rain's cheeks, but she wouldn't let her sister distract her. She looked at the women. "I'm sorry. You have to go. You can't be here. You can't show me kindness."

"Why not?" Alexis took a cookie from the plate Snow set on the table.

"You don't know about my curse?"

The werewolves shook their heads.

Rain's heart warmed. Chase hadn't told her secret. "Any witch who shows me kindness will suffer. Even if you have a little bit of witch blood, you're at risk. Being here, doing me a favor like this, you could end up getting run over by a bus."

Snow nodded. "It's happened to me. Well, it was more of a bump than a complete run-over, but it hurt like hell."

Rain gave her sister an apologetic look, but she waved it off. She'd lost count of how many times Snow had fallen victim to her curse, but every incident added another ounce of guilt to the weight she carried on her shoulders.

"Good thing we're not doing this for you, then," Alexis said around the cookie in her mouth. "We're under orders from the alpha."

That could've been a loop-hole, saving them from the curse, but it was best not to take chances. "You should leave."

"Are you kidding?" Alexis took another cookie. "I'm a rogue, and even I know better than to disobey an alpha. I leave, and I'll never be allowed back in New Orleans again. Especially since you're—"

"We'll be fine." Macey gave her a reassuring smile. "We're doing this for Luke…and for Chase." A funny look flashed in her eyes before she focused on the album. "I like this one, but it will have to be bigger, I'm afraid. Can you make this to feed four hundred?"

Rain let out a breath. Hopefully her curse would spare these women. They couldn't go against their alpha's orders. "Believe it or not, that one fed two-fifty. I can make it a little bigger. Is that the one you want?"

Alexis laughed. "She *wants* to elope and get married on a beach somewhere private."

Macey glared at her sister. "I'm adjusting to all the… people in my life. Before I joined the pack, it was just me and my parents. Now my family has grown by two hundred members."

Rain looked at Alexis. "You said you're rogue? Why aren't you in the pack?"

Her smiled faded. "Long story."

"And how is it that you and Luke are already mates but you aren't married?"

Snow set a tray of coffee on the table and cleared her voice. "Stop drilling them with questions. Some things are private."

Macey smiled and gave Rain that strange look again. "It's okay. I had a lot of questions in the beginning too." She pointed at a cake picture in the album. "Definitely this one."

"I'll write it down." Snow took the portfolio to the counter.

Macey folded her hands on the table. "Our parents died when we were very young, and we spent our childhoods in foster care. We didn't know we weren't human. Alexis ran away when she started shifting, and I got adopted shortly after. I had no clue I was a werewolf until I met Luke." Her eyes sparkled at the mention of her mate's name. "Being mates is different than being married. A couple can be mates without getting married because it's an oath you take before the pack."

Alexis took a sip of coffee. "It's binding. Marriage can end in divorce, but once a werewolf takes a mate, it's for life."

Macey nodded. "Normally, werewolves will become mates and get married at the same time. Luke was on a deadline. He had to be mated in order to become alpha, so we took the oath and then planned the wedding."

The look on Rain's face must have given away her confusion because Macey laughed. "Don't worry. The longer you're around Chase, the more things will start to make sense. Being loved by a werewolf is a gift to be treasured." The sparkle returned to her eyes, and Rain's chest tightened.

Did Chase's eyes ever sparkle when he talked about her? Rain's entire body tingled from thinking about him.

"Anyway..." Alexis said. "Tell us about the creature they're out hunting. Chase called it a tulpa. Where did it come from?"

Rain shifted her gaze to the last cookie on the plate. These women were risking their lives to protect her. They deserved the truth. "When I lived in Miami, I was in training for a spot on the national council. I had to complete a research project to qualify, so I was looking into an ancient form of magic that's no longer practiced. A tulpa is an entity created in the mind. It requires complete focus. The conjurer has to go into a meditative state for hours at a time, days and weeks on end. I thought it was impossible. A myth."

She looked at the women, who stared back at her intently. Snow pulled a chair beside her and rested her hand on her back.

"I was dating Isaac at the time...before I found out he was cheating on me and stealing my energy." A spark of anger ignited inside her, but she squelched it. Getting mad wouldn't do her any good. "I shared my research with him, and he apparently figured out how to make it work. I guess since he has the power to drain energy, his tulpa does too. It can shapeshift, and he can see through its eyes."

She shook her head. "But it doesn't really exist, so it can't be killed. Isaac is the only one who can destroy it."

Alexis lifted an eyebrow. "What if we destroy Isaac?"

"That would work too, but he's smart. He won't be easy to find."

"Have a little faith." Alexis crossed her arms. "Werewolves are excellent hunters."

She didn't lack faith. If anyone could find Isaac, it would be Chase and the other werewolves. But the fact that Chase couldn't shift had her trembling on the inside. That tulpa was fast, and Chase moved like a human. If he got hurt… His healing ability was bound with the rest of his magic. Did he realize that?

Macey put her hand on Rain's. "He'll be okay. They all will."

"Careful showing me kindness."

Macey gave her a sympathetic look and dropped her arm to her side.

"She's saying that to reassure herself." Snow looked at Macey, who nodded. "Her mate is out there too."

Rain's bottom lip trembled, so she bit it. She had to hold herself together. Becoming a blubbering mess would do nothing but make her look weak. Chase would be fine. They hunted in a pack, so the other werewolves would have his back. She took a deep breath and gave Macey an appreciative smile. "Can I ask you a personal question?"

Macey swallowed. "Sure."

"Are you and Luke…is he your fate-bound?"

Macey glanced at Alexis before focusing on Rain. "Yes. I didn't understand it at first…how someone could feel *that* deeply in a short amount of time."

Rain licked her lips and swallowed the dryness from her mouth. "Do werewolves ever mate with someone who isn't their fate-bound?"

"All the time," Alexis said.

"Why don't they wait? If their fate-bound is out there somewhere, why would they take someone else as their mate?"

Macey tilted her head. "There's no guarantee a were-wolf will meet their fate-bound. It's not a rare occurrence, but many don't. Love is love, whether fate brought you together or if you met by chance."

"That makes sense." Even if she wasn't Chase's fate-bound, he could still love her deeply. And if they became mates, he'd remain faithful for the rest of his life. "But what if a werewolf takes someone as his mate, and then he later meets his fate-bound? What happens then?"

Macey grinned. "I don't think fate would introduce them if he'd taken another mate. I'd have to ask Luke, but I've never heard of that happening." She looked at Alexis.

"I've never heard of it either. If fate has plans, you can't stop them from happening, can you, Macey?" She smirked at her sister.

Macey returned the look, something passing between them that even Rain knew better than to ask about. Her filter did occasionally work, though Snow would say otherwise.

Macey smiled at Rain. "You don't have to worry about that."

"I—" A *bang-bang-bang* sounded on the door, rattling it in its frame.

"Who the hell?" Snow paced to the front window and peered through the glass. "Oh, shit."

Rain's heart raced. "Who is it?"

The werewolves rose to their feet, Macey's hand hovering over the gun holstered at her hip.

"It's Calista and her band of merry meddlers. Six of them."

"Six?" Why was the high priestess of a coven she wasn't allowed to join knocking on her door at three in the morning? "You're sure it's her?"

"Come check their auras. Unless the tulpa multiplied, I'm pretty sure it's the coven."

Rain shuffled to the front and looked out the window. Calista banged on the door again, her deep-magenta aura sparkling with power. This couldn't be good. "It's her. I guess we better let them in."

Snow opened the door, and Calista pushed past her, marching toward Rain. She spun in a circle, taking in the room, her gaze pausing on the werewolves, her lip curling in disgust. "Rain Connolly, you're charged with the murder of three witches."

Ice flushed her veins. "What? No!"

"Subdue her." Calista jerked her head at Rain, and two of her subjects marched toward her.

Her mind reeled. Three witches? *Oh, no.* Isaac did drain another one to gain the strength to come here tonight. One strong enough to cast the binding spell he'd put on Chase. "It wasn't me."

Macey and Alexis moved in front of her before the witches could reach her. "She's not going anywhere with you." Macey kept her hand resting on her gun. "She's under protection of the pack."

Calista crossed her arms. "The pack would protect a murderer?"

"I didn't kill them. I've been here all night. I swear." She clutched Snow's hand. How could they accuse her of such an atrocity?

"A body was found in a dumpster behind Frenchman Street."

Rain cringed.

"We found the other one on your back doorstep."

The room seemed to turn into a vacuum, sucking the air from her lungs. It wasn't enough for her cheating ex to kill innocent people and hurt the man she loved. He'd set her up to be charged with the crime too. "Isaac was here. The one who did it. Please, if you'll listen to me, I can explain everything."

Calista put her hands on her hips. "You can explain from your holding cell when a council member arrives. You are the only witch in New Orleans with no powers of your own, so you're stealing them from others. Take her sister too. She probably lured Jason here."

"Jason Clements?" Snow squeezed her hand tighter.

Sadness filled Calista eyes before she hardened her gaze. "Yes."

The other two witches advanced toward them. Macey drew her gun. "The order of the alpha is that she remains in this building, unharmed, until he returns."

The high priestess inclined her head, looking down her nose at Macey. "You're his mate, right? I've heard your story. You almost tore the pack apart once; are you sure you want to be the reason we start a war?"

Rain clenched her jaw. Three people were dead, a little girl was sick, and Chase's magic was bound…all because of her. She couldn't let anything else happen. "Stop." She wedged her way through her werewolf guardians. "I'll go peacefully."

"Rain, don't." Alexis took her arm, but she pulled away.

"You don't need to start a war over me."

Snow's eyes widened, but she stepped around the werewolves to stand by Rain's side. "I'll go too."

Macey holstered her gun and nodded. "Luke's not going to be happy about this." She narrowed her eyes at Calista. "Expect to hear from him soon."

The coven allowed Rain to lock up before leading

Snow and her to the back seat of a black Mercedes. "Anything I do for the rest of the night that seems like kindness," Snow said, "is actually emotional support for myself." She flashed a small smile. "Just so you know."

They remained silent on the drive to the coven house, Snow gripping her hand the only thing keeping her grounded.

If the national council believed Calista's accusations, Rain was as good as dead. She'd been warned when they cursed her that the next step would be execution. Was that Isaac's plan all along? Not to be the one to murder her, but to let the council do it?

Flanked by four witches, Rain and Snow followed Calista into the house and down a flight of steps to the coven's makeshift prison. A single cot sat against one brick wall, and two lawn chairs occupied the center of the small room. Someone shoved her from behind, and Rain stumbled inside.

Snow rushed in with her and caught her by the arm. "Was that necessary?"

Calista straightened her spine. "The spell on this room neutralizes magic, and guards will be posted outside. Don't make this difficult by trying to escape."

Rain crossed her arms to hide her trembling. "There's nothing behind my building but a trash can. How did you know the body was there?"

"His girlfriend tracked his phone when he didn't come home." Calista mirrored her posture.

"Jason was my friend," Snow said. "We didn't do it."

"Save it for the council." Calista closed the door, and the sound of the magic lock clicking into place pierced the silence like a nail in a coffin.

Rain looked at her sister. "You knew Jason?"

Tears pooled in Snow's eyes, and her bottom lip trembled as she nodded. "Yeah." She wiped her cheeks. "He was powerful too. Whatever spells Isaac cast with Jason's magic will be hard to undo."

Rain sank onto the cot, dropping her head in her hands. "He bound Chase's power."

"Oh, no." Snow sat next to her.

"No kidding."

"I'm so sorry."

Rain let out a dry chuckle. "Looks like neither one of us will be getting our magic back anytime soon. If ever." She dragged her hands down her face. "He'll lose his rank in the pack. The council will have my head on a plate. The only good thing about this situation is that Isaac can't get to us in here."

Snow rubbed her hand across Rain's back. "There you go. Way to look on the bright side."

CHAPTER NINETEEN

Chase stopped at a red light and ground his teeth. They'd searched every damn inch of a five-mile radius around the spot where Isaac had latched on to him the first time, and they'd found nothing. Not a trace of the tulpa or the bastard who created it. Chase would still have been out there searching if Luke hadn't called them back in.

They'd split up, each of them taking a third of the area, so he'd managed to keep the fact that he couldn't shift to himself so far. Sooner or later, though, he'd have to fess up and admit his problem. Sure, he might lose his rank in the pack, but he didn't give a damn about rank. Unlike witches, a werewolf would never turn his back on one of his own. He could go it alone or he could have the support of the pack at his back. His choice.

He'd keep it to himself for the time being though, to protect Rain.

How long was this damn light going to stay red? He needed to get back to his woman. With thoughts of running it skittering through his brain, he lifted his foot from the ground as his phone buzzed in his pocket. He checked the screen and found a message from Luke: *Get to the bar. Now.*

Cursing, he hung a right on St. Philip and headed to O'Malley's.

At six in the morning, the place sat empty, save for a few men on Luke's crew having breakfast. He nodded to the morning bartender and shuffled through the side door toward Luke's office.

As he entered the room, he found the alpha sitting in a chair behind the massive oak desk, his mate perched on the edge of the surface, holding his hand in both of hers. Alexis occupied a green vinyl chair facing the desk, and they all looked at him with grim expressions as he closed the door behind him.

A feeling of unease expanded in his chest like rising dough. If they were here... "Where's Rain? Is she okay? If that bastard got to her—"

"She's not hurt. She's..." Alexis looked at Luke.

"The coven has her. Two more witches were drained, and they're blaming Rain and her sister."

"What? That's insane." His nostrils flared, and he clenched his hands into fists as he focused on Alexis and then Macey. "How could you let them take her?"

"Watch your tone." Luke growled in warning.

Chase lowered his gaze, swallowing down his frustration. "Sorry."

"We weren't going to let them." Macey's voice held sympathy. "She chose to go with them to avoid a confrontation."

That sounded like Rain. The pack would go to war to protect one of their own, and since he'd let them know she was his fate-bound, she was included. Rain would never let a war happen over her.

But she didn't have a choice.

He turned and grabbed the doorknob.

"Where are you going?" Luke's voice held an edge of warning, reminding Chase he hadn't been dismissed.

His muscles tensed, and he squeezed the door knob tighter. "To get Rain."

"You can't bust into the coven house and take her by force. She's one of them. They have jurisdiction in this."

"She's not one of them." Frustration raised his voice, so he took a deep breath to calm himself. Luke might have been his best friend, but he could tear Chase's ass apart if he didn't show the alpha respect. "She's not allowed in the coven because she's cursed. If a witch shows her any kindness, they'll suffer for it. They're terrified of her, so there's no telling how they're treating her."

Luke glanced at his mate. "I'm aware of her problem, and the fact that I had to hear the information second-hand is another issue." He stood and walked around the desk to lean on the edge. "They found a body behind her building. It does look suspicious."

"I was with her all night, man. Don't tell me you believe them." He balled his hands into fists. If his own alpha wasn't on his side...

"I don't, but you need to go in there with a clear head and defend her logically."

Chase straightened his spine. "Yeah. Of course. I will." His head was as clear as spring water. His fate-bound needed his help, and he'd do anything to save her.

Luke cupped Macey's cheek in his hand and gave her a quick kiss. "Get some sleep today. I love you."

"I love you too." She cast a worried glance toward Chase. "Be safe."

"Always." Luke nodded to the door. "Let's go."

Chase eyed the coven house as he marched up the sidewalk. No one would guess one of the best-kept houses in the Quarter housed a prison for witches in the back. Of course, no one would guess the quiet Irish pub on St. Philip held a prison strong enough to contain a werewolf either. New Orleans was full of dirty little secrets.

He stayed two steps behind Luke, silently thankful for his best friend's grounding presence. If Chase had come on his own, he'd have done exactly what Luke told him not to —busted in and taken his woman by force.

Alan, the witch he'd threatened in the alley, greeted them, crossing his arms and widening his stance in an attempt to look intimidating as he blocked their entrance. "Come to beg for your woman's release? Not so tough now, are you?"

Luke straightened to his full height, and Chase crossed his arms, mimicking Alan's posture. He'd show this asshole tough. A hint of fear flashed in the witch's eyes before he huffed and stepped aside, allowing them entrance.

Calista clicked into the foyer, wearing a pressed suit, her hair twisted into a neat knot on the back of her head. She appeared polished, but the dark circles beneath her eyes betrayed her. She'd lost sleep, whether from dealing with Rain or the loss of some of her own, Chase couldn't be sure.

Frankly, he didn't care. She had his love, and he wanted her back.

"Where's Rain?" His voice came out more hostile than he'd planned, but he couldn't hold back his anger. "If she's hurt…"

Luke put a heavy hand on his shoulder. "We'd like to negotiate her release."

Calista inclined her head. "I'm not releasing her. As soon as the hour is decent, I'll be placing a call to the national council and recommending immediate execution. We've put up with the murderous bitch and her curse long enough."

A deep growl rumbled in Chase's chest, and Luke tightened his grip on his shoulder. "She didn't kill those witches."

"Can you prove it?"

He attempted a step toward her, but Luke held him back. "I was with her all evening."

"You don't need to get your council involved in this." Luke dropped his arm to his side. "We know who's behind the murders, and we can stop him."

Chase moved closer to the witch. "We're not leaving without Rain and Snow. Let them go and no one has to get hurt."

Calista stiffened. "Call off your dog, alpha."

"Chase." Luke's voice was low with warning.

He needed to step lightly. Pissing off the high priestess wouldn't help his cause. He moved back, lowering his voice and speaking through clenched teeth. "Please let me see her."

The priestess regarded him, an amused smirk lighting on her lips. "She's special to you, isn't she?" She chuckled. "All this time I thought you had a grudge against witches, when it seems it's only me you can't stand."

Alan suppressed a chuckle. Calista cast him a sideways glance, and he stared at the floor.

Chase held her gaze, silently challenging her to continue mocking his emotions. He didn't have to explain himself to her, and he was done being civil. If she didn't take him to his woman within the next thirty seconds, he'd force his way in.

Luke must have felt Chase's intent because he stepped beside him, close enough to stop him from attempting anything stupid. "Listen to their story."

She shook her head. "How will I know they're telling the truth? Perhaps your second is in on it. Maybe he's an accomplice to her crimes."

"I'll vouch for him." Luke crossed his arms and gave her a challenging stare.

Her gaze danced between them before focusing on the alpha. "Luke, as much as I respect you, I can't..." She tapped a finger to her lips. "Although...I do know a way I could discover the truth on my own." She steepled her fingers beneath her chin and looked at Chase. "I offer you a trade."

"Name it." He'd do anything. Whatever she wanted was hers if she'd give him Rain.

"A pint of your blood. I can use it in a tracking spell to find the killer—whomever she may be—and I'll have enough left over for...future uses."

Her offer hit him like a meat cleaver to his heart. Of all the things for a witch to ask from him... No telling what she could do with that much blood. That much power. He swallowed the thickness from his throat and opened his mouth to respond.

Luke cut him off. "Not a chance. Werewolf blood is

sacred for a reason. No witch is getting a single drop from my pack."

Chase pressed his lips together to suppress a sigh of relief. If he'd have answered the way he'd intended, he'd be facing twenty years in the pit...if Luke went light on his punishment.

Calista shrugged and cast Chase a knowing look. "That's a shame. Worth a try though." Alan whispered something in her ear. She paused, looking thoughtful for a moment before squaring her gaze on Chase. "I like the idea, Alan. Unfortunately, spells that hinder free will are forbidden, even for the high priestess."

Damn, this witch seemed to know all his weaknesses. He couldn't give her his blood, but if he could get Rain back another way... "What kind of spell?"

"Alan suggested a truth spell. I have one; it's very easy to make, but the serum lasts twenty-four hours. You'd be forced to speak the truth for a full day."

"Give it to me. I've got nothing to hide."

She grinned and glanced at Luke. "What if I were tempted to make him spill your pack secrets?"

Chase answered, "If the pack has any secrets, I don't know them. I'm not first-family."

"Interesting..."

If she didn't wipe that shit-eating grin off her face, he'd be tempted to do it for her. He shoved his hands in his pockets to hold them still. His fate-bound was somewhere inside this house, and being this close without being able to see her grated on his nerves, making him want to snap.

She shook her head. "It's not worth the risk. Not when I'm about to get the council involved."

"Are there any side effects?" He couldn't let her dismiss it that easily. If he could get Rain back, he'd endure whatever the priestess threw at him. "Besides having to speak the truth for twenty-four hours, will anything else happen to me if I take the serum?"

She scoffed. "I'm a high priestess; no low-level witch could achieve a position like this. My spells do exactly as intended. Nothing more."

That was all he needed to hear. "You're not hindering my free will if I'm agreeing to it. I'll tell the truth for a day; no problem. Give it to me. I'll sign a release. Whatever you need."

"I'll sign it too," Luke added. "It appears to be the only peaceful way to solve this dilemma."

Calista narrowed her eyes. "I don't take kindly to threats."

Luke leaned toward her. "And I don't take kindly to you kidnapping someone who's under the pack's protection."

"She's not a werewolf."

"She's not a member of your coven."

She exhaled slowly and nodded to Alan. "Draw up the contract. I'll mix the potion."

Chase unclenched his fists as the tension drained from his muscles. Good thing this hadn't turned into a fight. A werewolf who couldn't shift wouldn't stand much of a chance against their magic.

"Lydia," Calista called to a woman down the hall. "Remove the dark-haired witch from the cell and take her and the werewolves to my office."

The mere thought of Rain being locked in a cell made his skin crawl. He followed the woman into the hall and down a short flight of steps. She opened a door and peered inside. "You come. You...stay put."

Rain shuffled into the hallway, and Chase swept her

into his arms. "Thank God, you're okay." He held her tight to his chest, relief flooding his veins as he breathed in her familiar scent. She was warm and safe, and there was no way in hell he'd leave this place without her.

"Chase?" Her words vibrated against his chest. "What's happening? Am I free? What about Snow?"

"Not yet." He loosened his grip so he could look at her, but he refused to let her go. "We have to negotiate your release with Calista."

"This way." Lydia motioned them toward the office.

"I'm glad you're okay." Luke patted Rain on the shoulder before following Lydia.

Chase wrapped an arm around his fate-bound's shoulders and held her tight to his side as they entered the high priestess's office. The same black cat from his last visit sat in the center of the desk, and it hissed at Luke, making a wide berth around the alpha before brushing against Chase's leg on its way out the door.

Luke flashed him a questioning look, and he held his breath. He needed to come clean about his powers, but now wasn't the time nor place. He was about to let a witch cast a spell on him for the fourth time in his life, and the thought soured in his stomach like two-week-old buttermilk.

"Calista will be right with you." Lydia closed the door, the unmistakable sound of the lock sliding into place penetrating the silence.

"Did you explain what happened? Has she called the council?" Rain clutched his shirt. "She wouldn't listen to me."

He rubbed her back, trying to calm her. "She hasn't called them yet. We're going to explain everything as soon as she gets here."

"I doubt she'll believe us. She's had it out for me since she found out about my—" She looked at Luke.

Chase hugged her. "He knows about your curse." He leaned down to whisper in her ear, "But not about mine yet."

She nodded. "I'm sorry to be so much trouble."

Luke leaned against the wall. "We take care of our own. It's no trouble."

"I know, but I'm not—"

"You're with Chase; you're one of us. Simple as that."

Chase's heart swelled with gratitude. One—that he didn't mention the fate-bound bit. He was waiting for the right moment to tell Rain. And two—that the alpha, and therefore the pack, had accepted her without confrontation.

Luke sauntered to the window and stared at the garden behind the house. "They're awfully trusting leaving us alone in this room. We could easily bust out and be done with this nonsense."

"I wouldn't leave Snow," Rain said. "And I doubt you could break out."

Luke looked at her over his shoulder, arching an eyebrow in disbelief.

Chase laughed. "She's right. They probably have a spell on the whole building. Nothing gets in or out unless they want it to. Rain had one on her shop."

"Snow made a new one, and she hid the totems this time," Rain said. "It's secure."

Luke gazed out the window. "What happened to the old one?"

"Damn tulpa tricked her." He took a deep breath and let it out in a huff. Since Calista was taking her sweet time, he might as well come clean. "It tricked me too."

Luke turned around to face them. "How so?"

He opened his mouth to spill the truth, but the lock disengaged and Calista sashayed into the room. The liquid inside the shot glass she carried glowed bright blue, and Rain tightened her grip on his waist.

The priestess offered him the glass, and though his throat thickened to the point he could barely breathe, he took it.

"What is that?" Wariness edged Rain's voice as she cut her gaze between Calista and the glass.

"A truth spell." Calista smiled triumphantly. "Your wolf-boy has agreed to take it in hopes of saving you from execution."

Rain's eyes widened, and she fisted his shirt in her hand. "Chase, no. You don't have to do that."

"Yes, I do." He lifted the glass, but Calista rested her hand on top of it.

"Not until you both sign the waver." She set a sheet of paper on her desk and plucked a pen from a wooden container.

Luke stepped toward the desk and took the pen. "You're sure you want to do this?"

Chase couldn't force the *yes* through his throat, so he nodded. Luke signed the paper and handed him the pen. He scanned the words on the page. He'd be promising not to hold Calista or the coven accountable for anything that happened because of the spell. *Anything.* "This doesn't say what the spell does."

The priestess narrowed her gaze. "It says it's a truth potion. Self-explanatory."

He shook his head. "I want it in writing. This contract absolves you of *any* harm done for any reason. I'm agreeing to a truth serum that you swore would only force me to tell the truth for twenty-four hours. If you're so sure of your magic, guarantee that's all that will happen to me in writing."

She glared at him before snatching the pen from his hand. "Fine." She scribbled the guarantee onto the page and initialed the change.

Chase took the pen, fisting it in his hand to stop his trembling. Taking a potion from Rain had been one thing. He trusted the woman with every fiber of his being. He couldn't muster a single iota of trust for the priestess, but he pressed the pen to the page and scribbled his name anyway. As he formed the final *P* in his last name, he hesitated, crushing the ball-point into the paper until black ink puddled around it. Calista pried the contract and the pen from his grip and shoved them into a drawer.

He looked at the potion in his hand. His stomach roiled, his breathing growing shallow as he lifted it to his nose to sniff. It smelled sweet, like cotton candy, and tiny bits of silver sparkled in the liquid.

His mind flashed back to his childhood. The witches, his so-called friends. The ritual. The pain he'd endured from whatever potion they'd convinced him to take. They'd almost killed him. His body swayed, the sensation that he stood in the center of a merry-go-round spinning out of control, making it hard to breathe.

Rain put her hand on his back, steadying him. "If there is anything other than a truth spell in that glass, Calista, I swear on my life—"

"If he doesn't drink the potion, you won't have a life much longer. I suggest you keep your mouth shut."

Was he being naïve again? Maybe. But Luke and Rain would have his back if this went south.

He closed his eyes and tossed back the potion. The

sticky, sweet liquid burned down his throat as if it took a layer of flesh with it to his stomach. He braced himself for the sensation to spread through his core, but the burning ceased.

Rain put a hand on his chest. "How do you feel?"

"I expected worse." Aside from a slight tingling in his head, he didn't feel any effects from the spell. "Are you sure you did it right, Calista?"

She sank into the chair behind her desk. "We'll find out, won't we? Have a seat."

He crossed his arms. "I'd rather stand." Sitting would make him vulnerable, and he couldn't give the priestess any more of an edge.

Luke looked him in the eyes, silently asking if he was all right. Chase nodded.

"Suit yourself." Calista leaned back in her chair. "I'll ask you a few test questions first to make sure it's taken effect."

Chase exhaled slowly. The smirk on the witch's face told him he wouldn't like what she planned to ask.

"You said you aren't first family. Luke has a cousin who is; why isn't he second in command?"

He ground his teeth and looked at Luke. Pack business wasn't *her* business, but what Stephen did was no secret. "He tried to kill Luke's mate."

She nodded. "Where is he now? Dead?"

He chewed the inside of his cheek, fighting the compulsion to spit out the answer. "Why do you want to know?"

"Answer the question, please."

The tingling in his head increased, willing him to tell her the truth. "He's in the pit. Our pack prison. Luke spared his life."

"Interesting." She folded her arms on the desk and leaned forward. "You said you and Rain were together all evening. Tell me what you were doing."

He clenched his jaw, hoping the sharp pain shooting through his temple would overpower the truth tingling in his brain. Answering with a question of his own seemed to be the only way to quell the confessions. "What do you think we were doing?"

Rain put a hand on his bicep. "That's none of your business, Calista, and it doesn't have anything to do with the murders."

She arched an eyebrow. "He'll answer the question or this meeting will adjourn and you'll be handed over to the council."

"We were having sex." He put his hand over Rain's and cringed at the indecent way the words sounded on his lips. It had been so much more than that.

Calista grinned. "Who was on top?"

"What the hell, Calista?" What kind of sick individual got their kicks from forcing people to talk about their sex lives? The tingling in his head intensified. Sharing his private, intimate experiences with anyone but the woman he loved appalled him, but the spell forced him to answer. "She was."

The priestess looked at Rain. "You got a werewolf onto his back. Impressive. With his attitude, I expected him to be more...dominant." She raked a heated gaze down his body. "I guess you're all bark and no bite."

Chase growled a warning, but what was the use? He'd have to endure her questioning if he planned to save his woman. "I respect her. What we do in the bedroom is a shared experience."

"I see." She flashed a wicked grin. "Tell me, Chase. If

your alpha hadn't been here to stop you, would you have given me your blood to save her?"

Anger seared through his chest like a blade taken straight from the forge. "Goddammit, witch." She was setting him up.

Rain gasped. "She asked for your blood?"

"She did." He looked at Rain, and her eyes grew wide in disbelief. Then he cut his gaze to Luke, who kept his expression neutral, though he probably knew Chase's answer already. Speaking the truth out loud would be admitting he'd disobey the alpha and pack law. He might as well walk his ass back to the bar and lock himself in the pit right now.

"Answer the question." Calista's voice grew impatient. "Would you have disobeyed your pack law and given me your blood to save this woman?"

The air in the room pressed down on his shoulders, threatening to crumble him. He'd have to deal with whatever punishment Luke deemed appropriate. He gnashed his teeth and growled out his answer, "Yes."

As he uttered the word, Luke faked a giant sneeze, the sound so loud it echoed in the small room. "I didn't hear what you said, and I'm giving you a direct order never to repeat it."

Calista inclined her head. "Well played, alpha."

"No more games, Calista. Get the information you need and nothing more." He pinned Chase with a heavy stare. "I'm going to wait in the hall."

As Luke stepped through the door and closed it behind him, Chase tipped his head back and closed his eyes for a long blink. Even as he'd admitted his disobedience, his solid friendship with the alpha had saved him.

Calista crossed her arms, narrowing her gaze as she

studied him. "Interesting. What would the punishment have been if you'd given your blood to me?"

"Whatever the alpha deemed fit." Was she playing some kind of power game? Trying to exert her dominance over the werewolves?

"I see. Yet, you were willing to endure whatever he could dish out to save a magicless witch. Why?"

He looked at Rain, and he couldn't have stopped the words from spilling from his mouth if he tried. "I'd do anything for her. She's my fate-bound."

Rain's breath hitched, and tears collected on her lower lids. "I am?"

He tucked a strand of hair behind her ear. "This wasn't how I planned to tell you, but yes."

Her bottom lip trembled. "How long...? Why didn't you tell me?"

"I was afraid I'd scare you away. I wanted to give you time to fall in love with me." The longer he spoke, the faster the truth tumbled from his lips. "I hope that you'll be my mate, but since you're not a werewolf, I was afraid this bond would overwhelm you."

She threw herself into his arms, burying her face in his chest. "It's not scary, Chase. I feel it too."

She couldn't possibly, but he'd let her believe it if she wanted to.

Calista let out a dry laugh. "If I'd known this juicy detail, I would've gotten *her* to ask for your blood."

He stiffened. "She would *never* ask for such a thing." He kissed her forehead as she slid from his arms. "She knows me too well."

"Can we get on with this?" Rain's brow furrowed as she sank into a chair. "Let us tell you what happened so we can stop anyone else from dying."

The priestess narrowed her eyes. "Fine. Tell me who's killing witches."

Chase explained the story of Rain's ex showing up in her shop and everything that led up to the event. Calista's pen flew furiously across a sheet of paper as she took notes. She asked for precise locations where they'd seen the tulpa each time, and he showed her on a map where Isaac had gotten hold of him in the swamp.

"I don't recommend sending any of your witches out hunting for him. He's proven he can kill. Let the were-wolves handle it."

Calista stared at the map and tapped her pen on the spot in the swamp. "You have twenty-four hours to *handle* it before I send my own team after him."

He grumbled. If the witches went hunting, they'd expose the whole damn magical community. They didn't care about secrecy. Didn't require it like the other super-natural beings living in New Orleans. "We'll take care of it."

Calista held his gaze, hesitating to let them go. "You'd better. For her sake. She is the reason this lunatic is here after all." She rose to her feet and motioned toward the door.

Chase didn't give her time to change her mind. He grabbed Rain's hand and tugged her to the exit.

Luke met them in the hallway. "And?"

"We're free to go. Let's get Snow and get the hell out of this place."

CHAPTER TWENTY

Rain leaned against the counter in her bakery, staring at Chase's magnificent backside as he conferred with Luke. Calista had activated the coven's emergency call tree, and every witch in New Orleans had been accounted for...all alive and well and on high alert for any suspicious activity. Isaac would be weak after the encounter last night. He didn't pose an immediate threat, which gave her mind time to ponder Chase's admission.

She was his fate-bound.

Her heart did a little flip in her chest. She needed to get him alone so they could talk about what this meant. He'd said he hoped she would be his mate, and she wanted to reassure him that she wanted the same. Of course, if she could get him alone, there wouldn't be much talking going on for a while.

Warmth bloomed below her navel, spreading through her body to chase away her fatigue. She'd slept maybe an hour last night, but she'd stay up all day if it meant sharing her bed with the sexy werewolf standing in her doorway.

She ran her tongue across her teeth, wrinkling her nose at the gritty sensation. She hadn't showered or used a toothbrush in more than twenty-four hours. A quick glance in the mirror revealed disheveled hair and mascara rings beneath her eyes.

She grabbed a napkin and wiped at the day-old makeup as Snow approached from the kitchen. "I double-checked all the totems. As soon as the guys get out of the doorway and lock it, the charm will be good to go."

Rain nodded, trying to wipe the grin from her face. She shouldn't have felt this happy when her life was in danger, but she couldn't help it. "I'm his fate-bound."

Snow smiled. "So I heard."

Chase looked over his shoulder and caught her gaze as he motioned for her. She pushed off the counter and stepped toward him, and he took her hand. "Tell him what you told me about the tulpa. How to defeat it."

"The only person who can stop it is Isaac, but he's not going to do it voluntarily."

Chase squeezed her hand. "But it's not real…"

She nodded. "It's a figment of Isaac's imagination that he's managed to make other people see, but in reality, it doesn't exist. As long as you can convince your mind it's not real…"

"Then it can't hurt you," Chase finished for her.

"Unless it gets ahold of a weapon. It can manipulate objects." She shivered. "It held a knife to my throat."

Luke cringed. "The blue moon tonight is good timing. Our wolves will be at their most powerful, so if we can find him, we can take him out."

Chase stiffened. "My wolf is bound." He looked into his alpha's eyes. "The bastard tricked me into taking a binding spell. I can't shift."

"Shit." Luke narrowed his gaze. "Why didn't you tell me this?"

"I was embarrassed. I...Crap." He looked away. "God-damn truth spell. I didn't want you to think any less of me. You and your old man...y'all saved my life. I wouldn't be here today if not for the pack, and I don't want to let you down. How can I be your second if I can't even shift?" He chuckled and wrapped his arm around Rain. "That's a truth I didn't even know myself."

Guilt snaked its way into Rain's chest, squeezing it tight. "I'm so sorry."

He pressed his lips to her hair. "It's not your fault."

Luke shook his head. "I don't have to tell you all the things that could've gone wrong when we went into that coven house...and I'd have been fighting alone."

"Not alone. I can fight." He leaned into her side. "I'm sorry, man. I let you down."

Luke inhaled deeply. "On the plus side, you won't have to fight the blue moon to take care of your woman tonight. You'll stay here with Rain. Macey will be your backup."

"Doesn't she have to work?" Poor Chase. She could tell he didn't like his friend thinking him unable to guard her on his own.

"Macey hasn't taken a vacation since she joined the police department. She's got plenty of days saved up." He clapped Chase on the shoulder. "We're hunting in turns. Call the bar if you need help. Someone will be around."

Chase nodded and tightened his grip on Rain as Luke strode out the door.

Rain locked it, activating Snow's protection charm, and turned to Chase. "What does he mean 'hunting in turns?'"

Chase shuffled to the counter and sat on a stool. "The younger, weaker wolves have a harder time fighting the shift on a blue moon. They'll hunt first. The strongest go last, since they can hold the beast longer. We can't have a hundred wolves hunting in the swamp at the same time, especially since the pull of the moon is so strong that we usually kill the first living thing we see."

She moved toward him, situating her hips between his legs and wrapping her arms around him, pushing the image of his last statement from her mind. "Luke doesn't think you're weak. You didn't let him down."

He sighed. "I did. I let you all down. I should've known that tulpa wasn't you. Anytime you're near me, I feel the bond in my heart, and now that I look back, I didn't feel it then. It didn't act like you. Hell, it wouldn't even speak. I let my guard down and got distracted, and I wasn't there for you when you needed me."

"Chase." She cupped his face in her hands, running her thumbs through his beard. "This is a ghost from *my* past. He's going after you to hurt me. I accept all the blame, and *I* am sorry for letting you down."

He smiled weakly. "You're pretty with your hair all messy like this." He ran his fingers into her mane and tousled her curls, but his attempt at flirting didn't mask the sadness in his eyes.

"Is something else bothering you?"

He pressed his lips together and lowered his gaze, obviously wanting to say no, but the truth spell wouldn't allow him to lie.

"You can trust me. With your secrets. With your heart. I will never hurt you."

"I know." He looked into her eyes. "Doesn't make it

any easier to admit weakness. I'm second in command of the sixth largest wolf pack in the country. I'm not supposed to show my pain."

She kissed his forehead. "Let me be your safe place."

"I've never missed the blue moon hunt. My wolf is bound, but there's a humming in my blood. An ache. And I'm under orders to stay here, but I really want to hunt the bastard down. I want to break this spell, remove your curse, and dammit...I want to live happily ever after with you. Beauty and the Beast did it. Why can't we?"

She smiled. The more he spoke, the more compelled he'd be to keep going. To spill all his emotions. It was how truth spells were designed to work. "I have to admit, I like all this raw honesty."

He blew out a hard breath. "You know I'd never lie to you. Truth spell or not."

"I also know you wouldn't willingly wish...out loud anyway...that our lives were like a Disney movie."

He chuckled. "You know me well."

"I have an idea." Snow strolled in from the kitchen with her hands clasped behind her back. An excited look danced in her eyes. "I think you can both have your happily ever after. Rain, you could create an unbinding spell to free Chase. Your magic is strong enough."

Rain rested her hands on Chase's thighs and shook her head. "No, Snow." A trickle of dread inched down her spine. *Please shut up. Not this. Not now.*

"I'm not sure if we can take his blood now, or if we need to wait until the sun sets." She glanced out the window. "We might as well wait. There's an hour of daylight left. What do you think?"

Oh, goddess, no. She said it.

Chase stiffened. "Who's blood?"

"Yours. Duh." Snow pranced toward them and held the unbinding spell in front of her. "And look. We haven't even collected the blood, and the incantation has already appeared with him simply being here."

"You...want my blood." He blinked at her, the incredulous look in his eyes piercing her heart. Sliding off the stool, he stepped away from her and took the spell from Snow's hand.

Rain's heart pounded against her ribs. "No, Chase. It's not like that."

Snow continued, apparently oblivious to the tension. "With Chase's blood, I can complete the spell and unbind your powers. Then, with your magic back, you can write a spell to unbind Chase's magic, and boom. Happily ever after for both of you. Isaac won't stand a chance against both of you with your magic intact."

Chase scanned the paper and read the words aloud. "Two drops of blood from a first-born werewolf, given willingly, beneath a blue moon." He dropped it on the counter. "All this time, you've been after my blood?" His eyes tightened, his brow pinching as his expression wavered between unbelieving and appalled.

Her hands trembled with the need to touch him, to comfort him, but as she reached for him, he stepped away. "No. I mean...yes, the unbinding spell requires werewolf blood, but I wasn't going to ask you for it after..."

"But you *were* going to ask me for it before, weren't you?" The confusion in his eyes tore her heart to shreds. "Is that why you agreed to date me? So you could get my blood for your spell?"

She could have denied it. Sworn she'd never intended

to ask, but she couldn't lie to him. "Originally, that was the plan."

"Well, shit. And there just happened to be a blue moon around the corner, so you thought you'd..." He raked a hand through his hair and turned away from her. "What the hell, Rain?"

"This isn't coming out right." She curled her arms over her head, clutching at her hair as she looked to her sister, widening her eyes in a *help me out* look.

Snow chewed her bottom lip and drummed her fingers on the counter. "She's been hot for you since you met. The fact that you're a werewolf and can break her curse is a bonus."

He growled.

"I'm not helping, am I?"

Rain glared at her. "No." She stepped toward Chase and put a hand on his arm.

He jerked away. "Don't."

Her breath lodged in her throat at his rejection. "Please let me explain." She reached for him again but let her hand drop to her side. She had to make him understand. "I've been living with this curse for seven years. When the council sent me the spell to break it, I was over the moon. The ingredients have been revealed one by one as I gather them, and the final one appeared the day after I met you."

The muscles in his jaw flexed as he ground his teeth, but he let her continue.

"Seeing werewolf blood as the final ingredient, I thought I was doomed. I'd never find a werewolf willing to give me his blood. But you know how fate works. Was it really a coincidence that a werewolf couple wanted me to make the cake for their wedding right before a blue moon?

Then you came back to apologize, and I thought maybe..."

He let out a hard exhale and narrowed his eyes.

She hurried to finish before he stopped listening. "But then I got to know you, and I fell in love with you. And when you told me your story...with what happened to you when you were a kid...I knew I could never ask you for the same thing that hurt you back then."

He looked at the door. "Maybe I wasn't wrong to distrust witches."

"Chase, please." She took his hand, and he didn't pull away. "I wasn't going to ask you. I should have told Snow I didn't plan to ask." She looked over her shoulder at her sister.

Snow lowered her head. "I'm sorry."

"I love you, Chase."

His phone rang from his pocket, and he slipped from her grasp to answer it. "Hello?"

He paused as the other person spoke.

"What happened?"

Another pause. "All right. I'll leave as soon as Macey gets here."

He shoved his phone into his pocket and looked at her, his eyes finally softening. "There's been an emergency; Luke needs me at the bar."

"What happened?"

"I don't know. He sounded weird. Called from a number I don't recognize, so it must be important." He jerked his head toward the door at the sound of Macey knocking. Disengaging the lock, he swung the door open, stepping past Macey as she entered.

"I thought I was your backup, not your relief," Macey said.

"I have to go." He stopped outside the door and turned to Rain. "Macey will take care of you." Shoving his hands in his pockets, he turned and strode away.

"Everything okay?" Macey shut the door and turned the lock.

Rain opened her mouth to answer, but no words came. Nothing was okay. The man she loved thought she was using him, and she hadn't tried to stop him from walking away. Her deranged ex-boyfriend was killing innocent people to make her suffer. What if the emergency Chase had to attend to was dangerous? Would he do something stupid trying to prove himself and wind up getting hurt? "I have to go after him."

"Hold on." Macey put her hands on her shoulders. "You're supposed to stay put until the threat is neutralized."

"Yeah, Rain." Snow shuffled around the counter. "I'm sorry for blabbing about the spell. I thought you guys had talked about it already."

"Well, we hadn't." Her voice came out as a trembling whisper.

Macey let her go but didn't move from the doorway. "Whatever it is, I'm sure you'll work it out when he gets back."

"I'm not." Pressure mounted in the back of her eyes. "I'm going to take a shower and lie down for a while." She turned on her heel and trotted through the kitchen to her bedroom. Grabbing her robe, she headed to the bathroom and turned on the shower.

She had to get through to Chase somehow. To make him believe he could trust her. That she wasn't just another witch out for his blood. She stood beneath the stream, setting the water as hot as she could stand it and breathing in the steam. The warm moisture filled her nose, opening her airways and clearing her mind. She'd make this right somehow.

With her skin pink and softened from the heat, she shut off the water and slipped on her robe. She padded to her bedroom, pulled on a pair of sweatpants and a T-shirt, and gazed at her disheveled sheets. Her heart ached at the memory of sharing her bed with Chase. Picking up a pillow, she pressed her nose against it and inhaled deeply. His musky, masculine scent lingered on the soft fabric, and a sob caught in the back of her throat.

A tapping sound drew her gaze to the window, and she glanced out the glass in time to see a shadow dart from right to left.

She started for the window, but her phone chimed from the bedside table. She picked it up, and a message from an unknown number lit up the screen: *I have your boyfriend. If you want to see him alive, come to the swamp. Alone. My tulpa will guide you.*

Isaac. Her hand trembled, and the phone slipped from her grasp, landing on the bed. The screen dimmed, extinguishing the message as terror twisted in her gut. She couldn't let him hurt Chase. She would never forgive herself if anything else happened to the man she loved. To anyone.

Tiptoeing to the kitchen, she peeked into the storefront. Snow and Macey sat at the table, drinking coffee, so she grabbed a chopping knife from the block, padded back into her bedroom, and slipped it into her shoulder bag before shoving her phone in her pocket.

Before she could talk herself out of it, she snatched the bride and groom cake topper from beneath the dishtowel on her table and broke the couple apart, shattering the protection charm Snow had placed on the building. Opening the window, she crawled outside and ran to her car. Her hands trembled as she shifted into drive and headed to the swamp.

Tonight would probably end with one of them dead, and she had to make certain it wouldn't be Chase.

CHAPTER TWENTY-ONE

Chase pushed open O'Malley's front door and shuffled into the pub. Amber stood behind the bar, and his sister sat on a stool near the corner.

Bekah spun in her seat to look at him, her face contorting into a mask of concern as she met his gaze. "What happened?"

"Noth—" The word got stuck in his throat. Damn it, he couldn't even lie and say "nothing."

"None of your business." That was the truth. "Luke in the back?"

Amber furrowed her brow. "He's not here."

"Shit." He plopped onto a stool and checked the clock on his phone. Whatever this emergency was, Luke had better get there fast. Chase had bigger problems on his plate.

Honestly, when the call had come through, he'd been relieved to get away from the bakery. Away from Rain. A million thoughts spun through his head, but he couldn't seem to catch onto any of them. And with the truth spell active in his system, he might've said something he'd regret if he'd stayed.

Then again, truth spell or not, the thought that he should be there protecting her anyway clawed at the edges of his mind.

Bekah sat on the stool next to him. "You look like death warmed over." She put her hand on his. "You feel like it too. What happened?"

He pulled from her grasp. The last thing he wanted to do was talk about his feelings with his sister. "Where's Emma?"

"Mom took her to Shreveport to see the Imagination Movers show. They're spending the night in a hotel."

He nodded and checked the time again. Where the hell was Luke? As mixed up as his thoughts were about Rain, he didn't like leaving her when a madman was after her.

Bekah narrowed her eyes. "Did you break up with Rain?"

"Not yet. I…"

"Not *yet*?" Amber stepped toward him and rested her hands on the bar. "You can't break up with her. That's not how I felt your future."

Damn these women and their empathic abilities. He let out a dry chuckle. "How do you *feel* the future, anyway?"

Amber crossed her arms. "Tell us what happened, Chase."

His head tingled, the truth rolling through his brain and out his mouth before he realized what was happening. "She needs my blood for a spell. She's wanted it all along."

Bekah's eyes widened. "Does she know about…?"

"Yeah, she knows. She knows everything." He fisted

his hands on the bar. "I trusted her, and she betrayed me. All this time I thought she was falling in love with me, but in reality, she wanted my blood. Turns out my disdain for witches was well-founded after all."

Bekah pursed her lips, tilting her head. "She does love you. I felt it in her the last time she was at the house."

A flutter of hope shot through his heart, but he squelched it. "She loves what I can do for her."

"What can you do? Why does she need your blood?" Amber asked.

He clamped his mouth shut as the truth spell tried to force the words from his lips. What the hell? If he stayed with her, the pack would find out about her curse eventually...and if he left her, what did it matter? "She's cursed. Her powers are bound, and two drops of my blood can break the spell. Apparently, werewolf blood is a highly coveted ingredient for potions."

Bekah gave him a confused look. "So you're upset with how she asked you? I don't understand the problem."

"She didn't ask."

"Then how do you know she needs your blood?"

"Her sister showed me the spell. Two drops of blood from a first-born werewolf, given freely beneath a blue moon." A sour sensation formed in his stomach. "Rain said after she learned about my past, she didn't plan to ask me, but..." He balled his hands into fists, unable to stop the truth from flowing. "Why would fate bind me to someone who wanted to use me?"

"Exactly," Amber said.

"Fate wouldn't." Bekah put her hand on his shoulder. "You're bound to her because you're supposed to be together. Because you need each other. I think you should give it to her."

How could she even suggest that, knowing what the punishment would be? He shook his head. "It's against our laws. Calista asked for some in exchange for Rain's freedom earlier today, and Luke forbade it."

"He wouldn't let you give it to *Calista*," Amber said. "Rain is your fate-bound, he won't stop you from giving it to her." She looked him hard in the eyes. "I know my brother...and you know him too. Stop using the alpha as an excuse."

He let out a slow breath and mumbled, "I'm scared." *Damn this truth spell.*

Bekah laughed. "I doubt two drops will hurt her."

"It's not that." He stared at the bar and traced the wood pattern with his finger.

"What are you scared of then?" His sister leaned an elbow on the bar. "You found your fate-bound. That's pretty damn special."

His shoulders drooped. "But she's not a were, so it only works one way." Shaking his head, he huffed and lifted his gaze. "My heart is bound to hers for the rest of my life, but she could walk away at any time. That would crush me. What would I do then?" Hell, where had that come from? What else had he been lying to himself about?

Bekah laughed. "Wow. This is the most emotion you've ever shared out loud."

He glared at her. "Don't get used to it."

"She's not going to walk away." Amber put her hands on her hips. "Fate wouldn't bind you to someone who would. Besides, my premonitions about your future have been strong. Your heart is bound to hers forever. I think she's worthy of receiving your blood."

Who was he kidding? He couldn't walk away from Rain if he wanted to. And deep down, he didn't want to.

He loved his witch with every fiber of his being, and if his blood would break her curse, why wouldn't he give it to her? He'd give her the moon if he could pluck it from the sky.

"Do you believe her?" Bekah asked. "That she wasn't going to ask you for it?"

"I do." He pressed his fingers to his temples. "She was willing to sacrifice her unbinding spell to keep from hurting me."

Amber gave him a pointed look. "That says a lot about her character."

"You're right. There won't be another blue moon for two years. I can't let her live with her powers bound another day. Not when I can do something about it."

As soon as he finished whatever Luke needed him to do, he'd go to the bakery and break her curse. He checked the time again. "Where the hell is Luke? He told me to meet him here."

Amber furrowed her brow. "Luke took a group of teens out for the first hunt. I'm surprised he didn't ask you to chaperone too."

"He called me half an hour ago. Said there was an emergency."

"He was already in the swamp by then. He wanted to have the kids away from civilization before the sun set, so they didn't do anything stupid."

His stomach tumbled into his boots. The odd quality of Luke's voice. The unfamiliar number the call had come from. "Shit." He shot to his feet.

"What?" Bekah asked.

"If Luke comes back, tell him to call me ASAP." He darted out the door and climbed onto his bike.

Peeling off the curb, he sped down St. Philip toward

Royal, weaving his way around taxis, narrowly missing a pedestrian who stumbled into the street. When he reached the intersection of Bourbon, a crowd of partiers stood in the street, oblivious to the line of cars trying to get by.

The driver of a Mercedes laid on the horn, and a couple of people shuffled out of the way. A belligerent drunk man yelled a string of profanities at the driver and gave him a one-fingered salute.

"Hell, I don't have time for this." Chase revved his engine and wound around the string of vehicles. His shoulder bumped the drunk, knocking him out of the way of the Mercedes as he sped past.

Hanging a right on Royal, he plowed onto the sidewalk in front of the bakery and parked against the wall. Snow and Macey sat at a table inside the store, and Snow padded toward the door as he pounded on it.

"Where's Rain?" He pushed through the entrance and marched through the storefront, into the kitchen.

Snow followed. "She's sleeping."

"Are you sure?" He flung open her bedroom door and found it empty. His stomach churned as he stepped into the room.

"Maybe she's in the bathroom." Snow ducked out and returned a few seconds later. "You don't think she…"

"She went after Isaac." He picked up the broken wedding cake topper he found lying in her bed. Half the groom's arm hung from the bride's hand where the two pieces had been connected.

Snow's eyes widened. "She broke my totem. The circle of protection." She took the bride half of the figurine from his hand. "Why would she go after him alone?"

His throat thickened. "She did it for me. To prove that I can trust her." He dropped the totem on the bed. "Damn it. The bastard lured me away so he could get to her." He brushed past Snow and stormed into the storefront.

Macey stood by the door. "What's the plan?"

"I have to go after her." He dialed her number, and it rang five times before going to voicemail.

"I can track her phone." Snow pressed a few buttons on her screen. "She's here." Pointing at the map, she angled the phone for him to see. "There's nothing out there but swamp."

"That's where he's hiding. I saw his tulpa there the night he tried to drain me. Shit." He clenched his jaw. He couldn't shift. He could handle the witch himself, but that damn tulpa was another story. Real or not, it could do some major damage. "If Rain had her magic, could she beat him?"

"Goddess, yes. She was the most powerful witch I've ever met. Are you willing to give us your blood?"

He glanced at Macey. She'd be obliged to tell Luke, but dammit, he didn't care. "I told you I'd do whatever it took to break her curse. Give me a knife."

"Hold on." Snow took a wooden box from a shelf and pulled out a copper bowl. "She has to pay me for mixing each ingredient or the curse will get me. If you give me your blood now, I might not make it out the door." She poured a thick liquid from the bowl into a small glass jar. "We'll do it when we find her. If she drinks the potion as soon as it's mixed, the curse should lift before it has time to affect me." She capped the jar and stuffed it in her pocket as she strode to the door. "I'm coming with you. I've got the incantation memorized."

He nodded and looked at Macey. "Will you stay here in case she comes back?"

"Of course."

"If you hear from Luke…"

She nodded. "He'll understand."

"Wait." Snow darted behind the counter and took a cookie from the display case. "Eat this. For clarity."

He looked at the blue-frosted question mark and shook his head. "I know exactly what I need to do."

She held it toward him. "Rain said that if you can convince yourself the tulpa isn't real, it won't be able to hurt you. This will help. Trust me."

Last time he ate a magic cookie, he lost his wolf. He cut his gaze between the cookie and Snow and clenched his teeth. Without the ability to shift, he'd need all the help he could get. He shoved it into his mouth and chewed. A tingling sensation spread across his tongue and down his throat as he swallowed.

Snow grabbed one for herself and followed him to his bike. He tossed her a helmet. She put it on and climbed on behind him, wrapping her arms around his waist. "We'll find her."

God, he hoped so.

Rain exited the highway and parked behind a cypress tree. With the cover of night and the dense forest, no one would notice her car in the trees until morning, and hopefully she'd be out of here before sunrise.

She climbed out of her car and clicked the door shut before peering into the trees. The blue moon hung high in the sky, casting the swampy forest in a silvery glow. Spanish moss wept from the branches of towering cypress trees, and a bullfrog croaked in the distance. The dank scent of rotting foliage hung in the thick, wet air, and as her eyes adjusted to the darkness, she caught sight of a shadow bounding through the trees.

Hopefully it was the tulpa and not a werewolf. She shook her head. Did she really hope the monster lurking in the trees was the slave of the man who lured her out here to kill her? According to Chase, Isaac and his tulpa weren't the only predators in the swamp she needed to worry about tonight.

She crept deeper into the trees, carefully placing each step to avoid slipping and breaking an ankle. Her shoes squished in the mud as if she walked on a wet sponge, the ground becoming soggier the deeper she ventured into the woods.

Her heart thrummed. Was Chase already dead? Had Isaac called her into the swamp to watch him bury the man she loved before he killed her too? She couldn't think that way. Not if she wanted to stand a chance against Isaac.

A rustling in the brush sounded off to her right, and she jerked her head toward the noise. The shadow rushed her, knocking her into a tree before darting off to the left. Her arm scraped against the bark with stinging pain, but she caught a glimpse of the dull-gray aura before the tulpa disappeared into the darkness.

She leaned her back against the tree and tried to calm her breathing. What was she thinking coming out here alone? Without her magic, she'd have to rely on strength and wit to outsmart the man who'd spent seven years planning his revenge. She'd rushed out here with no plan. No idea how to stop him.

Slipping her hand into her shoulder bag, she gripped the knife handle and tiptoed in the direction the shadow had run. Maybe she could reason with Isaac. Maybe she could convince him to…what? Let Chase go? Forgive her for sending him to a fate worse than death?

She stepped around a thick tree trunk, and her breath caught in her throat. Isaac stood in the clearing, his spine straight, the skin that clung to his bones filled out as if there were muscle beneath, the lifeless body lying at his feet evidence he'd fed.

Her heart stopped for a moment, but the form was too small to be male. He'd drained a woman, using her life energy to rebuild his own body, gaining temporary access to whatever magic she possessed.

"Rain, you're just in time." Isaac smiled as the tulpa scooped the woman from the ground and tossed her body into the murky water.

"Where is Chase?" She tightened her grip on the knife in her bag.

Isaac laughed. "I've changed my mind about your boyfriend. I'm going to kill you first, so you can leave this world knowing that even your death couldn't save the ones you love from suffering."

Her lungs tightened until she could hardly breathe. "Why hurt them? It's me you want."

He tilted his head. "Because hurting them hurts you, my love."

Her jaw clenched, and the nails of her empty hand dug into her palm. "Don't call me that. You never loved me. You loved my magic."

"That's where you're wrong. I was infatuated with you from the moment I saw you, but you weren't the slightest bit interested in me. You were too focused on your goals. Opening your bakery. Gaining your place on the national council. I wasn't skilled enough to cast a love spell; you know how hard those are to create. An obsession spell, though…" He stepped toward her, clutching his back as if the movement caused him pain. "It wasn't an easy task, but it worked." He laughed again. "Boy, did it work."

The tulpa hovered next to her, inching closer, making her palms sweat. *It's not real. It can't hurt me.*

The shadow swiped a fist toward her face, and its hand turned to mist, disintegrating around her head and reforming behind her. She swallowed the bile creeping up the back of her throat.

Isaac narrowed his eyes, and the tulpa grabbed her bag, twisting it around her shoulder and pinning her arm behind her back. She held in a groan as sharp pain shot through her arm. She wouldn't give him the satisfaction of seeing her cry.

"He can still manipulate objects, whether you believe in him or not." The tulpa used her bag to throw her to the ground.

She landed on the same shoulder, and another wave of pain shot through her body. Using her hands, she pushed into a sitting position. "Let's talk about this, Isaac. You don't need to hurt anyone else."

"We could have talked about it when you caught me draining you…before you tried to kill me. Now, it's too late."

"I wasn't trying to kill you. I was trying to make the one you loved most hate you. How was I supposed to know you loved your power more than anything? I never would have done it if I hadn't been under your spell."

"We aren't so different, you know?" He took another step toward her and grimaced as he clutched his hip. "You loved your power more than anything too. You didn't have time for love until I made you make time."

"That wasn't love." She crab-walked backward until her shoulder smacked a tree.

"Obviously not."

Using the trunk for support, she pushed to her feet. "We've both suffered."

"You call your little curse suffering?" He spat out a dry laugh.

"I can fix this. The council...they sent me a spell to break the curse. If I get my powers back, I can undo the spell I put on you. We can both be free."

He paused, rubbing the raw skin on his jaw. Confliction clouded his eyes, his brow furrowing as he contemplated her offer. The tulpa reached into her bag, yanking out the butcher knife, and Isaac's gaze hardened. "We can both be free? Is that why you brought a knife?" The tulpa pressed the tip against the base of her throat.

She swallowed, and the sharp point pierced a shallow layer of skin. "It was a precaution," she dared to whisper.

"The council may think you've served your punishment, but I'll watch you burn in hell for what you've done."

With the blade pressed against her neck, she couldn't convince her mind the shadow wasn't real. It grabbed her arm, wrenching it behind her back, and forced her to her knees.

CHAPTER TWENTY-TWO

THE SIGHT OF RAIN ON HER KNEES WITH A KNIFE TO her throat sent Chase's heart into overdrive, and he charged toward Isaac, barreling into him and knocking his boney body to the ground.

His concentration broken, Isaac's control of the tulpa slipped, and Snow dragged Rain away from the shadow. Chase drew his arm back to slug the bastard in the face, but the tulpa hurled the knife, jabbing it into his back.

Searing pain spread through his muscles, and he staggered to his feet, reaching behind, barely grasping the handle and yanking it from his back. His head spun. Blood gushed from the wound, and the muffled sound of Rain's scream reached his ears before his knees gave out.

Isaac scrambled into a sitting position, clutching his arm and grinding his teeth so hard that blood dripped from the corners of his mouth.

Gripping the knife, Chase advanced on the sadistic witch. The tulpa charged, knocking him to the ground again. The impact knocked the breath from his lungs, and electric pain shot from his wound through his chest. The edges of his vision darkened, and nausea churned in his stomach.

"It's not real, Chase," Rain called.

He squinted through his tears to find Snow clutching her arm, holding her back.

"It can't hurt you without a weapon," she said. "Use the magic from the cookie."

The shadow sat on his chest, a two-hundred-pound weight crushing his ribcage. "I don't believe in you." Chase closed his eyes and focused his mind. The magic from Snow's spell tingled behind his forehead, bringing his thoughts into crisp focus. "You're a figment of this sick bastard's imagination." The weight of the shadow lifted, and Chase stood, passing through it like a mist.

Using the trunk of a tree for support, Isaac clambered to his feet. He stumbled forward, narrowing his eyes in concentration, and the tulpa lunged for Chase again.

It's not really there. Chase stopped, closing his eyes briefly as the shadow passed through him yet again. He chuckled. "It's you and me now, Isaac."

Chase advanced on the witch, trying to ignore the searing pain ripping through his back. If his magic hadn't been bound, he'd have healed by now. Instead, he could barely get enough air into his lungs, and stars danced before his eyes as he closed in on the man trying to hurt his fate-bound.

The *snap* of a tree limb breaking barely distracted him from his target. He raised the knife, and something hard smacked into his back, knocking the air from his already starving lungs. He went down, the knife slipping from his grip and landing somewhere in the mud. The tulpa lifted the branch to strike him again.

Rain screamed and charged toward them. She grabbed

onto the branch, engaging in a tug-of-war with the imaginary being, giving Chase a chance to stumble to his feet. His head spun. The world tipped on its side and his stomach roiled, but he grabbed a branch to hold himself upright. It was time to end this.

Isaac leaned against a tree, his body too damaged to move, but his mind agile enough to control the tulpa as if it were an extension of him.

Where the hell was the knife?

"Chase." Snow lifted her hand from the murky water and tossed him a two-foot-long icicle with a razor-sharp point. The intense cold stung his hand like dry ice, and a thin mist rose from the makeshift weapon like a magical aura.

Rain grunted as the tulpa spun around, pinning her between the branch and a tree. "Chase." His name came out as a squeak as the shadow pressed the air from her lungs.

He paused, momentarily paralyzed as the primal need to save his fate-bound fought to control his movements. Instinct to hurl himself at the shadow propelled him forward, but the only way to stop this monster stood behind him.

He turned to Isaac and hurled the frozen spear at him, piercing his chest. The witch gasped, his eyes widening in disbelief before he crumpled to the ground.

A strangled gurgling sound emanated from Isaac's throat as the tulpa dropped the branch, and it splattered in the mud. The entity reached for something on the ground and lunged for Chase.

The knife sank into his chest, an explosion of searing pain sending him to his knees.

"No!" Rain screamed and ran to him.

His vision tunneled, and he fell to his side and rolled onto his back. The tulpa rose behind Rain, lifting a branch above its head.

Chase gasped for breath to warn her, but he couldn't suck in any air. The sound of Isaac's hacking cough echoed in the night. Then it ceased. The tulpa dissolved, and the branch thudded to the ground.

———

Rain knelt by Chase's side, her head throbbing as if her heart had leapt all the way up to her skull. This couldn't be happening. Her mind reeled, a million thoughts ricocheting around in her brain, scrambling for coherence.

She put her hands on his chest. It barely rose and fell with his shallow breaths. "Oh, goddess, no. Chase? Talk to me, please. You're going to be okay."

"We need to get the knife out so he can heal." Snow grasped the handle and ripped the blade from his chest, and the wet, sucking sound of metal leaving flesh made Rain's stomach turn.

He groaned, his head rolling from side to side, his eyelids fluttering as blood gushed from the wound. Rain pressed her hands to the gash, trying to slow the flow, but blood pooled between her fingers, the deep-orange glow pulsing as his magic tried to break its bond.

"Why isn't he healing?" Snow's voice tipped with panic. "He's a werewolf. He should be healing."

Tears streamed down Rain's face, her heart wrenching in her chest. "His magic is bound. He's not going to heal. We need to get him to the hospital."

"No." His voice was barely audible as he put his hand on hers. "Take my blood. Break your curse."

"My curse is the last thing I'm worried about. I'm calling an ambulance." She fumbled for her phone and found it dead, the screen cracked, her distorted, tear-streaked reflection staring back at her from the blank surface. "Dammit!"

She looked at Snow, who held a small bottle in her hand. "What are you doing?"

"He offered his blood, so I'm taking it. There won't be another blue moon for two years."

Why were they both so concerned with her curse? Her soulmate lay dying. Saving him was all that mattered.

Chase coughed, sending more blood oozing from his wound. Rain pressed harder on the gash. "I don't care about my curse." She couldn't live without this man. He meant the world to her and spending a single second without him by her side would be unbearable.

"Take it, Rain." His voice was raspy and strained. "Fate bound us together for a reason, and it wasn't so I could die without helping you. I'm meant to break your curse."

"No." Hot tears stung her eyes. "Our hearts are bound because we're meant to spend forever together."

He gripped her hand. "Some forevers aren't that long."

A sob bubbled up from somewhere deep in her soul. This wasn't how it was supposed to end. She should've been the one lying on the ground, bleeding out. *She* was the one who deserved to die.

Snow lifted his shirt and pressed the bottle to his side beneath a stream of blood. The first drop fell into the nearly-completed potion, and nothing happened. Then the second drop splashed into the liquid, and a burst of light filled the bottle with shimmering orange sparkles.

Chase's eyes fluttered shut as Snow whispered the incantation.

Panic surged through Rain's veins. "Chase?" She took his face in her hands. "Don't die, Chase. I need you."

His lids opened into slits. "I love you, Rain."

"I love you too. Please don't leave me."

His eyes closed, and it felt as if the knife were driven into her own chest, filleting her heart into a million microscopic pieces.

Snow grasped her hand and closed her fingers around the bottle. "Take it, Rain. Don't let this all be for nothing."

She looked at the shimmering liquid in the glass. The cure for her curse. If she had the ability to heal, she'd down the potion in a heartbeat and use her powers to heal her werewolf. But she didn't. Her magic was useless against the wound draining the life from the man she loved.

She sucked in a breath. She couldn't heal Chase...but his wolf could.

Her heart was bound to his like a tether, their souls intertwined as if they were two parts of the same whole. Maybe...

She tugged on his chin, parting his lips and holding the bottle to his mouth.

"What are you doing?" Panic laced Snow's voice. "The spell was written for you. It won't work on anyone else."

"It will work on him. Fate didn't bind us together to rip us apart." She poured the potion into his mouth. "Swallow it, baby." She rubbed his throat, encouraging him to let the magic flow into his body. "Please. For me."

Nothing happened. His chest stopped moving. The potion glowed deep-orange inside his mouth, but he didn't swallow it.

Ice flooded her veins. "Chase?" She patted his cheek as

a sickening nausea churned in her stomach, reaching up to tangle with the pieces of her shattered heart. "Swallow the potion, Chase." She moved his jaw to close his mouth and tapped on his throat. "Swallow it, dammit."

Snow grasped her shoulders. "He's gone, sweetie. I'm so sorry."

"No! He's not gone." She wrenched from her sister's hold and threw herself on top of him. "He can't be gone. He can't!"

With tears flooding down her cheeks, she sat up and positioned her hands over his chest. Locking her elbows, she pushed down forcefully, sending blood spewing from his wound. She pushed again, willing his heart to beat.

"Rain, please." Snow rested a hand on her shoulder. "You're making it worse."

"You're. Not. Leaving. Me," she said between chest compressions. Her entire body trembled. She couldn't get enough air into her lungs. Collapsing on top of him, she sobbed into his shirt, fisting the material in her hands. He couldn't be gone. Not after everything they'd been through. She squeezed her eyes shut as a gaping hole tore in her chest, hollowing her heart, ripping her world apart.

She gasped for breath and choked on a strangled sob. "No, Chase. Don't leave me."

CHAPTER TWENTY-THREE

RAIN PRESSED HER FACE INTO CHASE'S CHEST AND slid her hands to his cheeks. He couldn't be gone. She refused to accept it.

His arm jerked, and she sat up. The muscles in his throat contracted, and he gasped, choking on the potion. His lids slammed open, his eyes wide with confusion as a coughing fit wracked his body.

"Chase!" Rain's heart lurched into her throat, beating a frantic rhythm as she stroked the hair from his face and leaned over him. "It's me. You're okay." She ran her hands across his forehead and down his cheeks before pressing a kiss to his head.

"Rain? What?"

She lifted his shirt, her eyes widening in astonishment as the knife wound began to heal. The fibers of his skin stitched themselves back together, closing the gash and stopping the bleeding instantly.

He rose onto one elbow and felt his chest with his other hand. "How?"

Fresh tears streamed down her cheeks, but this time, they were tears of sheer joy. "I gave you my unbinding spell."

Snow knelt next to her. "Unbinding spells release your magic in a gush of power. That's why you healed so quickly."

He sat up, and she reached for him, wanting more than anything to hold him in her arms forever.

But he put his hand on her shoulder, gripping her tightly. "My wolf."

Her shoulder ached. Apparently, his strength had returned in that same rush of power. "You're hurting me."

His face pinched, and he yanked his hand off her arm. "Get away from me."

His words stung, but she refused to move. "What's wrong?"

"I can't control my wolf."

"Oh, shit." Snow shot to her feet and yanked Rain up by the arm. "He's going to shift. We need to run."

"No, we don't. I've seen him shift before." She planted her feet and pulled her arm from her sister's grasp.

"It's a blue moon. Werewolves attack the first living thing they see. He said so himself." She tried to drag her away, but Rain held her ground.

Chase's body shimmered, engulfing him in magical light as he transformed into a massive wolf with dark-chocolate fur rolling over his body. He bared his teeth and let out an ear-splitting howl.

"Crap, those teeth are big." Snow's voice trembled.

"Stay behind me." Rain took a step toward him. "He won't hurt me."

He growled as she approached, and her heart sprinted

in her chest. She reached a shaky hand toward him and stroked the soft fur on the side of his face. "You need to hunt?"

He exhaled a huff through his nostrils.

"I love you, Chase. Go."

Lowering his head, he turned and bounded into the trees.

Rain let out her breath, and a strange mix of relief, exhilaration, and shock tumbled through her system, making her limbs tremble.

Snow moved to stand next to her. "Holy crap. I can't believe that worked."

Rain laughed and threw her arms around her sister. "He's alive."

"And Isaac is dead. It's over." She took Rain by the shoulders and held her back to look into her eyes. "Are you okay? You may never get rid of your curse now."

"I don't care. Chase is alive, and that's all that matters. I'll gladly spend the rest of my life cursed, as long as I get to live it with him."

Snow smiled. "I suppose his life is worth whatever the curse decides to throw at me for completing the spell without getting paid."

Rain cringed. Her sister would pay dearly for what she had done. "I'll write you a check as soon as we get back to the bakery. Maybe that will be good enough to spare you."

She nodded. "I'll call Macey and see what she wants to do about these bodies."

"Good idea. I—" Her stomach quivered like a swarm of moths had been turned loose inside her. Her head spun, and she pressed a hand to her temple.

"Are you okay?"

"I...don't know." The fluttering spread to her chest and down her limbs, buzzing and humming with a familiar power, though the intensity felt like her veins would explode. She gripped Snow's arm for support as her magic unfurled in her core, filling her with energy that rolled over her body in waves.

The hum spread, connecting her soul to her element, every molecule of water in the air buzzing with her magic, preparing to do her bidding.

She laughed, straightening and throwing her arms to the sky, sending her energy into the clouds. The water obeyed her command. Drop by drop, she collected the elemental liquid, drawing it toward her as if she were magnetized. Thunder clapped, and the sky darkened as she gathered the storm.

Snow backed away. "Did you get your magic back?"

"It sure feels like it." She unleashed an explosion of energy, and rain poured down on them. It washed away the blood and the muck, cleansing her body and soul as the energy welled inside her. Another burst of electricity flew from her fingertips, and thunder boomed from above.

"Can you rein it in?" Snow asked. "I don't want to get struck by lightning."

The overwhelming sensation rolled through her body, awakening her cells, filling her heart with exuberance. "I can't, but I'll try to take it with me."

Snow smiled. "I'll take care of the mess here, and I'll meet you at the car when you're done."

Rain nodded and strode deeper into the trees, running her hands along the rough trunks, breathing in the fragrance of the storm, *feeling* things as if she were feeling them for the first time.

An act of selflessness would end her curse. She'd saved

Chase at the cost of never breaking the spell, putting his life above everything else.

She wandered through the woods to a clearing and stood in the center, looking up at the sky. As her burst of magical energy waned, the sky began to clear, the pouring rain relenting to a light shower, with the blue moon peeking from behind the clouds.

Chase bounded through the forest, the elation of having his wolf back driving him to run harder than he'd ever run before. He'd hunted, his instinct guiding him to his alpha to assure Luke everything was okay. Now that the beast had been satiated, the man needed to be with his woman.

She wasn't hard to find. He simply followed the downpour to its center, where his fate-bound stood beneath the falling droplets, lifting her face toward the sky. Soft moonlight glinted off her dark curls, giving her a magical glow.

He shifted into human form and stepped into the clearing as the rain lightened into a fine mist that hung in the air like a fog. She met his gaze and smiled, and he stood there for a moment, absorbing her beauty. Water dripped from the ends of her hair as it cascaded over her shoulders. Her wet shirt clung to her curves, the fabric darkened from the downpour.

A peacefulness settled around her, and she put her hands on her hips, looking more comfortable and complete than he'd ever seen her. "How was your hunt?"

"Good." He moved toward her, taking her in his arms. "I figured with your name you had some kind of water power, but...you can really control the weather?" He gazed into her dark-gray eyes, reveling in the magic energy dancing across her skin.

"I can only make it rain."

"Impressive." He leaned down, touching his lips to hers, and electricity shot through his body, the combination of their magic and their emotional chemistry mixing into a whirlwind of desire. "Thank you for saving my life."

"Thank you for breaking my curse." She held him close, resting her cheek against his shoulder and running her fingers through the hair on the back of his head.

He kissed her temple and sighed as he memorized the perfect way she fit in his arms. The vapors in the air settled on the ground, and he inhaled the sweet scent of clean air mixed with the feminine fragrance of the woman he loved.

She pulled from his embrace and cupped his cheek in her hand. Her touch was warm. Soft. Her eyes brightened with her smile as she placed a tender kiss on his lips. "Snow is waiting for me at the car. Will you come home with me?"

He laced his fingers through hers and kissed her palm. "I'd go anywhere with you."

He led her through the swampy forest toward his bike, making a wide berth around the place they'd defeated Isaac. The tulpa had disintegrated, so Isaac had to be dead, but Chase wasn't taking any chances.

He was still high on adrenaline and magic, and he knew the perfect way to expend his energy.

With the way Rain looked at him, she seemed to have the same idea. "There are so many things I need to say to you, but I can't seem to form a coherent thought."

"We'll have plenty of time for talking. Right now, let's just ride."

They reached the road and found Snow leaning against

the hood of Rain's car, an amused grin lighting on her lips. "Hey, you two."

Rain squeezed his hand before releasing him and running to her sister. She hugged her tightly, and Snow laughed. "Since you seem to have another way home, I'm going to wait here for Macey. Give me your keys, and I'll drop off your car at the shop later today."

Rain handed her the keys, and Chase pulled Snow into a hug. "Thank you. For everything."

She patted his back and whispered, "Anything for my future brother-in-law."

He chuckled. "I like the sound of that."

"Me too."

Rain gave him a curious look. "The sound of what?"

He took her hand and led her to his bike. "I'll tell you later. Let me update Luke, and we can head home."

He grabbed his cell phone from a pocket on his bike and dialed his number. "Hey, man. Checking in."

"Everything's under control on this end. You okay?" The smile behind Luke's voice was evident.

"Never better."

"Take the night off. I'll handle the rest."

"Thanks." He shoved his phone in his pocket and tossed Rain a helmet. She put it on, sat behind him, and wrapped her arms around his waist.

They flew down the freeway toward the French Quarter, the crisp air biting into his skin, his wet clothes intensifying the chill. With Rain hugging him from behind, his body blocked most of the wind from her, but she shivered as he exited I-10 onto the frontage road.

As he stopped at a red light, she loosened her grip, resting her hands on his thighs. He squeezed her fingers. "We're almost home, *cher*."

Without saying a word, she slipped her hands beneath his shirt, tucking the tips of her fingers into the waistband of his jeans. The magic on her skin tingled against his stomach, tightening his muscles and hardening his dick. Holy hell, he couldn't wait to get her home.

The light turned green, and he sped into the French Quarter, parking in the alley next to the bakery. Rain slid off the bike, and when Chase dismounted, chunks of mud fell from his pants legs onto the cobblestone walkway.

"We can't walk through your kitchen like this. We'll make a mess." He kicked off his boots and set them next to the door.

Rain stepped out of her shoes and peered at her legs. With a wicked grin, she slipped her pants off, dropping them in a heap next to her shoes. "Better?"

His pulse quickened. "Getting there."

She unlocked the door as he shoved his pants to the ground and stumbled out of them, wrestling to yank the wet denim from his legs. She'd disappeared into the building by the time he got the damn things off.

He stepped into the dark kitchen, and the door slammed shut behind him. He spun around in time to catch Rain as she flung herself into his arms. She kissed him hard, slipping her tongue between his lips and moaning into his mouth.

Her taste. Her scent. The vibration of sound moving across her lips. It was enough to drive him mad. Between the unbinding spell unleashing his magic in a rush and the power of the blue moon, his instincts had sharpened to a fine point. He needed her to be his and his alone. To belong to him, like he belonged to her.

He broke the kiss, trailing his lips to her ear. "Rain?"

She stepped back and grinned. "I feel dirty."

His heart thudded. "What kind of dirty are you talking about?"

She took his hand and tugged him through the kitchen. "Shower with me."

The thought of his hands on her naked body, slick with soap, hardened him even more...if that were possible. He followed her into the bathroom. "I still don't know what kind of dirty you mean."

She laughed as she took off the rest of her clothes and stepped into the shower. Tipping her head back, she let the water flow down her body, drenching her from her hair to her toes. It ran in rivulets over her soft curves, caressing her skin as it washed away the grime from the swamp.

Damn, she looked good wet.

"Are you going to stand there or are you going to come help me get clean?" She lathered the soap between her hands and ran them down her stomach and up to her breasts.

Holy hell. He stripped and joined her in the shower. His fingers twitched with the urge to touch her, but watching her washing herself...touching herself...sent his heart racing. Warm water beat down on his shoulders as Rain slid her hands to her throat, leaving a trail of suds along her skin. She closed her eyes as she massaged her neck and glided her hands to her breasts again, cupping them and circling her nipples with her thumbs.

She opened her eyes. "Want to help?"

His stomach tightened. "I want to watch."

She lathered more soap in her hands and continued washing herself, putting on the sexiest show he'd ever seen. As she bent to slide her palms along her legs, her hair brushed his dick, sending a jolt of electricity to his core. He didn't want the sensation to stop.

Straightening, she looked at his hand gripping his cock and grinned. "Like what you see?"

He chuckled. "How'd you guess?"

She wrapped her fingers around his hand, moving it up and down his shaft. "It's kinda obvious."

He shuddered. Her hand on his, guiding it on his dick, helping him pleasure himself...he wouldn't last long like this. He'd never had a woman show him how to jerk off before, but damn it if she wasn't better at it than he was. She knew exactly how to move, how much pressure to squeeze with, the perfect spot to twist her grip. He ground his teeth, staving off the orgasm coiling in his core.

As if she felt his climax building, she released her hold and ran her hands up his chest. "Not yet."

He let out a shaky breath and put his hands on her hips. "You're good at that."

"I'm good at a lot of things." She poured more soap into her hands and spread it over his torso. Her soft touch raised goose bumps on his skin, and he closed his eyes, memorizing the way her hands felt on his body.

Her magic tingled on his skin as her fingertips caressed every inch of him, setting his soul on fire.

"All clean." She pushed him under the stream, and bubbles spiraled down the drain.

He glided his hands along her slickened curves, holding her close as the scents of soap and Rain filled his senses. Everything about this moment felt so right. The woman he loved in his arms. Their magic intertwining, dancing across his skin, seeping into his being.

Though they stood skin to skin, he couldn't get close

enough. He needed her. To be inside her. To become one with her.

With her back against the wall, he pressed his body to hers, his cock sandwiched between their stomachs, aching to fill her. He nipped at her collarbone, gliding his tongue along the delicate skin of her throat to find her mouth.

She tangled her tongue with his and moved her hand between their bodies to grip his dick. Heat flushed through his veins, igniting his nerves with electricity.

"I love you, Chase." Her words pierced his soul, filling him with emotion, weakening his knees with their sincerity.

"I love you too." His voice was thick, and she must have sensed his need because she hooked one leg around his hip and guided him to her entrance.

He pushed inside her, delicious wet warmth squeezing him as he filled her, and she let out her breath in a slow, satisfied hiss. Holding still for a moment, he gazed into her stormy eyes and ran his hand over the creamy flesh of her thigh. He pulled out slightly, and her breath hitched, her lids fluttering before her focus returned.

Her foot slipped, and he caught her leg, lifting her from the floor to settle his cock deep inside her. She moaned and leaned her head against the wall, arching her back toward him to take him in even farther.

Holding her ass, he rocked his hips, sliding in and out and creating a delicious friction that awakened every instinct inside him. She moved with him, using the wall as leverage to match his thrusts beat for beat.

Gripping his shoulders, she cried out his name as she came, her body writhing against him and her sounds of ecstasy dancing in his ears. She was a goddess. An angel... no, an elemental witch.

His witch.

He buried his face in her neck, pinning her against the wall as she clutched his back, thrusting his hips harder and faster until his orgasm coiled tight like a spring and exploded through his body.

Her breath came in pants as she clung to him, resting her head on his shoulder, trembling from her own release. He leaned into her, stroking the hair from her face and trailing kisses along her neck.

Unwilling to break their intimate union just yet, he pushed deeper inside her. "You're mine, Rain Connolly."

She lifted her head from his shoulder, and a tiny smile played on her lips. "I know."

Slowly lowering her legs to the floor, he slipped out of her but held her close. She shivered as the once warm water of the shower turned cold, and she stepped out of the stream. "I suppose we've wasted enough water."

As he reached for the faucet, Rain lifted her hands, palms up. The water stopped, droplets suspended in midair as if she'd pressed a pause button on the flow.

"This is incredible." He ran his hand through the water as if the drops were glass beads, holding steady to their spots in the air. Taking one between his thumb and forefinger, he plucked it from the stream and rolled it in his hand. Squeezing it, the droplet crushed, returning to its liquid state and dripping from his fingers.

He looked at the amazing woman before him and smiled. He'd known she was powerful the moment he'd met her, but to control an element? "Amazing."

"Can you hit the faucet?"

He turned the knob to shut off the flow, and Rain released the droplets from their semisolid state. They splattered on the floor of the shower and cascaded down the drain.

"I'd forgotten how amazing my powers were...are." She grabbed two towels from a rack and handed him one before patting herself dry. "When I was young, it was all I really cared about. Elemental witches are rare, but for some reason, my power never seemed like it was enough."

She hung the towels over the shower curtain rod and guided him to the bedroom. "I always wanted more. I thought getting a seat on the national council would be my greatest achievement, but I doubt I would have even been satisfied with that."

Chase climbed into the bed with her and pulled her into his arms. "There's nothing wrong with wanting more. Ambition is a good thing."

"Maybe, but spending seven years cursed and powerless helped me get my priorities straight. Power and position won't make me happy. I know that now, thanks to you."

He kissed her forehead. "Me? What did I do?"

"You have power...and position, but that's not what makes you tick. Your pack...your friends and family... they're what matter most to you. From now on, they're what matter most to me."

His heart pounded. "Speaking of my pack...and family." He rolled to his side to face her, taking both her hands in his and entwining their legs together. "You are my fatebound."

She smiled. "I know. That's why the unbinding spell worked on you, even though it was created for me." Holding his hand, she touched his palm to his own chest and then to hers. "The bond works both ways. You're stuck with me."

He held her gaze, losing himself in the deep-gray of her eyes. The raging storm had settled, and now all he could see when he looked at her was the rest of his life. "Will you be my mate? My wife?"

Her eyes sparkled as she smiled and rested her hand on his cheek. "All I can promise you is forever."

He laced his fingers through hers and kissed her palm. "Forever is all I need."

EPILOGUE

Rain took a deep breath to calm her sprinting heart as Chase stood beside Luke near the alter. She sat in the audience, on the second row next to Bekah, with little Emma situated between them.

Chase caught her gaze and winked as he adjusted the lapels of his jacket. Though her husband looked damn fine in a suit and tie, he'd be ripping at his collar by the end of the night. She bit her bottom lip as thoughts of helping him out of the confining garments danced through her mind.

They'd been married and mated for a month, living in the apartment above the bakery for three weeks. Though Chase was second in command of the pack, since he didn't belong to the first family, his wedding hadn't required the pomp and circumstance of the alpha line. He and Rain had taken their mating vows beneath the last full moon, and Luke's father officiated the marriage ceremony immediately after.

She grinned. That was the first time she'd helped Chase out of an uncomfortable suit.

With her curse broken, she'd finally reunited with her parents. Though she missed them, New Orleans was her home now, and Chase's pack had welcomed her as if she were one of them. Like family.

The organist began the wedding march, and Rain stood, along with the other four hundred or so wedding guests, to watch Macey walk down the aisle.

Emma giggled and tugged on Rain's hand. "She looks so pretty."

Rain smiled and put a finger to her lips, reminding the little girl to stay quiet.

Luke held his eyes wide as Macey approached. From her view in the audience, it appeared as if he fought back tears.

Rain understood the feeling. She hadn't been able to stop her own tears from flowing when she married Chase. She'd barely been able to keep the rain from falling from the clouds that had gathered like they tended to do when she was in a state of heightened emotion. The love of a werewolf was intense, loyal, and unwavering, and she thanked fate every day for leading her to Chase. She was the luckiest witch alive.

Rain ducked out as soon as Luke and Macey said their vows, and she headed to the ballroom for the reception. Snow was putting the finishing touches on the cake display when she arrived, and Rain stood back to admire the massive wedding cake she'd created with her sister.

Frosted in buttercream, with an intricate basket-weave design, the five-layer cake was topped with an array of yellow roses that cascaded down the sides in a waterfall pattern. She'd accented her classic vanilla-almond cake with a raspberry cream filling that Chase swore was the most decadent thing he'd ever tasted.

Snow adjusted a flower and stood next to her. "It's our best one yet."

"We should take some pictures for the portfolio before the guests get here."

"Good idea." Snow ducked behind the table and pulled her phone from her purse.

As she snapped pictures of the cake, Rain turned to survey the ballroom. Dozens of tables drenched in white linen filled the space, and a band had set up on a raised platform at the end of the room. A set of wooden steps led up to a series of French doors that opened onto a balcony overlooking the French Quarter.

As the first guests entered the ballroom, the band started in with some smooth jazz. The people mingled, mostly werewolves, but mixed with the leaders and other important people from the entire magical community.

Calista caught her gaze and gave her a warm smile as she approached. "The cake is beautiful."

"Thank you." Rain braced herself for the questions. With her curse lifted, and her true powers revealed, the high priestess had tried to become her best friend.

"Are you sure you won't join the coven? We could use an elemental witch in our group."

"I told you I haven't made up my mind yet. Until I get settled into my new life, I'll keep paying the fee to operate a witch business." Her acceptance into Chase's pack increased her number of customers ten-fold. She made more than enough money to pay the rent on the shop and her new apartment, along with the fine for not joining the coven.

Calista inclined her head. "My offer stands. A seat on the board is yours if you want it."

"Thank you. I'll keep that in mind." A few months

ago, she'd have jumped at the chance to be on the board. It wasn't the national council, but it was prestigious in its own right. Now though, the position wasn't the slightest bit appealing, especially since the person offering it had previously wanted her dead. Rain had her bakery, her husband, the support of a werewolf pack, and her sister. She didn't need anything else.

The wedding party arrived, and she sat next to Chase at the head table. The werewolves dined on filet mignon, and Rain had a goat cheese ravioli with pesto sauce.

When they finished dinner, Rain stood next to Chase on the dance floor as Luke and Macey swayed to the music —their first dance as husband and wife.

As the song ended, Chase tugged her into his arms for their own dance. He held her close, his hard body pressed to hers, his masculine, woodsy scent filling her senses, making her head spin. Would she ever get used to the way this man affected her? She hoped not.

He took her right hand in his left and ran his thumb across the small tattoo adorning the inside of her wrist—a wolf head centered on a fleur-de-lis, like the one on Chase's shoulder. The tattoo wasn't a requirement of joining the pack, but getting it seemed…right.

Since she'd broken ties with the Miami coven and her powers had been unbound, her magical crest had dissolved from her skin. This tattoo was made of mundane ink and would be a part of her forever. She would be a part of this pack…be Chase's mate…forever too.

She ran her hand over his shoulder and down his jacket lapel. "This suit looks good on you."

He chuckled. "It'll look even better on the floor when we get home."

"Hmm…" She leaned back to take in his form. "I think you're right."

They danced to a few more songs before Luke called Chase to the stage to give a toast.

Alexis stood next to Rain and bumped her with her elbow. "That cake was amazing."

"Thanks." Rain glanced at Alexis, but the werewolf focused her attention on something across the dance floor. She followed her gaze to what had intrigued her friend. "Macey's partner is cute, isn't he?"

Alexis's cheeks flushed pink. "Bryce?" She looked at the floor. "He's okay. He's human."

"There are a lot of humans here."

Alexis nodded. "Macey grew up in the human world." Her gaze drifted back across the dance floor.

"Bryce seems like a nice guy."

Alexis drew her shoulders up. "I'm leaving town tomorrow. Don't know when I'll be back."

Rain smiled. She could take a hint. "Take care of yourself."

"I'll see you around." The toasts ended, and Alexis strode toward her sister, pulling her into a hug.

Chase hopped off the stage and met Rain on the dance floor. Taking her by the hand, he led her up the steps and out onto the balcony, where soft moonlight painted the city in a silvery glow. She leaned on the railing and looked at him, and so much love filled her heart she couldn't help but smile. "Luke and Macey leave for their honeymoon tomorrow. Are you ready for two weeks as pack leader?"

His hazel eyes sparkled as he returned her smile and shook his head. "Five years ago, if someone had told me I'd be married to a witch and running a pack, I'd have laughed in his face."

"And now?"

He wrapped his arms around her waist. "I'm ready for whatever fate has planned. It hasn't steered me wrong yet."

"Fate does have a way of leading us to the things we need most, doesn't it?"

"That it does."

The balcony door opened, and Bryce shuffled through. "Sorry, guys. Didn't mean to interrupt. I needed some fresh air."

Chase slipped his hand into Rain's. "No worries. You going to make it without your partner for two weeks?"

"I'll be fine." Bryce gazed through the window into the ballroom. "I can call you if we come across anything weird?"

"You've got my number."

Rain tugged Chase toward the window and followed Bryce's gaze. Alexis stood on the edge of the dancefloor, laughing at something James said. A lopsided grin spread across Bryce's face, and a look of longing sparkled in his eyes.

Rain nodded toward Alexis. "Macey's sister is pretty."

Bryce's grin widened. "She is cute, isn't she?"

ABOUT THE AUTHOR

Carrie Pulkinen is a paranormal romance author who has always been fascinated with things that go bump in the night. Of course, when you grow up next door to a cemetery, the dead (and the undead) are hard to ignore. Pair that with her passion for writing and her love of a good happily-ever-after, and becoming a paranormal romance author seems like the only logical career choice.

Before she decided to turn her love of the written word into a career, Carrie spent the first part of her professional life as a high school journalism and yearbook teacher. She loves good chocolate and bad puns, and in her free time, she likes to read, drink wine, and travel with her family.

Connect with Carrie online:
www.CarriePulkinen.com

Made in the USA
Middletown, DE
07 February 2020